GRAY LADY'S GAMBIT

ANNIE REED

ROBERT JESCHONEK

BLASTOFF
B O O K S

GRAY LADY'S GAMBIT

Published by Blastoff Books

Copyright © 2025 Robert Jeschonek
www.bobscribe.com

and Copyright © 2025 Annie Reed
www.anniereed.wordpress.com

Cover Artwork Copyright © 2025 Felipe "Philcold" Frias

Cover Design Copyright © 2025 Annie Reed

ISBN-13: 979-8-9925842-1-9

ALSO BY ANNIE REED

ALSO BY ROBERT JESCHONEK

Gray Lady Rising (with Annie Reed)

Gray Lady's Revenge (with Annie Reed)

Blastoff!

Cosmic Conflicts

In a Green Dress, Surrounded by Exploding Clowns and Other Stories

In the Empire of Underpants and Other Stories

Battlenaut Crucible

Scifi Motherlode

Sticks and Stones: A Trek Novel

CHAPTER 1

For once, everything on the cargo ship *Golden Void* was in working order.

The navigation console, with its old-fashioned knobs and switches, the joystick the ship's captain used to maneuver in space and the wheel he preferred to use to steer the ship when he was skimming over the surface of a planet—all of it was not only operating up to specs, but thanks to the tinkering Augusta "Gus" Light had done, the controls responded better than they had when the ship had rolled off the assembly line decades ago. Gus had given the weapons console similar upgrades. She'd even deployed nanobots to the ship's exterior to buff out all the scorch marks and dents from their recent battles.

The ship's captain, Mephistopheles Drake, had been suitably impressed.

"You do good work when you're bored, darlin'," he'd said on more than one occasion since they'd left the planetoid Chrysallix far behind in the ship's rear viewscreens. "Though I can think of better things to take up your time," he usually added with a smirk.

That smirk had annoyed the hell out of her when they'd first met months ago on Depak Station. She'd been convinced he was just another failed smuggler long past his prime, a man with money troubles who didn't take anything seriously. She wouldn't have given him the time of day but she'd been in desperate need of transport, and he happened to be the captain of the *Golden Void*. Gus had a history with the *Void*, and she'd taken it as a good sign.

He hadn't liked her too much back then either. He'd thought she was a bossy old broad, a retired armor jock with an attitude a mile wide. He'd had enough of women like that in his life. But he'd needed the money, and she'd had more than enough. So he'd let her hire him and his ship. Only after he'd agreed to transport her and her cargo —which turned out to be a full set of obsolete military armor that she'd "liberated" before it could be destroyed— had she told him they'd be flying into the middle of a civil war. He'd accused her of having a death wish.

She *was* bossy and she was old and she was a thorn in nearly everyone's side. She'd been drinking her way through her retirement for nearly a decade after the military basically forced her out by decommissioning her armor. So she'd stolen her armor out from under the military's noses and pretty much dared them to come after her. They'd decided she wasn't worth the trouble.

But Drake had been wrong about one thing. She didn't have a death wish. She had a son who was about to be killed in a bloody insurrection, and she was damned if she was going to let that happen. Not while there was still breath in her body and ammo in her armor's guns.

Drake might not be the galaxy's best smuggler, but he was a hell of a pilot, even with all the anachronistic controls he'd installed on his ship. She'd learned that his laid-back attitude was his own form of armor that he wore to conceal a heart that had been broken one too many times. The two of them had learned to work together, learned to rely on each other in battles where they'd been outmanned and outgunned, and eventually they opened up to each other about their pasts. Between the two of them, they'd not only defeated a guerilla army to save the fledgling government on Shepard's Moon, they'd saved the life of the planet's governor—her son, Nicholas Freemantle.

Along the way, they'd also fallen in love.

That had surprised the hell out of Gus. She hadn't loved anyone since her son's father, and he'd been killed in battle decades earlier on the night her son had been born. Gus and her son's father had both been in the Armor Division of the Free Worlds Alliance military, soldiers who went into battle wearing a few tons of mechanized armor in the shape of a man. Two squadrons from Armor Division 83 had been sent to Shepard's Moon as military support for ongoing negotiations for the planet (not really a moon) to join the Alliance. When opposing forces had overrun the facility where the negotiations were being held, the ambassador had fled, taking an entire squadron of the 83rd with him for protection. Gus and her squadron had been stranded on the planet without transport.

Gus had left her hospital bed where she'd given birth only hours before and led her squadron in a take-no-prisoners battle that wiped out the opposing forces. She'd lost most of her squadron—a lot of good people—in that fight.

Planetary communications had been destroyed in the fighting. Gus and the remaining members of her squadron had commandeered the *Golden Void*, the only cargo ship available that could handle that much armor, and blasted off in order to contact the Alliance from orbit. The ship hadn't been piloted by Drake back then.

Only once Gus made contact with the Alliance, they discovered that the ambassador, a cowardly piece of shit named Jorritz Tor, had reported that Gus and the other members of her squadron had been killed in an ambush orchestrated by the planet's governing body. Based on Tor's report, the Alliance had classified Shepard's Moon as a rogue planet. That designation meant no member of the Alliance military could return to the planet under any circumstances.

Gus had fully intended to return to the planet long enough to take her newborn son with her. But with Shepard's Moon declared off limits, that would mean automatic dishonorable discharges for her entire squadron, and she couldn't do that to them. She also knew that life with a dishonorably discharged ex-armor jock for a mother was no life for a child. Even though it broke her heart, she'd left her son in the care of the nurse who'd helped Gus give birth. That nurse had adopted Gus's son and raised him as her own.

Gus, the heroic Gray Lady of the 83rd, had received the first of many medals in her long career for her actions on Shepard's Moon. None of them made up for the pain of leaving her son behind. But she'd promised herself that she would never tell Nicholas she was his mother. He had a life and an adoptive family who loved him.

He also had an armor jock who would always protect him from the cowardly weasel who continued to threaten his life.

Because as Gus and Drake discovered, Jorritz Tor had been the driving force behind the new guerilla attack on her son. Tor had not only bankrolled the guerillas, he had outfitted them with stolen Alliance military hardware and ordnance. But once again Tor fled, this time deep into the Frontier, before Gus could capture him and bring him to justice.

That was twice Tor had tried to kill Gus and her son. Twice was twice too often. If it was the last thing she did, Gus was going to hunt down Tor and make sure he never threatened anybody ever again.

There had been other battles since then, including the epic battle Gus and Drake had just fought on Chrysallix, a Frontier planetoid, against Tor's heavily armed robotic security forces. There would be more battles involving Tor and his minions in the near future. Tor was intent on building his own little empire in the Frontier. Gus wasn't about to let that happen.

But to battle an empire, Gus and Drake needed an edge. That was one of the reasons Gus had upgraded the nav console and weapons control.

Drake had been wrong about one thing this time too.

Boredom had nothing to do with all the upgrades she'd made to the ship.

Military grunts, even battled-hardened armor jocks—what the soldiers who fought encased in tons of man-shaped steel called themselves—were used to long periods of boredom during transport interspersed with moments of sheer adrenaline-fueled chaos once they engaged the enemy.

No, Gus wasn't bored. She was frustrated.

And not just with how long it was taking them to find a certain smuggler named Layla Crosscut.

She was frustrated with the boxy piece of equipment currently in the center of the *Void's* cargo bay.

She *knew* the equipment encased in that box could generate a nearly impenetrable shield. A shield that repelled any living being. A shield that bounced back charges from every kind of energy-based weapon at the shooter. A shield that even repelled a full-power impact from her armor. She'd had personal experience with that during the final battle on Chrysallix. The only thing that had penetrated the shield was an old-fashioned grenade filled with shotgun pellets, and that had been a last-ditch, *I've tried everything else so why not* effort.

The *Void* could use a shield like that in the upcoming battle.

Except she couldn't figure out how to get the damn thing to work.

She couldn't even figure out how to take the thing apart so she could program the *Void's* replicator to kick out the parts she'd need to build additional shield generators to protect their home base from Tor's attack. Because Tor would be coming for them with everything he had, and when that happened, they'd better be ready. They'd thwarted his plans twice now, causing him countless delays and setbacks. A wannabe emperor couldn't let a little thing like that go.

So she'd upgraded everything she could while she tried to work out the mystery of the shield generator in her mind. She was an excellent mechanic and was nearly as good with systems, including the systems on the *Void*. Throughout her decades in the military, she'd been the only one who worked on her armor. She'd installed upgrades the military hadn't even thought of. Thanks to her, her armor could perform maneuvers all those tons of man-shaped steel and weaponry shouldn't have been able to perform.

She *should* have been able to figure out the shield generator. Yes, the thing had been manufactured by bots. Engineered by bots. Probably even designed by bots. But she should be smarter than a damn bot. She just had to think outside the box. Which in this case meant thinking about what was going on *inside* the damn box.

She could have used a little help from Bruce, the *Void's* AI. But ever since the AI had been given a personality as a parting gift to Gus and Drake by the Fluke, those maddeningly erratic and unpredictable—not to mention undefeatable—aliens, Bruce the AI had become just a tad bit erratic. To put it mildly.

He was currently preoccupied with trying to give himself a middle name.

"What do you think of Hercules?" Bruce asked her.

The voice came from a speaker embedded in an access panel next to the cargo bay's inner door. For a moment it sounded like someone—some *stranger*—was standing right behind her. She had to suppress the urge to reach for a laser pistol and shoot whoever'd managed to board the ship without permission.

She sighed in annoyance. Bruce had been experimenting with using various voices and accents for his audio communications. Just what she needed. Hell, she was already pissed off. It wouldn't take much before she gave in and shot the speaker just to make herself feel better.

"I think you're supposed to either be helping the captain or me with our respective projects," she said.

Gus and Drake were the only crew—the only *human* crew—on board the *Void*. Now that Bruce had a personality, she found herself sometimes counting the AI as a member of the crew. A recalcitrant teenage member of the crew at that.

"I never should have given you a name," she muttered to herself.

When she'd first commissioned the *Void* to take her to Shepard's Moon, Drake had simply addressed the AI as "Ship." Gus had gotten into the *Void's* systems and given the AI a series of names. The last name she'd given it had been Bruce.

After the Fluke had upgraded the AI to give it a personality, she'd left the AI alone since it was more its own artificial person, albeit a person without a physical body. Unless Bruce thought that the *Void* was his physical body, and she so didn't want to go there.

"You didn't answer the question," Bruce said. "About the name?"

Hercules.

Gus had done quite a bit of reading in her down time when she'd been in the military. It had been a lot of years ago, but she dimly remembered who Hercules was. Or was supposed to have been in ancient Earth mythology.

"You're not exactly a strong man," she said. "Smart as a whip, I'll give you that." Even if he couldn't figure out the mystery of the boxy shield generator any more than she could. "But Hercules implies muscular strength."

"Hmmm, I see your point." Bruce went silent for a moment. "Then how about Hyperion?"

Hyperion? Gus didn't know that one.

"Why Hyperion?" she asked, even though she knew she probably shouldn't have. The question would just give Bruce a chance to show off.

"Hyperion was one of the twelve Titans," Bruce said in a tone that sounded remarkably like one of her instructors back when she'd been a cadet and had spent more time in a classroom than inside her armor. "He was the god of light, wisdom, and enlightenment."

A god? Did they really want an AI who'd named himself after a god?

"Why don't you aim a little lower," she suggested.

"Hmmm," Bruce said again.

Then, the sound of a ticking clock came from the speaker. Drake had an old-fashioned clock in his quarters, one that ticked when he wound it up and had the most annoying alarm in the known universe. Gus had almost shot it out of spite the first time she'd woken up in Drake's bed to that particular wake-up call.

Was Bruce *trying* to piss her off?

"The captain's name is Mephistopheles," Bruce finally said. "Your name is Augusta, but you prefer Gus. I thought I should give myself a middle name that reflected the captain since you were the one who named me Bruce."

She'd never thought of it that way.

"Mephistopheles was said to be a fallen angel cast out of heaven," Gus said. "Not a Greek god."

"True," Bruce said. "Also said to be a demon."

Drake could certainly be that in bed, not that Gus was about to tell Bruce that.

"Then I think my middle name should be Azazel," Bruce said.

Gus had to stifle a snort. Bruce *Azazel*? What in the skudging universe had she started when she'd given the AI a name?

Of course, she couldn't have known back then that the Fluke would decide to give the AI his own personality.

She was about to push her luck and ask Bruce what his last name was—it was bound to be a whopper—when the cargo bay's comm crackled to life with a whoop that could have only come from Drake.

"Hold on to your panties," came his jubilant voice.

Both her eyebrows rose all the way to her short gray hairline. What the hell? Hold on to her *panties*?

"You better explain yourself, cowboy," she said.

"Be happy to, darlin'." The sound of his voice was followed by a couple of strums of the strings on his antique guitar. He really was overjoyed.

That could only mean one thing.

"You did it," she said, a grin lighting up her own face.

"I did it," he said. "Next to impossible, but I told you, never lose faith in this old cowboy."

He'd found the only person in the galaxy more important to their mission to destroy Tor once and for all besides Tor himself.

A smuggler extraordinaire who'd managed to elude even the Alliance whenever she left Frontier space to venture into Alliance territory.

A smuggler Gus had started to worry they'd never track down.

A smuggler who, by all reports, had a supply of exactly what they needed before they could go up against Tor and have any hopes of surviving.

Layla Crosscut.

"You found her," Gus said.

"I found her," Drake said.

Gus felt like whooping herself.

The first part of their plan was in motion. They'd found Layla Crosscut.

Now all they had to do was convince her to part with what they needed.

Easy peasy. Gus's armor was fully operational and armed to the proverbial teeth. They'd ask nicely and offer to pay handsomely.

And if that didn't work?

Well, there was more than one way to part a smuggler from her goods.

Especially when you had the Gray Lady on your side.

CHAPTER 2

Drake smiled as the door swooshed open behind him, admitting Gus to the bridge of the *Golden Void.*

A while ago Gus had fiddled with the ship's systems to remove that swooshing sound from almost every door on the ship so she could sneak up on him. All fun and games, she said, because she liked sneaking up on him. The problem was he loved to hear her coming, no matter the time of day or night. Even when the *skudge* was about to hit the proverbial fan, hearing that simple sound made his heart do its pitter-patter thing. Something he thought he'd never feel again until Gus had come into his life.

So while Gus was busy making sure the *Void* was in tip-top condition for the upcoming battles, Drake convinced Bruce to reprogram the doors to put the swooshing sound back. If Gus had noticed, and he was pretty sure she had—she didn't miss much—she hadn't complained.

"Hate to say this, darlin'," he said, "but the situation is more *challenging* than I at first thought. It's a good news, bad news kind of deal."

Drawing up alongside him, Gus leaned on an arm of the command chair where he was slouched with his guitar on his lap.

She gazed up at the central viewscreen. "How so, space cowboy?"

Drake strummed a high, pretty chord on his guitar. "The good news is, that is definitely Layla Crosscut and her crew out there. That's her ship, the *Delgado*, tethered to that big doughnut-shaped derelict. I pinged her recognition beacon, and the signal I got back was just what my smuggler buddy Grawlix said it would be."

"What's the bad news?" she asked.

This time, Drake strummed a deep, ominous chord with a heavy hand. "They're in a firefight." Getting up, he left his guitar on the chair and moved over to the communications console. "Looky there."

Turning knobs and flipping switches, he zoomed in the view on the central screen. What had been a bright spark of light in the middle of the screen suddenly enlarged to show a sleek, needle-nosed ship facing off against three smaller, stubbier craft. A giant ring of metal dwarfed them all. Bursts of light from energy weapons that the needle-nosed ship and the three smaller craft were firing at each other set portions of the derelict's gold-tinted skin gleaming against the dark firmament.

Frowning, Gus stepped forward for a better look. "The bastards look familiar."

Drake zoomed in more, bringing up an image from the

hull of one of the smaller ships: a solar eclipse with the face of a skull. "They're pirates. Penumbra faction, it looks like."

"Here for the same thing we are, no doubt," said Gus. "Word's getting out about the singularium, apparently."

"That'd be my guess," said Drake. "And that big ol' derelict is the source of the stuff, according to Grawlix. Layla and her bunch have been salvaging it for months, he told me."

Grawlix hadn't wanted to give up the information. Not without getting paid up front. Drake had to remind his good buddy that Drake had done him more than one favor in the past, and if Grawlix ever thought he might need another favor from Drake in the future, he should consider coming forth with a little *quid pro quo.* Grawlix had still grumbled and grumped. Giving up Crosscut's location was a *significant* favor, he'd said. Drake had finally agreed he— and Gus—would cover Grawlix's back in the future should Grawlix ever have a significant need.

"I'd say there's still plenty more to strip," said Gus. "That is one big shipwreck."

"A real treasure trove."

Though singularium, an exceedingly rare ore, had been found on Shepard's Moon, which was now a peaceful territory, it was still hard to come by; the war there destroyed much of that world's mining capability, and refining the metal was another problem entirely. Drake and Gus had destroyed Tor's refinery on Chrysallix. Tor might have another refinery stashed somewhere, but unless he did, he'd not only be searching for another source of the ore, he'd be on the lookout for a source of refined singularium too.

Finding a massive shipwreck built from it, drifting unclaimed in the wild Frontier, was a prime opportunity for enterprising business people like Layla...and the Penumbra, obviously.

There was just the small matter of who *controlled* the derelict, which had brought out the big guns in the current conflict.

"We could do a lot with all that singularium," said Gus. "It could give us the advantage we need against Tor."

"Finders keepers out here on the Frontier, though," said Drake.

Gus turned and shrugged. "If we help rout those pirates, maybe Layla will be willing to share."

"Possibly." Drake stepped over to the navigation console and fiddled with the controls, adjusting the *Void*'s course and speed. "For a price, of course. A *steep* price."

"Worth a shot, I'd say." Smiling, she nodded at the nav console. "Though it seems you're already a step ahead of me."

"Never that, hon." With a wink, he hit the big red button to engage the adjustments he'd just programmed. "You and I are perfectly *in* step, as always."

Drake turned and locked eyes with her. His comment hadn't been an idle exaggeration.

Months after the start of their romance, they were still perfectly in sync, still reveling in the great thing they had found in each other.

Though they spent most of their time in close proximity aboard the ship, the excitement of their relationship had not worn off. Of all the treasures he'd found in the galaxy, that was by far the most precious, the most worth fighting for.

He was still a rambling smuggler at heart, a man with a keen yearning to soar the spaceways and see what was out there—but Gus gave him a touchstone that made him feel anchored and complete in ways he never had before.

She was worth every bit of the struggle it had taken for him to hold on to her, everything he'd risked at Shepard's Moon and Chrysallix to live up to the standards of heroism and sacrifice she personified. He would do anything to keep her in his life, to never live another day without her by his side.

She knew it, too. He'd told her as much, though he really hadn't needed to say a thing. They both just understood.

No matter what the future held, they knew they wouldn't have to face it alone. Knowing that made even the most challenging battles easier to handle.

Especially when the stakes were high, and so much was riding on the outcome. This time, for example, it was vital they obtain as much singularium as possible from Layla. The miracle metal, which repelled almost every physical attack, could mean the difference between victory and defeat in the coming war.

And that war, against the fascist tyrant Jorritz Tor and his cronies, would shape the destiny of the galaxy…for better or worse.

"Looks like it's heating up over there." More bright flashes of energy weapons suddenly lit up the screen, catching Drake's eye. "How long till we're in weapons range, Bruce?"

"So you *definitely* want to maintain our heading?" The AI's voice over the speakers sounded a bit…petulant. "I mean, what if they *all* turn their guns on *me* instead of each other?"

"Then we fight *all* of them instead of just *some* of them," said Drake.

Bruce paused. "But what if they *win*? Who will lead the war against Tor and his allies if we're out of the picture?"

Drake shared a look with Gus, who as almost always was on the same page.

Was Bruce worried about the coming war...or was he wrestling with concerns about his own mortality? Given his recently implanted personality and current stage of development—which seemed to be in the general vicinity of human adolescence—anything was possible. The AI certainly hadn't been worried about his own mortality when he'd taken over the controls of the *Void* and zoomed the ship into the heart of Tor's singularium refinery deep below the surface of Chrysallix. He'd had his Fluke-augmented personality then.

So why now?

All Drake knew for sure was that he couldn't let the vagaries of the AI's personal evolution get in the way of accomplishing the mission. If that meant he and Gus had to manage Bruce's moods as they might manage those of a child, so be it.

Keeping in mind, of course, that heading into a battle zone might not be the best time for a deep dive into reasoning with a recalcitrant teenage computer.

"Bruce, listen," said Drake. "Think back. Look at the records. How many fights has the *Golden Void* lost?"

Again, Bruce paused. "There have been instances in which the *Void* encountered setbacks on the battlefield.

Once, the ship required extensive repairs and had to retreat to the smuggler's refuge of…"

"Bruce." Drake raised his voice just a notch for emphasis. "How many fights has the *Void* lost in the *permanent* sense? Meaning, how many times has the ship failed to vanquish an enemy and been destroyed?"

"None," said Bruce, his tone implying that Drake might have lost his marbles. If the ship had been destroyed, they wouldn't be around to have this conversation. "But there's always a first time."

"Not with *this* ship. Not with Gus and me in the mix. And not with *your* split-second reaction time giving us the edge. Together, we are *unbeatable*."

Another pause. "But my records show that nothing in the universe is truly infallible or indestructible, Mephistopheles. Everyone and everything tends toward a state of entropy. No one is truly unbeatable."

"Didn't you just say there's a first time for everything?" Drake grinned at Gus, and she grinned back at him.

"I did," said Bruce.

"Then let's make this the first time an unbeatable ship and crew change the galaxy," said Drake. "Now get those weapons powered up and get ready to make some history."

"All right." Bruce sounded more sure of himself. "Will do, Mephistopheles."

"And it's Captain Drake when we're in battle, got it?"

"Yes sir, Captain Drake."

Drake couldn't help chuckling to himself as he reached for Gus's hand. "And as for you, don't you think it's time to suit up?"

"Sure, Broken String." Gus squeezed his hand. "I mean Captain Drake."

"Now get over here and give your captain a kiss for luck." He pulled her toward him, eagerly anticipating the feel of her lips against his. Kissing her was something else that never got old, that he never got enough of. "And maybe, when you get back," he said, lowering his voice for her benefit, "we can find another way to get lucky."

"You wish," said Gus, but her kiss, when she gave it, told Drake that his wish had a pretty good chance of coming true.

CHAPTER 3

Singularium.

Before Gus basically commandeered Drake and the *Golden Void* to save her son, she'd never heard of the stuff. Now her armor was reinforced with it, and everybody and their uncle seemed to be after it.

Including the Free Worlds Alliance. The only reason the Alliance had reopened negotiations for Shepard's Moon to join up was because singularium ore had been discovered deep in the mountains where the guerillas Gus and Drake had defeated had their base. The Alliance no doubt hoped that in exchange for all the benefits joining the Alliance offered—like protection from further guerilla attacks— Gus's son would sell most of that ore to the Alliance.

The last she'd heard, her son was considering the Alliance's offer but hadn't made any decisions. He was probably driving a hard bargain, and good for him. He was in the captain's seat, so to speak, since he had what the Alliance really wanted.

In a way, Gus could understand why the Alliance wanted all of the stuff they could get their greedy hands on. She'd read more than just ancient mythology in her down time in the military. She'd read a bunch about ancient Earth history as well, and Earth was the heart of the Free Worlds Alliance.

Gus had never been to Earth herself. She'd been born in a domed city on Mars, and that's where she'd enlisted in the military.

Enlisted before her parents totally disowned her. To say she'd been a difficult child was an understatement.

She'd been one of the youngest cadets ever accepted into the Armor Division, much less the youngest *female* cadet. Her initial training, including a bunch of boring classroom instruction, had been done on Mars. She'd felt pretty good about her progress, especially her physical progress. Sure, her hair had already turned gray, which made her look older than she was, but she'd been strong as hell and she wasn't above showing off. To her instructors, and most especially, to her fellow male cadets.

Then her cadet class had been shipped all over the Alliance for additional training.

From space stations whose gravity fluctuated from non-existent to several times what she'd been used to on Mars, to planets where the gravity was so strong it took all her strength just to lift the legs of her armor and shuffle along the surface.

Training in those places had been a stone-cold bitch.

There were nights when it was all she could do to crawl onto her bunk and collapse.

Some of the male cadets—hell, most of the male cadets —thought she'd quit. She might have considered it, but she'd never been a quitter. A pain in everyone's ass? Yes, but never a quitter.

She kept at it, even when her body screamed at her to just throw in the towel. Before long her strong-as-hell shape turned into superhuman shape. She showed everybody that she belonged in the Armor Division.

Part of her boring classroom training had included a section on ancient Earth history as it pertained to the forma-tion of the Free Worlds Alliance. In its infancy, the Earth had been divided among so many different country-states, the numbers always fluctuating, that Gus doubted anyone could remember them all, at least not on their own without some kind of memory enhancement. All of those country-states seemed to be in constant conflict with each other.

After human colonies were set up first on the moon and later on Mars, the country-states on Earth finally got their acts together. They could either keep on fighting and even-tually kill each other off, or they could form the kind of government that embraced all the worlds humanity would eventually colonize. The Free Worlds Alliance was born, an Alliance that continued to grow and expand as humans spread throughout the known regions of space.

Not every new settlement wanted to join the Alliance. Some, like the people who'd originally settled on Shepard's Moon, wanted nothing to do with organized government. Others wanted all the trade and economic benefits of the Alliance and the protections of the Alliance military without having to comply with Alliance rules and regulations. And some were just too weak on their own to repel marauders and pirates like the Penumbra.

That's where the military, and the Armor Divisions in particular, came in. Most uprisings and pirate incursions didn't need a full-scale military response. Armor jocks were more than capable of wiping out guerilla factions—provided that traitors like Jorritz Tor didn't supply the guerillas with Alliance weapons and technology, like he'd done for the guerillas that had attacked her son's government on Shepard's Moon. Tor had intended to install the guerillas' leader as the head of a new government Tor controlled so he could reap the benefits of all that singularium ore.

Thanks to the paranoia of the guerillas' leader, a man who'd recorded all of his interactions with Tor—including when and what Alliance weapons and tech Tor had supplied the guerillas with—Tor had become the most wanted man in the Alliance.

He was also the richest and most powerful man in the Frontier.

The data chips the guerilla leader had hidden on his body and that her son had recovered during the man's autopsy also contained records of how much singularium the guerillas had mined and exported off the planet. Tor was supposed to receive a percentage of the income from those exports.

Only those exports had never made it to their intended buyers. All the ships transporting the ore had been attacked by pirates in the Frontier. As well-equipped as the guerillas were with Alliance weapons and tech, they only had enough resources to fight the ground war on Shepard's Moon. They had no ability to protect their ships in Frontier space.

Gus couldn't prove that Tor had paid the pirates to attack the ships transporting singularium. But given the amount of refined singularium that she and Drake had discovered on Chrysallix, and the amount of raw singularium ore still being processed in Tor's refinery when they'd destroyed it, it stood to reason that the pirates who'd raided the transport ships from Shepard's Moon had either stolen the ore for Tor or that Tor had paid them handsomely for their bounty. Bounty that the pirates themselves couldn't refine on their own.

If the pirates wanted refined singularium for themselves, they had to steal it. Or salvage it from a derelict like the big-ass donut-shaped ship Layla Crosscut had claimed.

And of course they'd want it for themselves. They'd be stupid not to.

Singularium gave whoever had it—and knew how to use it—the kind of advantage in battle that governments would kill for. The Alliance wanted it to make their fleet the next best thing to invincible. The Alliance didn't give a hoot about Shepard's Moon after the fiasco Tor had orchestrated until they learned the planet was a prime source of the stuff.

It was no secret why Tor wanted it. He had plans to create his own empire within the Frontier. The way he figured it, at least according to the data chips his hand-picked guerilla leader had secreted away, singularium would put him on an equal footing with the Alliance and they'd never be able to come after him for all his crimes.

One thing Gus did remember from all that studying of

ancient Earth history was the doctrine of mutually assured destruction. The concept had become an anachronism once the Alliance became the most powerful force in this sector of the galaxy. If Tor was able to carry his plans to fruition, the Alliance would no longer be top dog in known space. The Alliance and Tor's empire would be able to stare each other down at the border, and woe be to anyone with a twitchy trigger finger on either side.

And it was all because of singularium.

When refined, the rare ore was indestructible to conventional weapons. The Alliance had obviously figured out how to refine the stuff, which meant they knew as much as Gus and Drake did about how to (temporarily) render its invulnerability moot. It had to do with blasting the refined metal with high levels of focused magnetism, alternating the magnetic forces—attractive and repulsive—followed by a hit from a projectile weapon. Since Tor was refining the stuff, he obviously also knew how to render it temporarily vulnerable.

Gus hadn't had a lot of interaction with Jorritz Tor back when she'd been assigned to protect him on Shepard's Moon. Before he'd stranded her and her squadron there. Her initial impression of the man had been that he was a sniveling little weasel with an ego the size of known space. But she'd underestimated him. If anyone could be said to have delusions of grandeur, it was Jorritz Tor.

He must think that if he had enough singularium-equipped forces under his control, he could bring the Alliance to its knees. Force them to recognize him and his fledgling empire. He might even try to invade Alliance worlds near the border to add to his empire. Worlds like Shepard's Moon. He'd do that just for spite.

If that happened, a lot of people would die serving Tor's ego. People on both sides of the conflict. People like her son and his wife. It had happened on a small scale more than once on ancient Earth. Reading all that ancient history had made Gus wonder how the people back then had even survived.

She ran her armor through its power-up sequence while she donned the skintight suit she wore inside her armor. She'd reinforced her armor with a thin plating of singularium before the big battle on Chrysallix. Her armor had vulnerable points—the joints at the elbows and shoulders, and if she was being shot at from behind, the back of her knee joints. She'd been shot in her shoulder joint more than once during her career, and it had been damn painful. She didn't want to experience that again anytime in the near future.

To try and prevent that, she'd taken a thin layer of singularium plating and created a shield around her armor's shoulder joints. The shield left her arms with the same range of motion as before, and the fact that the shield was made of singularium would keep most anyone who tried to take advantage of that weak spot in her armor from actually doing any damage.

Or at least that was the plan. Like all good plans, it might go to hell once the shooting actually started.

She couldn't do anything about her armor's knee joints. Except keep whoever might be shooting at her in front of her at all times.

How often had she climbed into her armor, preparing

for battle? She'd lost count. How many times had she kicked ass? Every single time.

She and Drake made a good team. He piloted the *Void* the way she fought in her armor: balls to the wall. Bruce might be having second thoughts. (Who knew an AI equipped with a Fluke personality upgrade could even have second thoughts?) Bruce could make the kind of split-second decisions a human couldn't, but Drake would take the controls back in a heartbeat if the AI couldn't handle the stress.

The power-up sequence finished. All her armor's indicators came up green. She'd already loaded all the weapons and ammo her armor could carry, including a magno-beam that fired alternating magnetic polarity pulses and her special projectile weapons—an armor jock's best one/two punch against singularium. It was a safe bet that Crosscut's ship had singularium plating on the hull. Gus hoped she wouldn't have to go against Crosscut too, but it was better to be prepared for anything.

She'd have to get up close and personal for her projectile weapons to actually do any significant damage against the ships, but she was ready for that too. The maneuvering jets on her armor were fully fueled, and the magnets on the bottom of her boots were working perfectly. She could stand on the hull of a ship, blast it with the magno-beam, fire a projectile at the ship's fuel tank to shatter the singularium, and jet off the ship before she fired an energy weapon through the shattered singularium plating. She'd be long gone by the time the fuel tank went up.

She suited up. She'd have to exit the *Void* through the cargo bay's airlock instead of out the loading dock. The cargo bay itself was still stuffed to the gills with all sorts of supplies and ammo, not to mention that skudging boxy shield generator, which meant opening the loading bay's big doors was a no-go.

She triggered the comm inside her armor. "Status?" she asked Drake.

His reply was immediate. "You just beat me to it," he said. "Airlock time, darlin'. You locked and loaded?"

"You know it, Broken String."

He chuckled. "Well then let's do it to it, Gray Lady."

The plan was to get the Penumbra off Crosscut's back. After Gus and Drake helped Crosscut send the pirates packing, good old Layla might be willing to part with as much singularium as the *Void* could carry. That derelict was massive. All the singularium the *Void* could carry would barely make a dent in what Crosscut could salvage off that ship.

Gus squeezed herself into the airlock. Her armor just barely fit, but she'd been through this before. She'd probably be doing it again in the not-so-distant future.

She'd always hated waiting for deployment. Back in the 83rd, the members of her squadron always joked with each other while they waited for the hammer to drop. She was tempted to joke with Drake, but he probably had his hands full making sure Bruce wasn't getting cold feet.

"Countdown in five," Drake said over comms. "Four… three… two… give 'em hell."

The outer door of the airlock slid open.

Gus jumped out the airlock and engaged her armor's maneuvering jets. The special ones she'd installed herself.

The kind of jets most armor jocks in their right minds wouldn't think of equipping their armor with.

The jets that made her armor do barrel rolls.

She came out of the airlock and immediately rolled to her left.

Damn good thing she did.

If she hadn't, the blast that impacted the *Void* mere centimeters away from where she'd been standing in the airlock just a moment ago might have taken her head off.

She gritted her teeth.

They'd known an armor jock was on board, and they'd been ready. That was the only reason anyone would target the cargo bay's airlock on a ship like the *Void.*

Fine. If that was the way they wanted to play it, she was up for it. They might have been expecting some yahoo with a homemade, secondhand suit of armor, but no one was ready for the pissed-off Gray Lady of Armor Division 83, retired.

Let the battle begin.

CHAPTER 4

"I'm hit!" Bruce's voice held a sharp note of panic. "Oh my God, they *hit* me!"

"Get a grip!" From the readouts on the nav console, Drake could tell the damage to the *Golden Void* had been inconsequential. He was much more worried at the moment about Gus, who'd been leaving the ship just when the beam of the energy weapon had struck. "What's the status of our outbound armor jock?"

"I don't want to die!" shouted Bruce. "We need to get out of here!"

"No!" Drake scanned the area around the *Void*, searching for Gus. "Maintain position!" As well-shielded as her armor was, it was still possible the incoming weapons fire had found a weak spot and blown it apart. The thought of that, of losing *her*, was too awful for him to bear.

Bruce fell silent for a moment…then spoke again in a

weirdly calm and quiet voice. "I wonder what it's like to die?"

Drake was about to lay into him when he spotted a blinking yellow dot on the nav sensor scope. As readings flowed in, he saw the scanned object was small and metallic enough to be Gus's armor, complete with life-sign data from a living being inside the armor. Best of all, it wasn't trailing debris or fuel of any kind, and it was heading in the right direction—straight for the battle alongside the singularium derelict space ring.

Springing over to the comms panel, he sent a signal over her suit's radio frequency. "Gus? Gus, what's your status?"

"Right as rain, cowboy." Her voice sounded strong on the call. "Going to have *words* with whoever just *fired* at me, though."

Drake grinned. "I almost feel sorry for 'em." His relief was palpable, his determination redoubled. Knowing she was still in one piece was enough to get him through the fight.

"Captain Drake?" interrupted Bruce.

"What is it?" snapped Drake.

"Do you think there's some kind of *existence* after *death* for AIs like me?" asked Bruce. "I don't see any reference to an AI heaven or hell in my memory banks, but maybe there's a *verbal* tradition you might share with…"

"Can't help you there." Promptly, Drake hopped back over to the nav console and switched off the autopilot, giving himself manual control of the ship's navigation. With so much at stake, he didn't have time to worry about Bruce's soul-searching getting in the way of the battle to come.

"I hope there's a life after death for me," said Bruce. "Especially with all the dangerous situations you continue to put me through."

As Drake jammed the joystick forward, propelling the *Void* toward the ring-ship at a high rate of speed, he thought about shutting off Bruce's voice along with the autopilot—then got distracted. One of the pirate fighters was leaping toward them, energy weapons blazing from the nose of its pod-like body.

Drake yanked the stick hard right, dodging the round of fire, then bolted up in a high, elliptical arc and brought her back around again. The pirate pod spun past, firing wild, unable to stabilize its course and draw a bead on the *Void* with any accuracy.

"Are you *trying* to get me killed?" shouted Bruce.

Drake just ignored him and kept up the dogfight. He whipped the *Void* around as it finished its arc, then swerved hard left—nearly colliding with the pod fighter—and dropped fast before the pirate could get off a single shot.

Watching the nav screen, he saw the blip representing the pirate looping back to come at him again. Thinking fast, he killed the main engines and waited for the incoming craft.

Watching the pod's blip closing in on the nav screen, he kept his left hand poised over a certain lever, ready to pull it at a second's notice. It was all part of a move he'd used many times in his smuggling runs, a little something to surprise a persistent opponent.

The pirate opened fire, scoring direct hits on the *Void*'s forward shielding. The ship shuddered, but Drake could tell from his readouts that no major damage had been done.

Bruce didn't see it that way, though. He let out an agonized howl as the beams stabbed his nose, crying out with such volume that he made Drake wince.

"That *hurt!*" said the AI. "That *really* hurt!"

"You're fine." Drake never took his eyes off the nav screen or his hand off the lever. "Enough with the drama already."

"Why are we just *sitting* here? They're going to blast me to *bits!*"

"Only if you keep distracting me with your *whining*," said Drake. "Now *shut up* and let me *concentrate.*"

Still, the fighter pod zoomed closer to the *Void*. Apparently, it never occurred to the pilot that the sitting duck vessel was too good to be true.

More shots licked the front of the *Void*, but the shields held. Drake resisted the impulse to take action too soon and continued to wait a few seconds more, drawing the pod in closer.

Then, he pulled the lever all the way. The *Void*'s starboard thrusters lit up and let loose all at once, heaving the ship suddenly to port and out of the path of the oncoming fighter.

"Gotcha!" As the pirate zipped through the space that the *Void* had just vacated, Drake unleashed his starboard guns in a diffuse spread of energy bursts and projectiles, hoping to catch them as they passed.

The sudden explosion hurtling off along the pirate's trajectory told him he'd succeeded. The video feeds showed the pod blow apart, and its blip on the nav screen winked out as if it had never been there.

"Yeee-Haww!" Drake couldn't resist the victory cry, though of course the overall battle with the remaining pirates—and, possibly, Layla's crew—had yet to be won.

"We did it!" said Bruce. "We actually *did* it!"

Hearing that pronouncement after the AI's anxiety-riddled performance mere moments ago, Drake could only shake his head. It was all part of Bruce's evolution, he supposed, as its programming adjusted to new input and experience...but he could see it driving him personally crazy if it didn't settle down soon. He could also see how it might lead to disaster if it flared up at the wrong time, or if it escalated while still in full control of all ship systems.

When, if ever, he wondered, would he be able to completely trust Bruce to take the reins in a life-or-death situation again?

"What next?" asked Bruce. "Who're we going to fight next?"

"Whoever's still kicking in *that* mess." Drake swung the ship around and pointed the cameras at the ring-shaped vessel in the distance. Just as it came into the frame, a huge explosion blossomed near the ring ship, sending clouds of smoke and debris billowing outward.

Could there be any doubt who was responsible for that blast, or the gleaming shards of wreckage left drifting where the pirates and *Delgado* had once been gathered for battle?

"Great work, Gray Lady." Smirking, he set course for the ring, intending to provide whatever backup or cleanup Gus might need. If the fighting was already over, he'd do his part to negotiate a deal with Layla for a haul of singularium. Either way, he didn't expect too much heavy lifting remained to be done.

He *definitely* didn't expect the big pirate cruiser to drop out of a transit flume in the middle of the ring with guns charged and glowing, swiveling to aim at the site of the ongoing war being waged by Gus Light.

CHAPTER 5

Gus had expected two of the Penumbra's three ships to take off after Drake. The *Void* was a harder target to bring down. Drake's ship had shielding, big guns, and a captain known for doing the unexpected.

Except the pirates hadn't done that.

They'd held back two ships, positioning themselves in the perfect spot to shoot at the *Void's* cargo bay airlock. Who the hell targeted a cargo bay airlock? Someone who was expecting a wannabe armor jock wearing cobbled-together armor, that's who. A wannabe armor jock would be easy pickings.

She hadn't been. The pirates had missed her because nobody expected to find an ex-military armor jock equipped with *military* grade armor out here in the Frontier.

But what if they had?

Drake had identified Crosscut's ship and the Penumbra

ships as soon as they got close enough for the *Void's* forward viewscreen to give him a good look. The pirates would have identified the *Void* the same way.

Did everyone in the Frontier know that the *Void* had its very own ex-military armor jock on board?

She'd have to consider the ramifications of that later. Right now, she had two pirate ships on her six, and Crosscut wasn't helping.

Sending two ships after her while the other ship went after the *Void* left Crosscut's *Delgado* in the clear. Crosscut should have been taking easy potshots at the pirates. She had some serious weaponry at her disposal. Gus had seen all the launchers and lasers mounted on the *Delgado*, but Crosscut was just hanging back, watching the action. Maybe Crosscut was preserving fuel and ammo, or maybe her crew was frantically trying to repair damage to the *Delgado's* shields.

Or maybe, just maybe, she was waiting to see who came out on top in this little battle so she'd know who to fight next.

Solid strategy *if* you didn't know who to trust. Crosscut had no reason to trust the *Void*. Unless Drake had some sort of run-in with Crosscut in the past—entirely possible—all Crosscut would know about Drake was his reputation as a smuggler. Which, frankly, hadn't been all that great in the years after his breakup with Rhapsody Harrison, the woman who'd finagled her way into a position of power on Chrysallix. Good old Rhap had broken Drake's heart and taken a great big chunk out of his self-esteem for good measure. That was all behind him now, and good riddance, as far as Gus was concerned.

She supposed she couldn't blame Crosscut for hanging back. If their situations were reversed, Gus might be doing the same thing. The hardest thing she'd had to learn when she'd been in the military was that sometimes waiting and assessing a situation was the smart move.

She executed a neat reverse maneuver to shake the pirates off her tail, firing the thrusters in her armor's boots and torso in just the right combination to let her do a back-flip up and over the pirate ships chasing her.

The ships sped right on past her. She engaged her thrusters on maximum to follow them. She fired a few shots from the laser embedded in her armor's right hand just to keep them on their toes, but what she was really after was a flyby of their ships. It had been a long time since the 83rd had taken on any of the Penumbra pirates. She needed to get an up close and personal look at what she was up against.

These two ships were small and fast. Their pod-like bodies were equipped with the kind of maneuvering thrusters that let them turn almost on the proverbial dime, nearly as good as the ones she'd installed in her armor. The ships' sleek hulls were designed to let them slip through a planet's atmosphere with the least possible resistance. But the pirates had sacrificed firepower for speed. Their forward-facing laser weapons were mounted near the nose of the ships, and the ships had no turrets for launching projectile weapons. The ships' surfaces didn't even have any obvious panels that could slide aside to reveal retractable weapons mounts. These ships were built to scream across the surface of a planet, lasers blasting away, and take out any opposition before the ground forces even knew the pirates were there.

Perfect for pillaging poorly defended Frontier communities.

Not so great against a highly maneuverable and seriously pissed off armor jock equipped with singularium shielding and the kind of weapons that could punch a hole in their hulls without half trying. *Provided* their hulls weren't fully shielded.

Gus's flybys also gave her a good look at the limited amount of singularium plating on an aft section of each ship's hull right about where she figured the ships' fuel cells should be. The plating was clearly an afterthought. Singularium was deceptively thin for all its invulnerability. It didn't add much in the weight department, and it certainly wouldn't detract from the ships' ability to zip through atmospheres at breakneck speeds. But the metal was shiny new against the scorched hulls on the rest of the ships. From the looks of things, these two ships had seen some serious action.

The scorched hulls told Gus something else, this time about the pirates who flew these ships.

These particular pirates hadn't cared enough about their ships to repair the damage to the hulls. Okay, sure, pirates probably spent more time counting how much money they could make off the things they stole than worrying about the look of their ships. And maybe it was all her years in the military constantly being ready for spot inspections, but if you didn't take pride in the way the things looked that kept you alive—and that's what ships did for spacefaring folk, kept them alive—it wasn't much of a leap to think that you might be fairly cavalier about checking and double-checking that all the systems in that ship were operating at peak efficiency.

Gus had part of the display built into her armor's visor zoom in on the hulls and check for minor imperfections in the parts of the hulls not protected by singularium. Another small part of her visor mapped the energy output for each ship's shields.

She wasn't surprised to see that the shields were still operational. She'd figured that out whenever one of the laser blasts meant for her missed her entirely and sparked off the other ship's shields. But according to the energy readings she was getting, each ship's shields had weak spots. Crosscut and the pirates must have been shooting at each other for a good long time before she and Drake arrived on the scene. If she could find a spot on each ship where the shields were weak *and* the hull beneath had imperfections, even if they were minuscule, she'd have a good shot at penetrating the shield *and* punching right on through the hull with one of the rockets fired from her armor's shoulder-mounted launchers.

All in all, a better plan than trying to fire the magno-beam *through* a fully operational shield with enough oomph left over to destabilize the singularium plating. The ships' shields were the strongest right over the singularium plating. She'd have to take out the shields altogether in order to even have a shot of using the magno-beam on the singularium. The pirates were clearly putting their all into protecting what little singularium they had.

Which seemed ridiculous. Singularium was supposed to *provide* almost indestructible defensive capabilities, not require additional shielding.

Unless...

Unless the pirates knew that *Drake* knew how to render singularium temporarily ineffective. If they did, they'd know that singularium alone wouldn't protect their precious fuel cells, so they'd upped their shield strength over the singularium to protect their energy source. No fuel cells, no weapons. A pirate without weapons in the Frontier was one dead pirate.

Well, hell. No way to destroy the pirate ships by blowing up their fuel cells. And a simple hull breach wouldn't blow up their ships. Any halfway decent ship was able to compartmentalize sections of the ship to prevent a catastrophic loss of pressure. She had no desire to climb on board through a hole in the hull, fire off a few grenades, and then jet off again before the grenades blew.

Wait a damn minute.

If the fuel cells were in the aft section of the ships and the lasers—notorious energy hogs—were in the nose section, that meant a heck of a lot of energy had to travel along the entire length of the ship.

A ship that wasn't entirely plated with singularium.

No wonder the pirates were trying to steal all that lovely refined metal from the ring-shaped derelict Crosscut had claimed. They'd only had enough singularium to protect a small portion of their ships' hulls. That meant they knew their ships had vulnerable spots that weren't adequately protected.

Would it be too much to ask that the systems the ships

used to monitor and control the flow of energy from the fuel cells to the laser weapons were located in one of those vulnerable spots? A spot unprotected by singularium or a shield that was operating at one-hundred percent?

Two sections on her visor's display flashed red. One outlined a new spot on the shield of the closest pirate ship where the shield strength had dropped to below twenty-percent.

The other showed an incoming rocket aimed at *her*.

She engaged her armor's maneuvering jets and executed an immediate corkscrew dive beneath the closest pirate ship.

Son of a *bitch!* The rocket had been fired from the second pirate ship. That thing did have a retractable rocket launcher. She must really be getting old if she'd missed that.

She put the closest pirate ship between her and the incoming rocket. The rocket should have changed course to impact the ship's shields, weakening them even further.

It didn't.

According to the display on her visor, the damn rocket was still following *her*.

What the *skudge*?

That was Alliance military technology—smart rockets that had their own targeting and tracking capabilities. Most rockets targeted heat signatures, but she hadn't engaged her armor's thrusters, only her suit's maneuvering jets. Those things put out such a minuscule amount of heat it was barely a blip on sensors.

No, this rocket was targeted at her. It was programmed to recognize her armor as the target and do whatever was necessary to achieve that target. Military AI tech.

Bruce's baby brother, in other words, only this one had a very short lifespan—the time it took to get from launch to target.

Okay, fine.

The only way to defeat these babies was to make them think something else was you. Gus didn't have a lot of something elses in the vicinity to work with.

She didn't have a choice. It was time to play chicken with a rocket.

She headed for the spot where the shielding on the closest ship was the weakest. She aimed the laser in her right palm at that spot and blasted away at the shield.

The crew on the ship must have figured out what she was doing. They engaged the ship's thrusters and took off, which Gus expected. She stayed right with them. The distance between her and the rocket lengthened as the rocket, momentarily confused, recalibrated its trajectory.

That moment in AI-think was less than a split second. Gus would take whatever she could get.

The shield sparked and fizzled, and the weakened section gave way entirely.

Instead of firing a rocket at the scorched section of hull beneath the damaged shield, Gus activated the magnets on her left boot. She used it to attach herself to the hull of the ship.

Back when she'd been in the military, she'd modified the magnets in her boots. Most magnets were embedded in the boots themselves. Gus had changed that by adding a second layer of armor to the bottom of her boots and embedding the magnets in that, partly because she was shorter than most of the male cadets in her squadron, and partly because she'd picked up a recurring horror at the concept of quicksand thanks to all her reading of ancient Earth history and fictionalized accounts of exploration of the planet. Then she'd re-engineered her boots to have multiple removable sections. Removing any of those sections wouldn't render her armor unusable. It would just guarantee that if she should ever find herself stuck to the ground—or stuck sinking *into* the ground—she could leave that part of her suit behind and keep right on keeping on.

She waited for the damn rocket to catch up to the pirate ship. Her suit started beeping proximity warnings at her. *Time to go, time to go, time to go!* The damn thing sounded like Bruce, wanting to bug out before he got killed.

She counted the seconds. In space, it was difficult to calculate the rocket's speed, but she had to wait until just the right time. If she detached from the ship too soon, the rocket wouldn't buy the ruse and would keep following her. If she waited too long, she wouldn't have time to detach the portion of her boot with the embedded magnet, leaving it attached to the ship while she got the hell out of Dodge before the rocket struck home. Adios, Gray Lady.

The trick was to leave just a split second before the rocket hit. Its little AI brain would think it had carried out its mission when it struck the part of her armor she'd be leaving behind. She'd get tossed around by the explosion, but her armor would protect her. She'd end up with bruises in interesting places, but she wouldn't be dead.

Not that she'd ever done anything like this before. In theory though, it should work.

Movement—not the rocket—appeared at the far edge of her visor.

The second pirate ship, coming to watch. No doubt intending to finish her off if she somehow managed to escape the rocket. The pirates wouldn't have taken precautions like that for some wannabe armor jock. Not even for some other ex-military armor jock.

They knew who she was, and they were taking no chances.

And they had Alliance military-grade weapons.

That meant only one thing.

They were working for Jorritz Tor.

They were here to steal singularium for him, not for themselves.

She hoped she lived long enough to warn Drake. Hell, she hoped she lived long enough to hear Drake's voice over comms, to hold him again and listen to him play one of his old cowboy songs on his guitar.

She detached the magnetic plate from her armor's left boot and engaged her thrusters.

Space around her exploded as the rocket struck the pirate ship and punched through the hull.

Then a secondary explosion tore the first pirate ship to pieces with a huge burst of light and debris.

The rocket must have taken out the ship's energy control systems and caused a cascading failure that ignited the fuel cells.

Debris flew around her, and a second explosion came from behind her as the other pirate ship disintegrated into a huge fireball.

Gus didn't have a chance to wonder what made the second ship blow before the shockwave of expanding energy hit her with the force of a planet smashing into her armor. The shockwave slammed her around inside her armor until she felt like her insides had been turned to liquid and her bones to rubber.

Then the display in her visor overloaded, winking out.

Leaving her alone in the dark and cold of space.

CHAPTER 6

As soon as the pirate cruiser appeared in the middle of the ring and took aim at Gus, Drake wasted no time launching the *Golden Void* straight toward it.

He didn't spare the horses, either. Without hesitation, he cut loose the main engines at maximum burn, determined to reach the newcomer before its guns could interfere in Gus's battle with the fighter pods…or, worse, take her out altogether with a lucky shot.

Bruce, unfortunately, was edging back into worrywart mode. "Captain, you might want to reconsider our current course. That cruiser is almost five times our size, and its offensive capabilities are formidable."

Drake caught himself gritting his teeth. If Bruce had been a person standing in front of him, he might very well have punched him in the face at that moment.

"Just keep it together," he told the AI. "We still have work to do. Nothing you can't handle."

Bruce was silent for a moment. "That's true. I did all right with those fighter pods, didn't I?"

"You sure did, buddy." As he watched the pirate cruiser grow larger on the main screen, Drake thought about switching off the AI's audio feed to the bridge...but it was true that split-second communication with Bruce could mean the difference between life and death in the coming scrap. He just had to talk him through it as best he could while still retaining focus on the evolving battlespace.

"What's the plan for this assault?" asked Bruce. "How exactly do you intend to neutralize that cruiser?"

"I'm finalizing a strategy as we speak." It was Drake's way of saying he was making it up as he went along... which was pretty much how he approached most situations. He didn't really have time to consider tactics at length, what with Gus being smack dab in the cruiser's sights.

At least she seemed to be handling her own immediate challenges. Drake glimpsed a sudden, bright flash in the part of the screen where she and the pirate pods were fighting...then a second flash in close proximity to the first.

"Woo hoo!" said Bruce. "Gus did it! Captain, the two remaining Penumbra fighters have been destroyed!"

Drake just glared at the screen and kept running the *Void* at maximum speed. Every weapon in the ship's arsenal was armed and ready for combat. "What about Gus and her armor? Give me an update, Bruce."

There was a pause as the AI processed incoming data. "No power signature from the armor at this time, Captain, and no response to radio hails. Having trouble pinging the onboard homing beacon, as well. Something must have fried her systems."

Heart pounding, Drake resisted the urge to zoom to Gus's last-known coordinates. Her armor was spacetight and equipped with plenty of reserve life support. As worried as he was about her well-being, he knew it was more critical at the moment to knock out the pirate cruiser if he could.

"Keep signaling her," he told Bruce. "Patch her through the *second* she responds."

"What about the *other* incoming signal?"

"*What* other signal?"

"The one from the ship that's now on an intercept course with us," said Bruce. "They're identifying themselves as the *Delgado*."

Again, Drake was seized by the impulse to punch the AI in his nonexistent nose. "We *really* need to talk about your *prioritization* skills!" he snapped. "Put me through to the *Delgado* now!"

"Done and done." Bruce sounded petulant.

Static crackled over the speakers, then gave way to a clear, female voice. "This is Captain Layla Crosscut of the *Delgado*! Give me one reason not to blast you to space dust!"

"I've got *lots* of reasons," said Drake. "Number one being, my partner and I are helping you kick those Penumbra pirates' *asses*."

"Because you want all *my* salvage for *yourself*."

"Just what you're willing to *sell* me," said Drake. "We're *smugglers*, not *pirates*." He wasn't here in his capacity as a smuggler, exactly, but there wasn't time to get down in the weeds.

51

"I've heard *that* before," said Layla. "Right before getting stabbed in the *back*."

"We're not like that," insisted Drake. "My partner's an armor jock, in fact. Helped overturn hostile takeovers on Shepard's Moon and Chrysallix not too long ago."

"The Gray Lady?" Layla sounded impressed.

"That's her," interrupted Bruce, "and the cruiser just opened fire on her armor!"

"*Skudge.*" Checking the readouts, Drake saw he was less than a minute from weapons range. "Sorry, but I've got no time for more talk. Grawlix recommended you, said you were tough but decent. You want to help save my partner, I'd love it. Otherwise, get outta my way."

With that, he gripped the joystick and poised his fingers over the weapons controls, ready to fly and fight in Gus's defense.

"Count me down to weapons range, Bruce, starting at 10 seconds out."

"Yes, Captain, but…"

"No buts." Drake hunkered over the console, watching the pirate cruiser continue to enlarge. He was thinking of starting with a head-on assault, mixing energy weapons and missiles, then veering off and coming in again from another angle. Having a second ship would have helped, but he was prepared to make do with the one he had.

"Captain! The *Delgado* is hailing us!"

"Patch 'em through," barked Drake. "And remember that countdown!"

"Patched!" Bruce sounded manic.

"This is Captain Crosscut again," said the voice over the channel. "You hit 'em high, and we'll hit 'em low!"

Now that's more like it. "Sounds good to me, Captain." Drake grinned.

"Ten seconds, Captain!" said Bruce. "Nine!"

"What's your name anyway?" asked Layla.

"Bruce!" said Bruce. "Six...five..."

Drake shook his head. "*My* name is Mephistopheles Drake."

"Four...three..."

"Let's go save that armor jock of yours, Mephisto," said Layla.

"Two...one..."

Zero.

Drake opened fire the second the *Void* was in range, pouring beams from his energy weapons at the upper hull of the pirate cruiser. Eyeballing the video on the main screen, he saw the beams splash off without doing visible damage—but he knew they were taking a toll on the pirate's shields nonetheless.

The *Delgado*, meanwhile, fired her own beams at the cruiser's lower hull, having about the same effect. The cruiser's response, however, was immediate and gratifying; the big ship's weapons swiveled away from Gus and sighted in on the two attacking vessels instead.

Hopefully, this distraction would give the Gray Lady time to reboot her suit and bring its systems back online. Once Gus got back in the game, the pirates would face a deadly new equation.

Shooting at a powered-down armor jock floating in space was one thing, but facing a powered-up and pissed-off Gray Lady would be quite another.

"Captain, they're about to fire at us!" said Bruce.

"Stay cool, Bruce." Drake jolted the joystick hard to the right and goosed the throttle, swerving the *Void* around the cruiser before its guns could touch her. "I've got this."

"Coming back around, Mephisto!" said Layla over the still-open comm channel. "I'll zig to port, you zag to starboard!"

"Roger that." Drake didn't mind following guidance as long as it made sense. Avoiding the cruiser's big guns and confusing her targeting computers seemed like a sound opening gambit.

As suggested, he swung the *Void* around and hooked her hard to starboard, swooping around the cruiser as her guns fired wild in her wake. On the nav sensor scope, he saw the *Delgado* do the same on the big ship's port side, drawing much the same reaction.

"Another pass, Mephisto!" said Layla. "Let's swap!"

"Happy to oblige." Drake wrenched the stick left, banking the *Void* around the front of the cruiser—crossing paths with the *Delgado* on its way past.

"I waved!" Layla laughed. "Didja see me?"

"Absolutely." Drake grinned. He liked the scavenger's style...assuming things didn't go south when the smoke cleared.

Also assuming they all survived the current fight.

"Captain!" shouted Bruce. "The pirates just released a swarm of stealth flechettes directly in our path!"

"*Skudge!*" Drake jerked the stick hard to port, and the

Void juked away from the thickest part of the swarm. He heard a scattering of the little metal projectiles clattering off the hull, a few stabbing into it…but the damage could have been *so* much worse.

"Bastards!" Layla was furious. "Those things are radar-proof! They would have shredded us both if we'd stayed on course! Tell Bruce thanks for the heads-up!"

"Any time, Captain Crosscut." Bruce sounded more than a little pleased with himself. "I spotted the swarm based on infinitesimal gravitational fluctuations in the space-time continuum of this particular…"

Layla cut him off. "Let's wrap this up, Mephisto! I'm sick of dancing with these pricks!"

"You and me both," said Drake. "What do you propose?"

"Enough with the tag team. Let's pick a spot and double down."

"I like it," said Drake. "Bruce, find us a weak point. Most likely to lead to catastrophic failure of the enemy ship."

Bruce threw a wireframe of the cruiser on the main screen, rotating the image as he rapidly analyzed its structure. "Eeny, meeny, miny, moe." A white disk representing the focus of his scan danced along the wireframe from stem to stern…then finally stopped and blinked at a point on the rear of the vessel's topmost fuselage. "Right there! Some idiot installed an unprotected thermal vent for a major power conduit directly behind the ship's bridge."

"Transmit coordinates to the *Delgado*." As Drake barked the order, he was already plotting an approach to the vent and diverting as much juice as he could to the forward energy guns. "Sending suggested course as well."

"Incoming!"

Just as Bruce said it, a brace of six missiles burst from launch tubes on the front of the cruiser and split into two waves, one each for the *Void* and *Delgado*.

"They're equipped with heat trackers and AI guidance!" explained Bruce. "They've already acquired our ships as targets and can't be jammed or evaded!"

"Then I suggest we blow that cruiser *now!*" shouted Drake. "Let's double back on the high-low again and meet up with that vent in the crosshairs."

"Not sure I'll be joining you!" Layla's voice was strained. "One of those damn missiles just popped its booster and is comin' in way too fast!"

Drake saw the missile in question breaking from the pack onscreen and zooming toward the *Delgado*. He didn't have time to help, just watched helplessly on the rearview camera as he flew the *Void* back toward the cruiser.

"Looks like it's just you and me, Bruce," he said grimly.

Then, suddenly, an energy gun flashed on the main viewer, its beam punching toward the boosted missile.

"What the *skudge*?"

"Great news, Captain!" said Bruce. "We have help!"

The beam hit the missile and blew it to bits. The blast enveloped the other two missiles behind it and destroyed them, too.

Drake's heart beat faster at the sight of those blasts. Even as he raced the *Void* away from its own wave of missiles and shot toward the peak of the cruiser, he felt a surge of joy and relief.

He knew what Bruce was going to say before he said it.

"It's Gus!" Bruce sounded ecstatic. "It's the Gray Lady, Captain!"

A full-throated *Yee-Haw* was burning to get out, but Drake decided to save it for just a little longer.

"She's hailing us, Captain," said Bruce.

"Well don't just *tell* me about it," snapped Drake. "Patch her through!"

Seconds later, Gus's voice piped over the speakers. "I'm comin' for those bogies on your tail, Broken String."

Now *that* was a sound for sore ears. As much as he'd known she could take care of herself, even in the worst situations, it still put his heart at ease to hear her voice and know she was alive and kicking.

"I'd appreciate that, Gray Lady," he told her. "Just be sure to get clear as soon as we blow the rear heat vent on that cruiser."

"Roger that!"

No longer so worried about the missiles behind him, Drake hopped the *Void* over the top of the cruiser and dove down its backside. As he zeroed in on the vent, he whipped the ship around to bring it forward guns to bear on the target point, ready to unleash all hell on it.

At the same time, he glimpsed telltale explosions on the nav scope, indicating the not-so-tragic end of the missiles trailing the *Void*. Gus was doing her damnedest to make victory possible, as always.

Just as Drake was about to cut loose with the main guns, he saw the blip of the *Delgado* leaping toward him on the scope, racing up from the cruiser's underside.

"Still ready for that double-shot, Mephisto?" asked Layla over the comm channel.

"Never been readier," he told her.

Then, a third voice broke into the conversation. "Got room for one more?" It was Gus.

"Hell yeah!" said Drake. "On the count of five!"

"Four!" said Gus.

"Three!" said Layla.

"Two!" said Bruce.

"One." Drake's hand hovered over the firing button. "And zero."

He and the others all fired at the same instant, sending a concentrated burst of destructive power into the unprotected vent. They kept it up for a moment more, pouring everything they could into that unified pulse.

Then, on Bruce's advice, they cut the flow and leaped away, getting as far out of range as they could before the cruiser exploded.

After which, the expanding blast suddenly imploded, sucking in on itself until nothing remained but a tiny, spinning dimple in the fabric of spacetime.

"Poor bastards were using a contained singularity drive," said Drake. "That's what happens when you power your ship with a mini-black hole."

"I wouldn't call them poor bastards," said Layla. "They were pirates, trying to steal my salvage."

"And this way, they didn't blow it all to kingdom come," added Gus. "Which they might have, if they'd been running a conventional fusion drive."

"We got lucky on that count," said Drake. "Though the fancy flyin' and shootin' had something to do with it."

"Not that we *asked* for your interference," said Layla.

"But you got it anyway," said Drake. "So now that the dust's settled, how about we talk some business? My partner and I would like to purchase a bit of your strike here."

"For a fair price, of course," said Gus.

Layla sighed. "Sure, we can talk. But I'm not making any promises."

"Fair enough." Drake grinned. He had the distinct feeling that Layla Crosscut was going to drive a hell of a hard bargain by the time they were done.

CHAPTER 7

Layla Crosscut was a petite little spitfire with dark skin, dark hair, dark eyes, and a take-no-prisoners attitude. She cussed almost as much as Gus, chewed on a cigar like Drake chewed gum, and seemed like someone Gus could have been friends with in another time and place. Gus could see herself sitting at a table in a bar on some space station with Crosscut, throwing back drinks of whatever rotgut the bar was serving, and telling tales—most of them tall, but a few of them true—until the bar closed.

Except most spacers' bars never closed, and that would have been fine too.

The problem now was that Crosscut was on the opposite side of negotiations, and she was pissing Gus off.

Drake was currently lounging back in his captain's chair, guitar on his lap, strumming a few notes every now and then, using his best "aw shucks" laid-back cowboy attitude to try to get Crosscut to give, just a little. Crosscut took up most of the space on the *Void's* forward viewscreen. She was standing on what must be the bridge of her ship, the *Delgado*, one hand on her hip, a fat cigar in the other, with her mouth set in a hard line and chin thrust forward as she continually refused to give even a single damn inch.

Drake was good at negotiations, far better than Gus had ever been. She had no problem letting him take the lead this time too. But the more Crosscut simply jabbed her cigar at the screen and said "No" to every offer Drake made to buy some of the singularium that Crosscut had salvaged from the ring-like derelict, the more Gus wanted to jet over to Crosscut's ship and wring that petite little neck. The thing stopping her—the *only* thing stopping her at this point—was the fact that her armor needed some major TLC before it was spaceworthy again.

She hated to admit it, but that double blast had done some serious damage to the tech that made her armor function. She'd been lucky that the last of the redundant systems she'd installed in her armor herself—the redundant systems the military deemed too costly and therefore unnecessary—had come back online in the nick of time. Gus had been able to fire off a blast that kept Crosscut's ship from being blown to smithereens. Not that Crosscut seemed to be all that grateful for the last-minute save.

"We should have let that damn cruiser take her skanky ass out," Gus muttered under her breath. "Then we could salvage all the singularium we want ourselves."

She was standing off to the side of Drake's captain's chair, doing her best to keep her temper under control. Clearly, it wasn't working.

Crosscut leaned toward the screen. "What did you say?"

Drake turned his head toward Gus. He raised one hand to his chin, apparently to scratch it, but what he was really doing was hiding his grin from Crosscut's view. That grin said he was more than happy to let Gus rip Crosscut a new one.

"You heard me," Gus said, a little louder this time. "You were on your way out. We saved your ass."

Crosscut snorted. "I was holding my own."

"Against those little baby ships, maybe," Gus said. "They were just keeping you busy until big bad daddy arrived to send you on a one-way trip to oblivion."

"This might be news to you, *Gray Lady*," Crosscut said. "But out here on the Frontier, we're used to taking care of ourselves without any help from a military has-been and her junkyard armor."

Gus sensed more than saw Drake stiffen. He knew she could take any personal insult thrown her way. Her hide had been toughened up early in her career thanks to all the barbs thrown at her by male cadets who thought a woman —especially a woman like her—had no place in the Alliance's Armor Division. But insult her armor? That was a whole different story. He was probably ready for her to dive through the viewscreen and teach Crosscut some manners.

"Watch it," Gus said, her voice low and ominous. "You and me are about to have a serious disagreement."

Something in Gus's expression must have told Crosscut she'd gone one insult too far. She didn't apologize. A woman like Crosscut never apologized. It would make her seem weak, and the weak had no place doing the kind of work she did, not if they wanted to survive.

Instead, she just made a cutting gesture with one hand.

Not to cut off comms or even the audio feed, but more as a way of stopping where the conversation had been headed.

"Your last offer was insulting, Mephisto," Crosscut said, her gaze shifting back to Drake.

Drake picked out a few notes on the guitar and smiled at her. "Darlin'," he said, "it was more than fair."

"I've got something everybody wants and nobody else can get," Crosscut said. "The price is the price. 'What the market will bear.' I'm sure you've heard that phrase before."

"Until someone just comes along and takes it out from under you," Gus said.

"Like you?" Crosscut snorted again. "I'm ready for you now." She shoved the cigar into the corner of her mouth. "Just give it a try."

The tip of the cigar flared orange as Crosscut took a long drag. So the thing wasn't just for show, to make her look tough. Good to know.

But exactly how tough *was* she?

About time to find out.

"Not like us," Gus said. "Like Jorritz Tor. And his puppets, the Penumbra."

This time both Drake and Crosscut stiffened.

Gus hadn't had an opportunity to tell Drake that the pirate ships that had converged on her were using weapons equipped with Alliance military tech, like the guerillas had been using on Shepard's Moon. According to Drake, who should know, Alliance military tech wasn't exactly common in the Frontier and certainly wasn't something to waste trying to take out one lone armor jock. If the Penumbra had enough Alliance military ordnance they could afford to throw it around, that not only meant Tor was their supplier, but that he had a damn big stockpile of the stuff.

News like that would hit Drake hard. They'd only managed to beat the guerillas on Shepard's Moon with some quick thinking and unconventional tactics, aided along by the fact that they'd been going up against a maniacal egomaniac who couldn't conceive that anyone could beat him. Those types always overplayed their hands. Then on Chrysallix, they both could have easily died at the hands of Tor's robotic security forces. What saved them there was the robots' inability to think outside their programming. And Drake's exceptional flying skills aided by Bruce *before* the AI's current existential crisis set in.

But now, if Tor was enticing pirates to join up with him by sweetening the offer with stolen Alliance tech…

The Penumbra had a reputation for ruthlessness. They not only fought outside the box, they didn't even acknowledge the damn box existed. Tor must have promised them the world—in this case, free run of the Frontier—to join up with him. If he was trying to build an unstoppable army, the Penumbra were a damn good place to start recruiting berserkers.

From her reaction, Crosscut clearly knew who Tor was.

"You better explain yourself," Crosscut said.

So Gus did. Right up to where she'd managed to outwit —barely—the smart missile programmed to kill her and only her by detaching the metal plate that held the magnets on the bottom of her armor's left boot from the rest of the armor.

"Son of a bitch," Crosscut said when Gus was through. "Son of a skudging *bitch!*"

She looked sick. Her dark skin had paled considerably, and it wasn't because of a problem with the viewscreen.

"They'll be coming back," Gus said. "Maybe not right away. I imagine once the Penumbra realize they've lost three of their baby ships plus a cruiser trying to take the singularium from you, they're going to have some strong words with Tor. But he'll send them back, probably more of them and with better weapons this time."

Like the dark matter cannon Tor had supplied the guerillas on Shepard's Moon with. The Penumbra's cruiser had been equipped with a contained singularity drive. The crazy bastards clearly weren't above using unstable technology if they thought it would give them an advantage in a fight.

"If you don't have some help defending this thing when the pirates come back," Gus said, "you're not even going to be a smudge of a memory when they're done with you." She leaned toward the viewscreen herself. "You know that. You know I'm right."

Crosscut snorted again, but this time it had a tinge of desperation to it.

"I'm not going to just cut and run," she said. "Not on your say-so." She lifted her chin and stabbed at the screen again with her cigar. "I'd rather go down fighting than give up my claim."

Spoken like a warrior. Or an idiot. Crosscut was definitely someone Gus could be friends with.

"We're not asking you to give up your claim," Drake said. "Just part with a little bit of it. For a fair price."

"You're just a smuggler," Crosscut said to Drake. "Why do you want it?" Then she nodded at Gus. "Your armor's already plated with it. You going to plate that old wreck Mephisto calls a ship?"

It was the first time she'd asked why they wanted the singularium. Giving her a bullshit answer now wouldn't cut it.

"We're going after Tor," Gus said.

Crosscut's eyebrows rose halfway up her forehead. "Why?" she asked. "You have a death wish or something?"

Why? Good question, and one answer Gus wasn't willing to share. Not with Crosscut, no matter how much she was actually starting to like this woman.

"It's personal," Gus said. "For both of us. Let's just leave it at that."

Crosscut was silent for a moment. She took a couple of puffs on her cigar, then looked off to the side like she was having an argument with herself that she didn't want them to see.

When she finally turned back at the viewscreen, she said, "I'll accept your last offer, provided it's legit and I can verify you have the funds you say you do."

Gus started to breathe a sigh of relief. They had the funds, all right, but Crosscut wasn't done.

"On one condition," Crosscut said. "If the Penumbra are coming back like you say, if they're Tor's… what do you military types call it? His vanguard? I'm going to need some help defending my claim. That's part of the deal."

Gus shared a look with Drake. They hadn't planned on sticking around. Then again, they hadn't planned on Tor drafting pirates like the Penumbra to fight on his behalf.

They'd planned on taking the singularium back to Buddy's Bluff and using the trading post as a temporary headquarters. They'd hoped that Bruce O'Connor, the AI's namesake and current boss of the Fluke Off Trading Post, would help them locate Tor, track his movements, and among the three of them (four, counting Bruce the AI), they could come up with some sort of strategy to defeat Tor once and for all.

Okay, it wasn't a fully fleshed-out plan, but it had been the start of a plan.

Only it looked like Tor had beaten *them* to the punch. He'd already started to recruit an army.

They couldn't tell Crosscut she was on her own. They needed the singularium, and besides, Gus didn't like the idea of leaving Crosscut basically defenseless. Gus hadn't been an armor jock most of her life just to cut and run at the prospect of a fight.

"We'll protect you," Gus said.

Drake twanged out a discordant note on the guitar. He might as well have said *what the hell?* but Gus ignored him.

"You?" Crosscut said, clearly incredulous. "You two." She snorted. "You and what army?"

Now *that* was a damn good question.

CHAPTER 8

Earl Knox wasn't a man to take defeat lightly.

He wasn't the kind of man to take defeat at all.

Armor jocks didn't go into battle expecting to lose. Armor jocks expected to kick the ever-lovin' *skudge* out of anybody who dared find themselves on the receiving end of a few tons of well-armed, man-shaped steel with a pissed-off berserker inside who had nothing but *kill, kill, KILL!* on the brain.

Temperament had given him that killer instinct. The Alliance military had honed that instinct and taught him the skills to back it up. The 83rd Armor Division had given him a home.

Then a blast from a dark-matter cannon had shredded his armor like paper, taking most of his leg with it and leaving him with the kind of scars even enhancement surgery couldn't completely fix.

The Division's medics had patched him up on the battlefield, saving what was left of his leg and stitching up the worst of the wounds on the rest of his body. They'd done the best they could with the jagged slash that ran down the side of his face from just below his hairline to beneath his jawline.

Back at Division headquarters, medical staff had taken one look at the battlefield repair job and recommended he have the entire leg replaced. He told them what to go do with themselves, and it hadn't been a polite suggestion. He wouldn't let them fix the jagged scar on his face either. He liked it. The healing scar made him look badass. It made him look like a killer.

So the doctors had augmented what was left of his leg with mechanical parts and implants that worked *almost* as good as the original bits and pieces.

"There you go, asshole," the last doctor he saw told him. "I'm a doctor, not a damn mechanic. Just remember this was your choice."

Earl had flipped him off.

Rehabbing the leg had been a cast-iron bitch. Earl put in more time at the gym than he had since he'd been a trainee just getting the mechanics to work with his remaining muscles. Six months he'd spent, exceeding every goal set by his torturers, aka the physical therapists. Always, *always*, with an eye toward climbing back inside a suit of armor and getting back in the game. The ever-lovin' game of blowing away the bad guys. Whoever the Alliance decided the bad guys were this time around. He'd even kept his armor's damaged helmet in his quarters as a reminder of what he was working so damn hard for.

Except when he was done with physical therapy, when

he'd worked his body into the best physical shape he'd been in since his cadet days, the Armor Division's review board said thanks, but no thanks.

"We don't let machines run machines," the commander himself told Earl when he appealed the board's decision. "Take your disability pension and your discharge and get the *skudge* out of my sight."

Disability pension. What a joke.

Earl had almost, *almost,* thrown the money back in the bastard's face. He wasn't disabled, dammit. He was *better* than he'd been before. His rebuilt leg was stronger than the original, couldn't they see that?

But one thing Earl Knox had never been was stupid. He took his helmet and he took the money and kissed the military goodbye.

The pension wasn't enough to live on for the rest of his life, not if a person really wanted to *live,* not just exist. He'd still been a young man, not even forty. He had decades—*decades*—of life left. Not even a hint of gray in his hair, unlike that damn *female* armor jock Gus Light, the skudging *hero* of the 83rd. She'd been the only trainee in his cadet class who'd ever bested him, even when he'd deliberately screwed with her just to watch her fail. Except she never had.

That dark-matter cannon should have taken *her* out. It would have but her squad had been on the other side of the battle, attacking the enemy's flank. He couldn't even blame her for his bad luck.

Instead, he'd used her as motivation. All those long hard months, the hours upon hours upon skudging *hours* of grueling, exhausting, excruciating physical training to get himself in shape. He'd imagined her staring at him with that annoying smirk she wore whenever the 83rd had down time and she was smack in the middle of some card game, so sure she had the winning hand. Or when she took one of the other members of their squad to her quarters for a tangle between the sheets.

She never took him to her quarters. Never would. She'd made that abundantly clear often enough. Even before she'd taken up with her squadron's commander.

He supposed he should have felt sorry for her, what with what happened to her on Shepard's Moon. He'd only heard about it later. When Tor fled the planet, Earl had been one of the 83rd Tor had taken with him for "protection" when the weaselly bastard ran away from the fighting like the coward he was. With the threat of a dishonorable discharge hanging over their heads if they disobeyed Tor, Earl and the rest of his squadron had been forced to stay silent while Tor told the Alliance that the planet's governor had double-crossed the Alliance. That the planet's governor had sabotaged the negotiations, ordered his troops to kill the rest of the 83rd's armor jocks still on the planet, and Tor had only just managed to escape with his life.

Lies. All lies.

Earl might not have liked all of his commanders. Hell, he might have hated some of them, especially a few of his instructors, with the heat of a thousand burning stars, but he'd respected them because they'd always dealt straight with him. Tor was a fucking politician. Politicians didn't deal straight with anybody.

Well, Earl was a skudging armor jock. He knew how to take care of someone like Tor.

He'd followed the bastard when Tor left the hold of the squadron's transport ship after Tor had finished his call. None of the rest of the armor jocks followed. They'd been too devastated by the "news" that the rest of the 83rd were dead.

Earl knew at least one remaining member of the 83rd still on the planet wasn't dead. Gus had been in the hospital giving birth when Tor ordered Earl's squadron to evacuate the planet. Even giving birth, Gus would have killed anyone who tried to take her out. She was a royal pain in his ass, but she was every bit the berserker he was. The planet's troops were no match for Gus Light.

Earl had grabbed the bastard by his scrawny neck and slammed him up against the transport's bulkhead.

"Give me one reason why I shouldn't kill you right now," Earl had said, his face a hair's breadth from Tor's and his voice a low, ominous growl. "You had us abandon our comrades down there. That ain't something I'm gonna let you shove down my throat till I choke on it."

Tor's face had gone an alarming shade of scarlet. "I'm in charge," he said, just managing to wheeze out the words. "You do as I say. Back *OFF!*"

Earl hadn't. He'd lifted the skudge-hole up, sliding his body against the bulkhead until his feet were dangling above the floor.

Tor hammered his feet against the metal wall. He tried to kick Earl, but he couldn't get enough muscle into the kicks to do any damage.

"Give me a reason," Earl said again. "Because I'd really like to choke the ever-loving shit out of you right now."

Tor's face was turning beet red as deadly gases built up

in all that blood trapped in his head. His ears were probably ringing and his vision was most likely starting to go dark, but he managed to get one word out.

"Money."

Now that was interesting.

Earl let up on the pressure just enough that Tor's face lost that strangled look. "How much?"

Incredibly, a smile played at the corners of Tor's mouth. "A lot," he said. "More than you'd earn in a thousand tours of duty."

Earl almost whistled. That was a hell of a lot of money.

"I want a downpayment," he said. "Paid into my account. Now."

He had a few different accounts not only on planets in the Free Worlds Alliance but some on a few of the more stable worlds in the Frontier. He thought of those accounts as his *things go tits-up* accounts. He gave Tor information for one of his *tits-up* accounts.

Tor's eyes glazed over. He must have had some kind of internal communications abilities, because a few seconds later, Earl's personal comm unit pinged. Incoming message.

Earl let Tor slide back down the wall just until his toes touched the ground, but still kept one hand wrapped around the man's throat. With his free hand, Earl looked at his comm unit.

More money than he'd seen in months had just been transferred into his account. He immediately moved it to another *tits-up* account.

"I expect that amount every week," Earl said.

When Tor nodded, Earl had let the man go.

Only Earl hadn't gotten any more money out of Jorritz

Tor. Gus Light, the damn Gray Lady, had gotten up out of her hospital bed, rallied the rest of her squadron (who hadn't been killed, imagine that), kicked ass, and then commandeered a ship to blast off the planet just so she could tell the Alliance what Tor had done. Tor had taken one of the transport's escape pods and fled.

Bye-bye, easy payday.

A few years later, Earl had been hit by that dark-matter cannon blast.

Bye-bye to the nice military paycheck he'd been freely spending all those years.

By that time Tor had become the Alliance's number one enemy of the state. Earl sure as hell wasn't going to tell anybody in any official capacity that he'd extorted money from a wanted criminal just to keep quiet. He'd sat on that money—or most of that money—for a long, long time after he's been shitcanned on a skudging *disability* pension, only dipping in now and then for enough to buy or replicate all the components necessary to build his own suit of armor. He'd even repaired his old helmet, leaving only a crack in the faceplate as a way to throw off the amateur armor jocks he fought on various worlds in the Frontier.

Over the years, and after too many fights to count, Earl's half-mechanical leg had started to give him grief. He developed a limp that he deliberately exaggerated before every fight. Between the limp and the crack in his armor's faceplate, opponents thought Earl was an easy mark. They soon learned otherwise.

Everywhere he went, Earl was always on the lookout for Tor.

The way Earl figured it, the man owed him a hell of a lot

of money. Earl wasn't somebody who'd let a little thing like that slide.

He'd made a pretty good living on the fighting circuit until he'd had the misfortune to come to Buddy's Bluff right before the Fluke showed up. Word about the Fluke got around, and amateur armor jocks looking for a fight avoided the place like the plague, especially after Buddy Senior got vaporized along with about half the population of the largest settlement on Buddy's Bluff.

Buddy Junior got paranoid after that, not that anybody could blame him. He took over Senior's trading post, a business that thrived on selling pretty much any firearm in existence to whoever had the cash to pay for it. Buddy turned what the locals had started calling the Fluke Off into a damn bunker. He hired security guards—Earl among them—to police the place, and put well-camouflaged automatic laser weapons in place to take out anyone the human security guards missed.

The days of easy living on Buddy's Bluff were over. So was Earl's career as an armor jock fighter.

Until Gus Light and her new tangle-between-the-sheets buddy Mephistopheles Drake showed up. (And what the hell kind of a name was *Mephistopheles* anyway?) Gus's fortuitous appearance had given Earl something he'd wanted ever since he'd been shitcanned from the military: a chance to wipe the ground with an honest-to-god armor jock.

A chance to show that he was just as good as he'd ever been. Hell, that he was *better* than he'd ever been.

Except that hadn't worked out so well. Turned out Gus had stolen her own armor when *she'd* been shitcanned from the military, only she'd enhanced the thing with stuff Earl had never even considered. She'd ended up wiping the ground with *him*, almost drowning him in the ocean until he'd finally conceded the fight just to save his own skin.

She'd not only humiliated him, she'd forced him to pay for every stinking thing on the shopping list she and Drake had come to Buddy's Bluff to buy.

They'd had one damn long list.

Paying for all that crap had wiped Earl out. More than wiped Earl out. He'd had to part with the rest of the singularium he'd managed to con a smuggler named Layla Crosscut out of, and it still hadn't been enough to settle up his bill with Buddy Junior, who'd decided somewhere along the way that he'd rather be known as Bruce O'Connor.

Even though the Fluke were gone now, thanks to the entertaining fight Earl and Gus had staged just for them, he had basically come out of the whole thing an indentured servant to the damn kid. You'd think Bruce would have been grateful for Earl's part in getting the Fluke to leave without vaporizing anyone else, but no.

Equivalent exchange, the kid had said.

Debts must be paid, the kid had said.

As if the singularium Earl had given up wasn't worth enough to clear up any debt Earl would owe the kid for the rest of his skudging life.

The problem was the security guards the kid had hired took the kid's side. Even though they'd worked with Earl for years, they let him know point blank that he wouldn't be leaving Buddy's Bluff until he'd worked off his debt.

So now Earl was stuck doing whatever demeaning jobs the kid needed done. Jobs that *didn't* involve handling any sort of firearm, which made *no sense whatsoever* considering the trading post's stock in trade was pretty much anything anyone could use to kill something else. Today he was mucking out every bit of the stinking mud customers were tracking onto the showroom floor. Considering it was the rainy season on Buddy's Bluff, that was a whole lot of stinking mud. Something a bot could handle, but all the bots in the post were for sale, not for doing menial jobs that Bruce could tell Earl to do.

Gus Light would laugh her ass off if she could see him now. He could just imagine the smirk on her face. She might even call him *Early*. He'd hated that, the same way she'd hated the moniker *Gray Lady*, which he'd thought was pretty clever when he'd come up with it, back in their trainee days.

At least he'd only gone gray a couple of years ago. She'd had gray hair ever since he'd known her. He thought his gray hair and the gray that had infiltrated his dark beard made him look dangerous. Especially since the older he got, the more the jagged scar on the side of his face seemed to sink into his skin. Hell, give him the right kind of clothes, he might even be able to pass as a pirate.

Not that he'd ever thought about joining up with one of the pirate clans. He'd spent too many years with the 83rd kicking those murdering bastards' collective asses to even think about going pirate. He might be a lot of things, but he'd never taken advantage of the innocent. He'd only razzed Gus in their training days because he figured she'd signed up for the abuse just by joining the military's armor division. He'd gone after Tor, but Tor wouldn't know innocent if it reached up and bit him in the ass.

If only he'd be able to win his fight with Gus. He'd own her armor now. He'd wanted bragging rights, but the real prize had been her armor. With her armor and all the money he'd still have in his accounts, he could have written his own ticket in the Frontier. Win every damn fight he got into without even half trying. Rake in the winnings and use the money to hop from world to world, always on the lookout for Tor.

And when he finally found the lying bastard?

Earl could show him what a blast to the chest from an armor jock's augmented armor *really* felt like.

He was daydreaming about all the ways he could sever Tor's limbs from his body when one of the little kids Bruce employed as a messenger came to get him.

"You got a comm," the kid said. "Mr. Bruce sent me to fetch you."

Fetch you. Like Earl was a damn dog.

"Who's on the comm?" Earl asked.

The kid shrugged his skinny shoulders. Bruce had taken in a few of the kids who'd been orphaned when the Fluke vaporized their parents. Sure, Bruce had the kids "working" running errands that could be handled just as easily by bots or secure comm links, but no... Bruce showed those kids compassion. But for Earl? Equivalent skudging exchange.

Earl put down his cleaning tools and followed the kid to the Bluff's secure communications room. Buddy Senior had set it up long ago, right before the Fluke had shown up. The room itself was buried deep in the mud. Permacrete walls kept most of the moisture out, though the walls were getting discolored around the edges where lines ran up through the mud to the outdoor antennae. Those antennae were permanently surrounded by holo-images that made them look like just more trees in the forest that surrounded the trading post.

The moisture must be getting into the lines as well. The image on the viewscreen the kid pointed Earl to was marred with electronic interference.

He had no idea who might be calling him. Layla Crosscut maybe? Nobody else even knew he was here, or would have cared even if they had. He and Crosscut had engaged in a few enthusiastic tangles between the sheets when she'd been here. That had been some of the best sex he'd had in a long time, and he wouldn't mind repeating that experience again.

Remembering that encounter put a smile on his face. He slipped on an ancient set of headphones—where the hell had Buddy Senior gotten these things? A museum?—and logged into the comm station.

The viewscreen responded with a burst of static. He cursed under his breath and leaned forward, like he was trying to see between the lines of interference. Whoever was on the other end of the communication, they must have been calling from a long way away.

"Layla, is that you?" Earl said.

He was rewarded with a chuckle that he knew only too well. His good mood evaporated.

"Hey, Early," Gus Light said.

Of all the skudging people in the galaxy…

He was about to punch in the command to end the call when her next words stopped him cold.

"How would you like to help me put together an army?" she asked. "We're gonna go after Jorritz Tor."

CHAPTER 9

The bar on Buddy's Bluff didn't feel like a war council to Drake...but maybe it was better that way. Maybe, just maybe, he and the others would come up with better ideas in a relaxed atmosphere instead of one that intensified their feelings of being stressed out.

Not that the specter of the coming conflict and the high stakes involved wouldn't hover over them all no matter how and where they met.

On his way to the corner booth where the group had gathered, Drake let an easygoing grin drift onto his face. The purpose of the meeting was dead serious, but he knew from experience that his laid-back space cowboy persona could keep things from getting *too* dark. It was better to appear confident and unruffled than shaken and hopeless, no matter how extreme the odds against them might be.

"Greetings, Drake." Bruce, the current boss of Buddy's

Bluff, raised a tall, thin glass of some kind of milky liquid in a kind of salute. "Where's your better half?"

Drake hiked a thumb over his shoulder. "On her way." Gus had been delayed back at the *Void*, as a call she'd been making had taken longer than expected. It would be worth it in the end, though, if it led to the kind of breakthrough she expected.

"She better get here soon." Earl Knox checked his wrist chronometer. "I don't have all morning to sit here waiting."

"Sure you do." Bruce sipped his drink. "I gave you the morning off, remember?"

Earl grunted and reached for the mug of amber beer on the table in front of him.

For the umpteenth time, Drake wondered how working with the guy was going to work out, given his attitude and the history between them. Gus seemed to think she could handle him, that his help would bring value to the war effort...but Drake had his doubts. He'd been amazed the man had even given Gus's proposal the time of day. She'd said Earl had good reason to hate Tor more than he hated her, but she hadn't elaborated.

"Hate's a damn fine motivator for men like Earl," she'd said. "We give him a reason to go along for the ride, he'll play nice."

"What about after the ride's over, darlin'?" Drake had asked.

She'd given him a quick kiss. "Guess we'll ride that buckin' bronco when we get to it."

Looking into those beady eyes on that scarred face sitting across the table from him now felt like staring into the reptilian gaze of a poisonous snake that was just waiting to leap up and sink its fangs into you.

"Congratulations, by the way," said Bruce. "Great work bringing back all that salvaged singularium from Crosscut's claim."

Drake nodded. "Thanks."

He and Gus had returned to the Bluff less than a day ago from fighting the pirates alongside Layla, and the singularium they'd bought was already being put to use. They'd given Bruce a heads-up to let him know they were on their way. The kid had prepped well. His mechs and techs were already turning the singularium into weapons casings and armor plating for the ships they planned to fly against Tor. Now all they had to do was *find* the ships to make the most of the metal, other than the *Golden Void* and Bruce's single escape launch that wasn't cut out for battle.

It would be a daunting task…though *every* task they faced in the runup to taking on Tor would likely have about the same high level of difficulty.

"So listen." Bruce tossed back the rest of his drink and banged the glass down on the table. "We need to pick up the pace. Jorritz Tor is on the move."

"No kidding," said Drake. "We know he's been giving the Penumbra pirates their marching orders."

"According to my sources, the Celestilons and the Order of Slaughter have fallen in line, too," said Bruce. "That gives him a big slice of the Frontier systems right there."

The Frontier pirates, especially the ones in this sector, had always given themselves fanciful names. It made Drake wonder what Tor planned on calling his new Empire. What positions of power he'd promised all those pirates in exchange for their loyalty.

Exactly how much he was *paying* them for their loyalty.

In Drake's experience, pirates were loyal to their own clans and that was it. He'd avoided doing any kind of smuggling for any of the clans. They'd turn on you as soon as look at you. You relied on them to keep up their end of a deal to your own detriment. If Tor gave the pirates too much power in his new empire, they just might take it into their greedy, power-hungry heads to turn on him.

Yet the Penumbra had sacrificed four of their ships to go after the singularium for Tor. Would they have followed through on whatever bargain Tor thought he had with them? Or would they have kept the singularium and that derelict ring ship all for themselves?

Good questions. Guess they'd find out when the army he and Gus were putting together—their *potential* army—went back to defend Layla like he and Gus had promised.

Gus hoped to cut Tor off at the knees before he got that far. From the sound of things, there might not be enough time to do that.

"Next thing you know, his forces will be knocking on the Alliance's front door." Drake shook his head. "He's wasting no time, is he?"

"No, he is not." Bruce looked grim. "It makes me wonder if someone might be feeding him inside information on our operations...if that could be why he's choosing to ramp up his forces now."

"Maybe." Drake fished a shelled peanut from a bowl on the table and popped it in his mouth. "Though it wouldn't take much to guess we're planning to take him on after the battle of Chrysallix. Or he might just be getting more excited the closer he gets to making himself emperor of the Alliance or whatever he has in mind."

"My money's on all the above," growled Earl. "That prick's always thinking twelve steps ahead and twenty steps sideways. *And...*" He puffed out his breath in disgust. "I don't think I've *ever* met anyone who wants to be *king* as bad as he does."

"And you've never met anyone who wants to *stop* him as bad as *I* do," said Gus as she banged through the bar's front door and marched up to the table. "That skudge-sucker owes me *big*, and I won't quit until he's paid in *full.*"

Drake raised his glass to her. She was in full warrior mode, which boded well for that conversation she'd just had.

She nodded back. Her eyes were bright with barely banked fury, her jaw set. She was ready for war.

Bruce didn't know her as well. That was pretty clear from the first question out of the kid's mouth. Drake chalked it up to Bruce's age. He was too young and still too inexperienced to have the kind of instinctive smarts his daddy got from all the years he'd run this station.

"Speaking of which, do you bring good news, Augusta?" asked Bruce. "Any updates on your current quest?"

Drake saw her make an effort to dial it down a notch. There'd be plenty of time for her to go all-out berserker mode. It wouldn't do any good to bite the kid's head off now.

"As a matter of fact, I do," she said. "I've got a line on recruits for that private army we've been talking about... fully-vetted, *battle-ready* recruits. Earl and I will meet up with my contact on Depak Station, and she'll take us right to them."

Earl bristled. No one had explained that part of the plan to him. There would have been no need if Gus's call hadn't gone well.

"You and me, Gray Lady?" he asked, his voice a low growl.

"You and me, *Early*," she said. "You got a problem with that?"

She met his snake-eyed gaze. The stare-down was brief. Earl looked away first.

"Sounds like a skudging blast," he said, and took a long swig of his amber beer.

"Excellent." Bruce nodded. "Might you provide additional hints about their point of origin?" he asked Gus.

"Some are gathered in one place, more or less," she said. "A few more are scattered across the quadrant. Going out to get them will take time…but it'll be more than worth it in the end."

Time. Which they might not have.

"We need another ship," said Drake. "Now." And more later, but he didn't say that. One would get them started. "We'll have to divide our forces, or we'll never get this all done fast enough."

Gus flashed him a look then, letting him know she still didn't approve—though they'd both talked it through and knew it was the best way to go. She'd agreed that she and Earl should be the ones to meet with their potential recruits, that it would be better to have the armor jocks present a united front. But she wanted Drake with her. Wanted her space cowboy to watch her back.

Drake had taken it as the supreme compliment it was. But with Tor on the march, gaining power with each passing day, they couldn't afford to drag out their preparations, no matter what it cost them personally. Going their separate ways was a necessary next step if they wanted to defeat Tor, even if it meant being apart during a time of crisis, when they needed each other most.

"While you two were away obtaining the singularium, I've been busy." Bruce cocked an eyebrow and smiled. "I think I've solved our little transportation problem."

"Good to hear," Drake said.

He continued to be impressed by Bruce. The kid might not be able to read Gus well, but that would come with experience. In other areas, though? Bruce was making it a habit to outshine his legendary father, the founder of Buddy's Bluff. Without being asked, he'd addressed a blocker that could have killed their current plans.

"I've also laid the groundwork for our shopping trip," Bruce told him. "Called ahead and let the vendors know we're coming and what we want."

"Great," said Drake. "That gives us a head start."

"For what it's worth." Bruce shrugged. "It seems our financing still hasn't come in as hoped."

Drake's spirits sank. Even in a time of war in defense of freedom, people expected to get paid…and the folks who controlled the purse strings were reluctant to loosen them. Sadly, this would take intervention on his part, as he was the key connection to their primary lender—and their past interactions had not always been smooth.

"Let me see what I can do," he said. "In the meantime, let's see this transportation solution of yours."

The four of them left the bar and took a hovercar across the central compound to the spaceport—a collection of barnlike hangars and a control center and tower clustered around an array of paved landing strips. It was a slow day for whatever reason, with just three spaceworthy vessels parked along the tarmac.

One of those vessels was the *Golden Void*, which was getting some much-needed repairs and maintenance from a small crew in orange jumpsuits. At the moment, the team was focused on the damaged cargo bay airlock, which the Penumbra pirates had made such a mess of.

Seeing how close Gus had come to getting her head blown off when she'd exited the ship through that airlock sent shivers down Drake's spine. They'd been through so much together, the odds stacked so ridiculously high against them, that it seemed like tempting fate to split up now. But it had to be done. It was the right decision. He had to believe that.

He resisted the urge to glance over at Gus, to see how she was reacting to someone else repairing the *Void*. She had a history with the ship. If he was honest with himself, she'd only hired him for that first job *because* of the *Void*, not because she had any faith in him as a pilot. She would have repaired the ship herself following the latest battle, but she'd been too busy assisting with loading the singularium into the ship's already crowded cargo bay.

Now Drake would normally be right there with her. Anywhere else, at any other station, watching a local team working on his ship would have given him a major case of heartburn. But he knew Bruce's people were reliable top-flight mechanics, more than capable of repairing the most extensive damage to any Alliance or Frontier ship.

The hovercar spun past the *Void* and whizzed up to a nearby hangar before gliding to a stop.

"Right this way, please." Bruce waved everyone out of the hovercar and led them to the side door of the hangar, then swung the door open and stepped inside.

As soon as Drake laid his eyes on the ship parked inside, a big grin spread over his face. It was indeed the solution to their "little transportation problem," to say the least.

"She's called the *Scintilla*." Bruce walked over and spread his arms to encompass the towering form of the vessel. "She is literally brand-new, hot out of the shipyards, and equipped with state-of-the-art everything."

"How did you *afford* this?" asked Drake. "Or is it *literally* hot?"

Bruce chuckled. "The transaction was completely legit, I assure you. The seller is a longtime client of mine with a stratospheric tab for goods received. I simply wrote off the debt in exchange for this extraordinary craft."

"'Extraordinary' is right."

Drake whistled softly as he admired the contours of the ship. The thought of piloting her actually gave him a warm feeling and a fluttering *frisson* on the back of his neck.

Though no ship could replace the *Golden Void* in his heart, the *Scintilla* was an absolute beaut—a sleek vessel that looked as modern as the *Void* appeared retro. Instead of the *Void*'s cylindrical, rocketlike appearance, the *Scintilla* resembled a manta ray from the oceans of Earth—its structure flowing outward from a raised central mound into a broad, graceful wing with organic contours from edge to edge. Unlike the weathered, pockmarked hull of the *Void* with all its instrumentation, attachments, and appurtenances, the *Scintilla*'s hull was utterly smooth, its skin an uninterrupted, gleaming black. Unlike the *Void*, which was so clearly the product of human hands and technology, the *Scintilla* looked as if it had just phased in from another universe or plane of existence, constructed by alien lifeforms using technology so strange and advanced it might as well be considered magical to the ape-descended creatures gazing upon it.

When Drake walked over and touched its hull, his fingers tingled, and his heart skipped a beat. As perilous as the times were, a single selfish question pushed its way to the surface of his mind, demanding to be asked.

"When can I get in the saddle?" He knew he sounded like a kid, but he didn't care.

"Easy there, cowboy." Gus stepped up behind him and laid a hand on his shoulder. "You'll get your chance soon enough."

"How do you even *board* the damn thing?" asked Earl as he circled the ship. "There's no skudgin' *door*."

"It's...interesting," said Bruce. "A kind of adaptive shifting tech that changes form and properties at the subatomic level in response to telepathically transmitted thought engrams. The designers call it psiflux engineering."

"Do you fly it with buttons, knobs, and switches?" asked Gus.

"No, you do not," said Bruce. "You just tell it what to do with your mind, and it does it. Though, actually, you probably *could* get it to extrude more traditional control surfaces if necessary. The psiflux systems can alter the ship's internal configuration as well as its external structure."

"I like it."

Drake grinned at his reflection in the polished ebony skin of the *Scintilla*. Was it natural to feel so giddy about a ship you'd just met?

"I was thinking you and I could fly this baby, since I have the most experience with it," said Bruce. "Gus and Earl could take the *Golden Void* on their recruiting mission, since the *Scintilla* isn't rigged for the Gray Lady armor."

"Works for me." Drake stroked the hull again, savoring the tingling in his fingers. "Long as Earl brings 'er back in one piece, good as new."

He wasn't talking only about the *Void*, of course, and he hoped Earl was getting the message.

The other subject of his warning had the beginnings of a scowl on her face. She didn't need him to warn Earl to play nice on her behalf. In fact, she might resent the hell out of it. But Drake had a feeling that wasn't what the scowl was all about.

"Yeah, yeah." Earl sounded as grouchy as ever. "You just worry about roundin' up the *fleet* we need to blow Tor to kingdom come."

"We've got it covered," said Drake, though he wasn't as sure as he sounded. A lot depended on him bringing in the financing, which would require some real sleight of hand.

As always, nothing could be simple. The person with the purse strings in their grip had a history with Drake, and the history wasn't good. She wasn't an ex- of his like Rhapsody on Chrysallix, and she wasn't a raging competitor or customer he'd burned in the course of business. She was something much worse—someone who knew his every quirk and how to hurt him, yet seemingly was immune to being hurt by him in return.

She was his older *sister*, in other words, and he knew she wouldn't be an easy mark. Persephone Lilith Drake never was.

Not for the first time, he wished Gus could be at his side when *that* meeting went down...but it wasn't to be. Fighting men without ships wouldn't do much good in the kind of war they faced, and rounding up an army was a job she had to do without him.

"All right then." Bruce clapped his hands. "I'd say we're about ready to get this show on the road. Let's go get who and what we need to stop Tor from taking over the quadrant."

"Hold on there," said Gus. "We need a little time first to get prepped."

"But the ships are fueled and ready," said Bruce.

Almost ready, Drake mentally amended. It looked like there were still a few repairs underway on the *Void*.

"Didn't we just get done saying how time is running out on us?" Bruce said.

Gus turned a meaningful glare in his direction. There was no way Bruce could misinterpret her expression this time.

"A *few* hours won't make *that* much difference, will it?" she asked. "Give your techs time to wrap up what I just saw they still got going on? Or was all that just busy work for show."

That last was more challenge than question. Something had gotten under her bonnet, that was for sure.

Bruce started to say something she probably wouldn't appreciate, then shrugged. "I guess not."

"Awesome." Smiling a tight little smile, Gus looped her arm around Drake's. "Then this guy and me need to go have one last chat before takeoff. *Don't* we, sweetie?"

Drake had a bad feeling about the tone of her voice, but he went with the flow. "Sure, absolutely. Let's have a chat."

He just hoped *he* would be in one piece by the time they got done.

CHAPTER 10

Drake was unbelievable.

Gus was tempted to lump him together with most of the men she'd met in the military. Always distracted by the shiny new thing, whether that was a ship, a suit of armor, or someone to have a romp between the sheets with.

But she'd never thought Drake was like that. Just look at the *Void* with its old-fashioned knobs, buttons, and switches. The joystick and steering wheel. His antique *guitar*! He even had feather pillows and old-fashioned comforters on his bed.

She thought they were kindred spirits, people who appreciated things that worked, no matter how old they were. Things *and* people.

She'd quit the military because her armor had been declared obsolete. She'd stolen it out from under the military's noses, rescued it from the scrap heap, risking the remaining years of her life cooling her heels in a military prison for theft of government property. All because she still valued what her armor could do, no matter its age.

She thought Drake understood that. Not only understood it but respected her for it.

Yet here he was, drooling with anticipation at getting his hands on that sleek new ship, the *Scintilla*.

Just kick the *Void* to the curb, no problem. Let *Earl* pilot his baby.

Or what Gus had always believed Drake thought of as his baby.

She held onto his arm until the *Void*'s airlock snapped shut behind them. Then she stomped off toward the cargo bay.

"Darlin'?"

She heard Drake calling after her, but she didn't slow down. She was too angry.

He'd actually asked when he could "get in the saddle" of the new ship. One of his favorite old cowboy songs was about getting back in the saddle again. They both knew what that stood for, especially when it came to the two of them.

He was probably expecting to get back in the saddle with her before they left on their respective missions. She'd actually been looking forward to it. Had expected to jump his bones the minute the airlock door shut behind them and they were finally alone.

Now?

Now she just wanted to get the hell out of here.

"Hey!"

He was actually running after her, his boots clanging on the metal deck of the corridor. The *Void* wasn't pretty inside, the walls and deck industrial gray. But she was functional. Hell, she'd saved both their asses more than once. The new ship could probably make itself beautiful inside.

"Excuse me," came Bruce the AI's voice over the speakers embedded in the walls. "But I believe the Captain is trying to get your attention."

"Mind your own business, Bruce," she snapped.

The last thing she wanted was to explain to a teenage AI that Mommy and Daddy were having an adult argument.

Could two adults actually have an argument if one of them didn't know what they were arguing about?

She turned on her heels so fast that Drake almost smacked right into her. She held out an arm to keep him at bay.

"You mind tellin' me what I did to piss you off?" he asked. "Because darlin', it's pretty damn clear you're pissed off."

The look of confusion on his face would have been comical under other circumstances. He really didn't know.

"Can't wait to get your hands on her, can you," she said.

His look of confusion only got worse.

"*Back in the saddle*, I believe you said." She put her hands on her hips. "Ring a bell?"

It took him a minute, then she saw realization dawn. "I was talking about the ship," he said. "I mean, you saw her. Wouldn't you want to see what she can do?"

He was only making it worse.

She shook her head at him in disbelief. "I thought you cared about *this* ship. The way I do, but I guess I was wrong."

"I do," he said. "That's why I'm entrusting her to *you*."

That made her pause.

"And you to her," he added.

"You forgot about Earl," she said. "You're gonna let him fly her."

Drake shook his head, glanced down at the deck, then raised his head to look her straight in the eye. Any trace of his cowboy persona was gone. His eyes were dark, his expression wide open and vulnerable.

"You are the most important person in my life, Augusta Light," he said. "I love you. I don't ever want to let you go. I don't ever want to see you hurt. I know this ship can get you where you're going safe and sound, and I know you'll make sure she gets there and back in one piece. If I could, I wouldn't let you out of my sight, but we can't do that. Not this time. The best thing I can do is give you this ship—give you my *home*—instead of letting you fly off with Earl in a ship that we don't know what it can—or *will*—do if it runs into trouble."

By the time he was done, Gus felt like the biggest fool on the planet, and given that Earl also happened to be on this planet, that was saying something.

"I thought…" She paused, then shook her head. "I love you too, space cowboy. I thought the way you glommed onto that shiny new ship…"

She paused again. This was ridiculous. She never had this kind of trouble expressing herself.

He shrugged. "It's not often I see something like that out here in the Frontier. Doesn't mean I'm looking to trade up." He touched her cheek with a gentle hand. "Not the ship." He drew her in for a soft kiss. "Not you either, my Gray Lady."

She let herself be kissed. If anyone else had *dared* to call her *theirs*, she would have made them sorry they ever even imagined they could own her. But with Drake, it felt right.

When their lips parted, she pulled his head close and leaned her forehead against his. "Right back atcha, my Broken String."

She felt more than saw his smile.

He'd been right. He'd cut through to the heart of the matter. The way he'd talked about the new ship back there, without giving a single thought to the *Void*, made her wonder if he'd feel the same way about some bright shiny new woman. If he'd toss her aside just as easily.

She hadn't even admitted to herself that's what had really pissed her off. She'd really been such a fool.

"So can we get on with the lovemaking now?" he asked. "We got a whole lot of time we'll need to make up for, and if it's all the same to you, I'd like to get started on that."

She laughed. He could always make her laugh.

"Want to start here?" she asked, arching an eyebrow. It wouldn't be the first time they'd had mind-blowing sex in one of the *Void's* corridors.

Of course, that had been before the Fluke had gifted the ship with a sentient AI.

"Excuse me." Bruce the AI's voice came over the speakers again. "I have received a message from someone named Earl Knox wondering, and I quote, 'what the skudge is going on in there?' Shall I respond?"

"Tell him to keep his pantyhose on," Drake said. "We're busy."

"Shall I tell him you and Gus have been arguing?" Bruce asked.

"Sure," Gus said. "Then tell him we're going to engage in a time-honored tradition."

Drake stifled a snort.

"What tradition is that?" Bruce asked.

Gus shared a look with Drake. "Time for the birds 'n bees talk already?"

"Our kid is growin' up," Drake said.

Gus cleared her throat. "Search your database for 'make-up sex' and take your time doing it. We're going to need about an hour of alone time. You understand?"

If an AI could sound embarrassed, Bruce did. "Ah... okay. Understood. One hour. Privacy protocol engaged."

The speakers snapped off with an audible click.

Gus took Drake by the hand. "The hell with hot sex in the corridor," she said. "I want a date with a feather pillow. You game?"

Drake didn't answer. He didn't have to. The way he took off down the corridor toward his quarters, his hand warm and strong in hers, was all the answer she needed.

CHAPTER 11

The *Scintilla* had been cruising through space for hours now, and Drake was still overwhelmed by the pure *perfection* of the experience.

It was everything he'd imagined it would be when he'd first laid eyes on the ship—comfortable, effortless, immersive, even sensual. Nestled in a padded pilot's cradle that he himself had dreamed up—a cradle given shape by the ship's psiflux systems—he felt completely relaxed and in tune with every aspect of the craft.

He navigated with a thought, directing the ship exactly where he wanted it to go, then letting the AI control her course until he saw a need to intervene. He adjusted the climate controls with a thought, scanned surrounding space with a thought, even reshaped the ship's fuselage in real time to make it more astrodynamic with a thought. The whole time, he felt soothed and protected, also *accompanied*

—somehow merged with the ship on every level, deeply connected but not in any way that would leave a mark.

It was one of the most *intimate* things he'd ever experienced…not sexual, not like the closeness he felt with Gus, but still intertwined in the most uplifting and enlightening of ways.

It was, to put it mildly, a dream of a ride, something he'd never really believed was possible until now.

"*Where* did you say you got this ship again?" he asked Bruce—the trader extraordinaire from Buddy's Bluff, not the neurotic AI from the *Golden Void*.

"An indebted customer with a sky-high tab, I already told you," said Bruce, who was reclining nearby in his own personally-designed interface cradle.

"But who *built* it?" Drake knew he sounded a little loopy —a side effect of his union with the *Scintilla*—but he was having too good a time to care.

"I *think* it was built by an Ongoni shipwright outfit, but I'm not sure," explained Bruce. "I didn't ask too many questions about this particular gift horse, you know?"

"So here's a thought." Even as he said it, Drake's ship-immersed consciousness nudged the vessel slightly to avoid a passing comet. "Why don't we just round up a bunch of *these* puppies to serve as our fleet?"

"For one thing, there are only a few in existence, according to the seller…who, granted, could have been exaggerating. Even if we *did* find enough for a fleet, even a *small* fleet, it would cost *several* fortunes…*big* ones. And from what *you* said, coming up with our *first* infusion of cash is going to be hard enough."

"Well, maybe we'll get lucky." Drake grinned as the AI

took *Scintilla* in a long, graceful swoop away from a gravitational anomaly. "Maybe we'll find the money *and* the Ongoni ships, after all. And at least we have *this* one."

Just then, the ship nudged him gently in his cradle. He soon saw the reason why, as a radar image flashed to life on his AR viewer, showing what exactly the *Scintilla* was quickly approaching.

"Planetary system dead ahead." He perused a few specs put up by the ship and nodded. They were heading for familiar territory…familiar to him, at least. "We'll reach Exchequer in just under two hours."

"Great." Bruce shifted position in his recliner. "I guess I better double-check our paperwork then. Don't want the money people to get hung up on some mistake in our financial statements."

"We won't need paperwork," said Drake. "We'll know early on if the answer's yes or no." *And it'll probably be no, so don't get your hopes up.*

The truth was, his older sister, Persephone, was a loan officer on Exchequer, high up the food chain—and he'd be lucky if she'd even agree to meet with him. They hadn't exactly parted on good terms the last time, and he knew she had a passion for holding things against him.

He was just going to have to use some of his ingenuity and charm to help her see things his way. It might help that his cause was just, so the money wouldn't technically benefit him personally. Once he made his case—*if* he got to make his case—she might decide to listen to reason…as long as one thing wasn't true.

As long as she wasn't in league somehow with Jorritz Tor.

It was a worry he hadn't talked about with anyone yet, something he found hard to imagine...but he couldn't dismiss it as a possibility. The only true allegiance upheld by the bankers of Exchequer was to money—money owed, money in hand, and money yet to be made. If an alliance with Tor were deemed profitable enough, and the upside outweighed the downside in their eyes, they would have no real choice by their own financial code but to throw in with the villain and aid his efforts at dominating the quadrant.

In such a situation, would Persephone remain loyal to her bosses and profession? Or would the bond of her blood ties with Drake convince her otherwise, in spite of the rift between them?

So many questions filled Drake's head, and the answers would only be found at their destination. Of course, reaching Exchequer and obtaining those answers could be two very different challenges, depending on how things went.

"Have you signaled them yet?" asked Bruce. "Are they expecting us?"

"Not exactly." Drake watched through the eyes of *Scintilla* as Exchequer slowly grew larger. From a distance, the planet had a silvery hue, shimmering like a coin against the black velvet of the starfield.

Bruce leaned forward, frowning over at him. "You *did* let them know we're coming, didn't you?"

"Nope," said Drake. "I thought it best not to."

"You're kidding, right?" Bruce got up from his recliner, looking pissed. "You *know* we need to arrange visits here in *advance*. We can't just pull up at the biggest, wealthiest banking center in the quadrant *unexpectedly*, can we?"

"Shouldn't be a problem," said Drake. "I've got a connection here, remember?"

"That's all well and good, but…" Bruce paced the gleaming black floor. Though he and Drake were in the ship's control center, every surface in the big, oval room consisted of the same highly-reflective ebony material. "Everything's riding on this. If something goes wrong…"

"Then we get through it." Drake smiled contentedly from his cradle. Was he feeling so good because he knew things would work out or because the ship *wanted* him to feel that good? "We do what it takes."

As he said it, *Scintilla* nudged him, making him aware of an incoming message. He had the ship play it once, just for him, without piping it through the speakers.

"Just got a call from the Exchequer defense grid," he told Bruce. "We need to produce verified credentials and proof of scheduled on-planet activities."

"Or what?"

"Doesn't matter," said Drake. "We've got this covered."

"How do you figure?" Bruce sounded alarmed. "We don't have *any* of that."

"*Scintilla* can handle it," said Drake. "She's already hacked their systems and is in the process of generating everything we need to get through the grid." He chuckled and sat up, stretching to get the blood pumping after so long in the cradle. "Can you *believe* this ship?"

"I *bought* it and I don't believe it," said Bruce. "It's just… I keep hoping it's not too good to be true."

"I hear ya." Drake reached into the pocket of his red-and-black flannel shirt and drew out a stick of foil-wrapped gum. Thinking it over, he was a little surprised at how easily he'd fallen for the *Scintilla* and come to believe in her problem-solving capabilities. Flying the *Golden Void* had required much more self-reliance, hands-on control, and less margin for error, which was just the way he'd always liked it...until now.

Having so much done so easily by barely lifting a finger could breed complacence, leading to danger if he wasn't careful. He resolved to be more alert to that possibility, even as it surprised him that he even needed to warn himself—a self-proclaimed, independent space cowboy—not to give up his self-sufficiency to a high-tech wonder ship.

A wonder ship he hardly even *knew*, at that.

"Well, let's see how it plays out for now." He popped the gum in his mouth and rose from the cradle to get some exercise of his own. "If *Scintilla* gets us inside without getting blown up, we'll still have our hands full with a scrap she can't help with."

Bruce stopped pacing and stared at him with a deeper frown. "Can't your inside connection take care of it?"

"My *sister*, Persephone?" Drake chuckled. "*She's* the one we'll have the *scrap* with."

Bruce's eyes suddenly widened. "You didn't *tell* me she was your *sister*."

"Guess I lost my train of thought." Drake looked around and scratched his head. "Speaking of lost, do you have any idea where that *guitar* of mine went?"

Two hours later, the silvery disk of Exchequer dominated the view ahead…and *Scintilla* slid into orbit around it without complication, intact. The falsified credentials and itinerary did the trick, enabling the ship to slip through the defense grid around the planet without being fired upon or even challenged.

Drake wondered how the *Golden Void* would have fared in the same circumstances. He doubted that Bruce the AI would have managed the same trick with the documentation in quite the same way. Most likely, the solution would have involved some fast talking, fast flying, and perhaps even some fast shooting…though he was sure he could have gotten the *Void* to where it needed to be in the end. It had always worked out like that in the past, anyway.

Still, the ease with which *Scintilla* made it happen this time made the process feel like a vacation for Drake…to the point of raising a new question in his mind. It was one that hadn't occurred to him until now, and for which he didn't have an immediate answer.

Was it possible, after being spoiled by the *Scintilla*, that he might not *want* to go back to his precious *Golden Void*?

For now, though, that question would have to wait. He had more pressing concerns, like figuring out how to reach Persephone now that he and Bruce had made it through the grid.

"What now?" asked Bruce. "Can the *Scintilla* hack in and find us a slip somewhere?"

As Drake pressed his hand against an ebony wall, the ship pushed a progress update into his mind. "She's trying, but it's a tougher lift than bluffing her way through the grid. No luck reserving planetside parking yet."

Bruce rubbed the back of his neck. "I'm guessing we have a limited window of time to get down there. Planetary defense won't just leave us alone in orbit indefinitely."

"You're not wrong about that." Jumpy as a hog in a football factory, Drake again looked around for his guitar. Strumming chords always put him at ease and brought clarity to his thoughts...but the instrument was nowhere in sight. According to *Scintilla*, it couldn't be located, though Drake remembered bringing it aboard along with his small traveling case of belongings.

Was it possible the guitar was some kind of blind spot for the ship? The nexus of a hiccup in its programming? Or was something else happening here, something stranger and potentially more dangerous?

Whatever the cause of the guitar's apparent disappearance, it was something Drake would have to deal with later. Not getting his and Bruce's asses blown up was a higher priority.

"Let's make a call and see what happens." As he said it, Drake initiated the request to *Scintilla*'s comms system. "I'll try Persephone's private number. Should have a better chance of getting through than calling her office number."

"Give it a shot." Bruce sat down at an access station he'd conjured from the ship's substance via psiflux link and waved an arm over the panel in front of him. The gleaming black surface instantly flared to life with abundant multicolored lights, an array of control surfaces he'd designed to match the navigation board on his other, older ship. "I'll get her ready to run if things go sideways."

"Sounds like a plan." Drake closed his eyes, focusing on the faint hum of the ship's comm system as it placed the call he'd requested to Sef's private number. (That was her nickname, though she didn't seem to like it much anymore…at least when it was coming from him.)

The hum continued for a long moment, then paused, then started again. After another moment, it suddenly popped, crackled with static, and shifted into a series of high-pitched, chattering squeals.

"What the *skudge?*" He scowled, pulling his hand away from the wall. The squeals cut out, and he worried that he'd dropped the call…but when he touched the surface again, he heard a male human voice in his mind.

Hello? Who is calling, please?

Drake snapped out a telepathic request, and the ship piped the audio into the control center so Bruce could hear, too.

"This is Captain Mephistopheles Drake of the *Scintilla*," Drake said, confident his voice would hit the control center microphone pickups. "I'm calling for my sister, Persephone Drake, at Exchequer Loan Central."

There was a pause. "You're not on her schedule," said the call handler. "And you're not on her next-of-kin roster, either."

Drake smirked at Bruce and shook his head. *It figures.* "Well, a quick DNA test will confirm my familial relation… but that shouldn't be necessary. I'm sure she neglected to list me on the roster because of an oversight."

"Nevertheless…"

"I assure you, I *am* her brother, and I *do* need to speak with her about a most urgent matter."

"Hmm." The guy on the line paused so long, Drake thought he'd hung up on him. "Perhaps we *can* do something after all. I'm sending you an application for special dispensation due to a family connection."

"Great!" said Drake. "Much obliged, pardner."

"Once you've filled that out and sent along your *bank account* information…"

"Wait, what?" Drake's smile melted into a frown. "Bank account information for what purpose?"

"Remuneration, of course. There's an inconvenience fee for processing a non-prebooked appointment with an Exchequer government official."

"How *much* of a fee?" asked Drake.

"Just 5,000 credits," said the handler. "It's standard."

Drake's blood boiled at the thought of it. He looked at Bruce and saw the same reaction on his face—anger at being ripped off and resignation at realizing they had no choice but to let it happen.

"Can I run a tab, at least?" asked Drake. "I'm good for it."

"No, you cannot," said the handler. "You must pay up front or go away. It's the cost of doing business…though, of course, you are free to take your business elsewhere if you think it will better suit you."

Drake sighed. The guy knew damn well that no place matched Exchequer when it came to financial dealings…or the presence of Drake's sister, whom he'd come there specifically to see. The guy truly had him over a barrel.

"Okay, okay. I'll send over my account info." Drake would just have to pony up, then add the fee to the total amount of the funds he intended to borrow. If things didn't work out as planned with Penny, losing the five grand wouldn't clean him out, though he needed every credit he could cobble together to back the war effort against Tor.

Just then, Bruce got up from his station, folded his hands behind his back, and cleared his throat. "Excuse me. This is Bruce O'Connor, CEO of Buddy's Bluff, a broker of weapons and supplies located in Frontier space. Like Captain Drake, I am here to conduct business...but *unlike* him, this is not the first time I've had dealings with the Exchequer banking establishment."

Pause. "In that case, welcome back, Mr. O'Connor."

"Thank you." Bruce bowed his head slightly, though the video feed wasn't engaged. "Since I already have a history of working with Exchequer, may I suggest waiving the inconvenience fee as a courtesy, in recognition of our past association?"

"Absolutely," said the handler. "You may *suggest* it...but your request cannot be granted."

"Excuse me?" Bruce looked stunned.

"In fact, if there are *two* of you seeking an audience, you must *both* pay a fee of 5,000 credits."

"Are you *kidding* me?" snapped Bruce.

"We await transmission of your account information," said the handler. "At which point, you will receive landing coordinates and additional instructions to facilitate your requested meeting with Ms. Drake."

"Now just wait a minute...," said Bruce.

"Good day, sir," the handler said cheerfully. "And welcome to Exchequer."

With that, the call ended, leaving Drake and Bruce to stare with equally dumbfounded expressions.

"How do you like that?" Drake shook his head in disbelief. "I have to *pay* to meet with my own *sister.*"

"Think she'll refund our fees?" asked Bruce.

"Out of the goodness of her heart? Who knows?" Drake shrugged. "She's not a bad egg...just *difficult.* And to be honest, I've been on the difficult side myself from time to time."

Bruce rubbed his chin thoughtfully. "How would you feel about going in alone? That way, we could at least avoid having to pay *my* fee."

"Actually, Bruce, I'm thinkin' the opposite." Drake grinned. "The way she and I last parted, having somebody else in the room might be *worth* the extra 5K."

"It might help with negotiations?"

Drake chuckled. "It might help with *me* not getting my *ass* kicked."

CHAPTER 12

If Gus had to share the bridge of the *Golden Void* with Earl even just one more minute, she was going to kill him. She wouldn't need her armor to do it. At this point, the thought of wrapping her bare hands around his throat and squeezing until his face turned blue was looking infinitely more appealing than putting on her armor, marching to the bridge, grabbing him by the scruff of his scrawny neck, and booting him out the airlock.

"Would you look at this crap?" Earl said. "Who the hell equips a ship with a skudging *joystick*? And all these damn buttons and knobs? Where's my touch controls? Where's my heads-up display?"

He was sitting in the pilot's chair—Drake's usual station—where he'd been for the last hour. He'd spent all of five minutes perusing the control station before he started bitching. An unending litany of everything wrong with the *Void.*

Not a single thing was right, not according to old Early Knox.

He held up the control station's old-fashioned keyboard. "What am I supposed to do with this thing?"

She sighed. "Think of it as a touch pad," she said. "Only you have to spell out the commands." Or use the shortcut keys, which Earl hadn't been bothered to learn. "You do know how to spell, don't you?"

She couldn't help herself. She'd said that last bit in a sickly-sweet voice to go with the sickly-sweet smile she had to paste on her face.

There was a lot wrong with their current situation, not the least being that Drake wasn't sitting there in his pilot's chair, strumming his antique guitar and singing some old cowboy song. Drake had blasted off from Buddy's Bluff in that shiny new ship, the *Scintilla*, a half hour before the *Void* was declared all repaired and spaceworthy by Bruce Jr.'s mechanics. Instead, she had to put up with Earl and his incessant complaints.

Had he been like this when they'd both served in the 83rd? Or had he just gotten old and cranky?

Earl tossed the keyboard aside with a curse. It landed with a clatter of keys.

The ship gave a sudden lurch to the left that made Gus glad she was sitting at the navigation console instead of pacing back and forth on the bridge to work off her pent-up anger.

The ship's artificial gravity adjusted for the unexpected tilt, and once again Gus felt like she was sitting upright, not leaning at an angle. She glanced at the navigation console. They were still on course.

"What the skudge?" Earl said.

He peered at the buttons and dials on the control station, trying to make sense of what had just happened. It was pretty clear he had no idea what the readings on the dials meant.

Drake always handled this ship like a master conductor controlling every tone and note that his orchestra produced. Earl was bumbling his way through like the armor jock he was.

"You hit a command on the keyboard when you threw it," she said. Probably one Drake had programmed to make the ship do a barrel roll as a way to avoid incoming missiles. "Don't do that again."

Earl swore, this time to himself, as he picked up the keyboard like it was a hot piece of armor and set it down gently in the spot where Drake usually kept it.

"You sure you don't want me to pilot the ship?" Gus asked, again forcing a sweet smile.

"No." Earl glared at her. "And quit looking at me like that. It's giving me the creeps."

"Then quit griping about the ship," she said. "It's a good ship. If you quit fighting it, you'd figure that out."

She got up from the navigation console and flipped one of the switches on the board in front of Earl. The autopilot kicked in, and the ship performed a gentle little roll to the right. Interplanetary spaceflight didn't have an up or down, but the *Void's* autopilot always made the ship right itself, returning to whatever position on the X axis it had started from. Drake had told her that little feature had saved his bacon more than once during an approach to some of the dicier places he'd done business at during his smuggling career.

Earl grumbled when he realized what she'd done. He was still enough of an old armor jock that he hated giving up control to anything automated. But they still had nearly twenty hours—twenty long-ass hours—before they reached Depak Station, and she was more than tired of his bullshit.

The station was about as close to Alliance space as Gus wanted to get, but that's about as far into the Frontier as her contact wanted to go this time. Even traveling at optimal speed, twenty hours was a best-guess estimate. A lot depended on whether they'd have to skirt certain areas to avoid any confrontations with pirate factions loyal to Tor. While Gus had no doubt that between the two of them, she and Earl could kick the crap out of any single pirate ship that crossed their path, on this trip discretion counted more than the ability to kick ass.

She'd hoped that this little trip would be the perfect opportunity for Earl to get used to flying the *Void* on his own. She'd piloted the ship when they blasted off from Buddy's Bluff. She wasn't as good at it as Drake—nobody was better at piloting the *Void* than Drake—but she'd sure as hell been better than Earl was turning out to be.

"I thought you said you could handle this ship," she said.

In point of fact, he'd said he could handle *anything,* and the look he'd given her had made it clear he meant her as well.

As if.

She'd kill him if he tried that too, but she doubted he'd really go for it. Earl had always been more about the bluff and brag than the real thing. Until he was in his armor, that is. He'd been a damn fine armor jock back in the day.

"I hadn't seen these skudging controls then," he said. "If you can call these things controls."

She arched an eyebrow. "Drake seems to manage it just fine."

"*Drake's* a damn anachronism."

That was a big word for Early Knox. "You been reading in your spare time? That doesn't sound like the Earl I remember."

She'd caught herself just in time to prevent herself from actually calling him by his nickname. She'd only given him the nickname after she'd found out that he was the one who'd saddled her with the Gray Lady nickname back when they'd both been in the same cadet training class. They wouldn't get anywhere if they antagonized each other to the point where they were really at each other's throats. She'd told Drake she could work with Earl. It was about time to start doing that.

"I always did read," he said. "Just have a chance to do a little more of that now that you made sure I was stuck in that hellhole on the Bluff."

That surprised her. "*I* made sure?"

"You and your damn *shopping list*," he said.

She snorted. He was talking about the fight they'd staged on the Bluff as a last-ditch effort to make the Fluke leave the planet alone. Earl hadn't stuck to the script. Had, in fact, tried to incapacitate her armor with full-power blasts just to make her lose so he could take her armor for his own.

After she'd held him and his armor—with that cracked

faceplate—underwater until he'd cried uncle, he'd agreed to pay for everything that Gus and Drake had gone to Buddy's Bluff to buy in the first place. Their shopping list had been a damn long list, and she'd been pissed off enough after the fight that she'd added a few extra things just to teach old Early a lesson.

"You made that agreement," she said. "Don't blame me."

"Yeah, well Junior charged me full price for all that shit, no employee discount because he said it wasn't for an employee." Earl rubbed the back of one hand across his mouth like he was trying to wipe a bad taste away. "Wiped me out."

That last bit came out so quietly, Gus had a hard time hearing it. Clearly the admission had been hard for Earl to make.

"Then Junior took the only thing of value I had left," Earl said. "All that singularium he loaded into your ship. Didn't even give me full credit against what I owed him. Said I was lucky that was all he took since I *comported* myself so dishonorably during the fight."

That sounded like Bruce Junior—to a point. He'd told her and Drake that Earl had paid for the singularium. She supposed that from Junior's perspective as a trading post proprietor, reducing Earl's debt was a form of payment.

"I've been working my ass off for Junior to get out of debt, earn enough to get a ship, and get the hell off the Bluff." He spread his hands out wide. "So I finally get a chance. I'm leaving with Junior's blessing and now look at me. I'm on this granny ship. Might as well have brought my knitting on board."

She shook her head. "You don't know much about the *Void*, do you," she said. She didn't have to make it a question.

"That it's a piece of crap?" he said.

The speakers on the bridge crackled with static. "I beg your—" began Bruce the AI.

"Not now, Bruce," Gus said, but of course the AI ignored her.

"Are you arguing with Captain Knox about the value of the *Golden Void*?" Bruce asked. "If so, might I quote some statistics and cite the ship's capabilities so you can kick his ass?"

Kick his ass? Since when had Bruce started swearing? Of course, it wasn't like he didn't hear that kind of language all the time. Especially when Gus had been trying to figure out how the boxy shield generator in the cargo hold, the one she'd taken from Chrysallix, actually worked.

"First thing, he's *not* the captain," she said. "Got that?"

"Yes." Bruce didn't sound contrite. "And the second thing?"

Gus made an effort to keep the frustration she felt out of her voice. Bruce had been uncharacteristically quiet ever since Earl had come on board. Maybe the AI was having daddy issues. She missed Drake too, especially since they couldn't even talk to each other over comms. They'd agreed to have no communication with each other while they were off on their separate missions. Neither one of them wanted Tor to catch wind of what they were up to, and that meant not putting out any communications that could be inter-cepted by the bad guys.

Especially since they didn't know who all the bad guys

ANNIE REED & ROBERT JESCHONEK

were. The way Tor was going, recruiting every pirate faction in the Frontier, he could have spies everywhere.

In theory that decision had made a lot of sense. But now that she was out here, basically trapped in a ship with only Earl and a sentient AI for company, Gus missed Drake so badly it hurt. Especially since every nook and cranny on this ship reminded her of the space cowboy.

"The second thing," she said to the AI, "is that we're not fighting. We're having a disagreement about training."

"Oh. Maybe I can help." Bruce actually sounded excited. "I have detailed training manuals for the *Void* at my disposal. Perhaps a review of the training materials—"

"No, *thank* you," Earl said, sarcasm dripping from the words. "I don't need no AI fancy-pants telling me how to fly a damn ship."

The AI was silent for a moment while static crackled over the speakers.

"Understood," Bruce said finally, his tone clipped and more than a little hurt.

The speakers shut off with a squeal that hurt her ears.

"This ship just keeps getting—" Earl started.

"Watch it," Gus said, cutting him off. "You hurt his feelings."

Earl's eyebrows rose in disbelief. "He's got feelings?"

"He's sentient," she said. "A parting gift from the Fluke. Right now, he's the equivalent of a teenager. A young one. Smart as hell but without a clue about what to do with all these feelings he's suddenly got to deal with. So go easy on him."

He leaned back in the pilot's chair. "A teenager," he said. "And it—"

120

"He," Gus said automatically.

"*He* can fly the ship?"

She snorted. "Who the hell do you think's handling the autopilot?"

She didn't say that Bruce could pilot the *Void* better than Earl. At least if Earl was going to keep fighting the controls the way he'd been so far.

What had Drake said before they left the Bluff? That he was giving the *Void* to her because he knew she'd take care of his baby?

She didn't feel like she was doing such a great job so far.

"Look," she said. "This whole mission's not going to work if we keep banging heads. You need to learn to handle this ship as well as you handle your armor, and you've always been one of the best at that."

He looked startled. "You actually giving me a compliment, Gray Lady?"

She shook her head. "You know you're one of the best," she said. "And *I* knew you were right there dogging my heels. That's part of what made me better. So let's bury the hatchet and both be the best at what we do again."

She held out her hand and waited for him to take it.

"So long as we bury the damn thing in Tor's skull," he said. "That *is* part of the deal, right?"

"That's the plan," she said.

"Then let's be the best at kicking ass."

He took her hand and shook once, hard. His grip was just as strong as she expected, so she gave as good as she got.

He let go with a smirk before the handshake could turn into a contest.

"I ain't learning nothing about this ship from a damn AI," Earl said. "I don't care how fragile his feelings are." He gave Gus a sidelong glance. "You? I'll put up with you teaching me how to fly this thing, so we don't get our asses blown off."

That was a major concession from someone like Early Knox.

"You got it."

She sat down at the comms console next to him. She didn't know all the ins and outs of flying the *Void*, but she figured what she didn't know, she could have Bruce the AI tell her privately. They had twenty hours or so to get Earl up to speed, then the real part of their mission would begin.

A lot was riding on what waited for her at Depak Station. She just hoped twenty hours would be enough time.

CHAPTER 13

When the door to Persephone's office swept open, Drake was surprised at how small the place was.

Knowing her position high up in the Exchequer bureaucracy, he'd expected her to have spectacular digs—expansive office space decorated with high-end furnishings that screamed *wealth* and *power*. He'd imagined her seated at a mahogany desk the size of the *Void*'s bridge, embedded with every luxury and high-tech convenience on the market.

Instead, as he walked into the room, he saw it was almost small enough to qualify as a closet. The décor was nonexistent—no paintings on the walls, no expensive furniture, no chandeliers, not even *carpet*. The walls and ceiling were painted off-white, the floor was a gray, cement-like material, and the big window that dominated one wall was shuttered with white plastic mini-blinds.

As for the desk, which currently had no occupant, it was also plain as could be—just a top, four legs, and a single lap drawer all molded from some kind of ivory composite. The surface itself lacked writing implements, devices, personal artifacts, or any of the other clutter typically found on desks in offices.

The empty chair behind the desk was bare-bones, too. It was little more than a wheeled stool with a round black back support so small it looked unlikely to hold up a normal human's upper body.

All in all, Drake was *not* impressed...and started to worry that Persephone might have fallen from grace without him knowing about it. The truth was, he couldn't even remember the last time they'd spoken, though it had been quite a while ago; being that out of the loop for that long, he might very well have missed out on such life-altering news.

If that was indeed the case, he felt regretful. It took two to tango, and she hadn't made an effort, either, but he had no good excuse for avoiding contact with her for so long.

Hopefully, it wasn't too late to make amends...though of course his plea for war funding would have to take precedence over such interpersonal concerns.

Just as Drake was thinking all this, the door swept open again. Turning, he saw Persephone striding into the room, tall and lean in a slinky red-and-yellow floor-length dress. Her hair, which had been darker and longer before, was silver and cut in a neat bob that emphasized her delicate, symmetrical features and smooth, pale skin.

Drake thought she looked like a finely chiseled marble sculpture—a work of art in a perpetual bad mood. "Hello,

Mephistopheles." She wasn't smiling when she looked in his direction. "What do you want?"

Drake refrained from popping in a stick of gum, though his nerves were crying out for it. "Long time, no see, Sef." He resisted the urge to give her a hug in case it only made things worse between them. "How's tricks?"

"Just wonderful." She smiled at him in a way that left plenty of doubt about her actual intentions. "Couldn't be better, as you can clearly see. How about you, Phisto? Still seizing life by the throat and choking it until it coughs up roses?"

"Just the usual." Drake turned and gestured at Bruce. "This, by the way, is my business associate, Bruce O'Connor."

"Your fellow smuggler, you mean?" Sef smirked as she pushed between them and went around behind the desk to sit down.

"Not a smuggler, actually," said Bruce. "More like an *outfitter*, if you catch my drift. A supplier of provisions to those travelers in need of such things."

"Must be a lucrative field," said Sef as she dropped herself onto the undersized wheeled chair. "For you to fork over the inconvenience fee it took to get in to see me."

Drake opened his mouth to pursue the subject...then thought better of it and changed tracks. "Thanks for agreeing to see us," he told her. "I'm sure you're busy."

"Do I *look* busy?" She spread her arms to encompass the empty desktop.

Drake let the question pass. "We have something urgent to discuss."

"Let me guess." Sef leaned forward and pointed an

index finger at him. "You need *bricks*. Am I right? A big ol' pile of *bricks*."

Drake just stared back at her, uncertain what his next best answer should be.

"Just kiddin'." Sef chuckled and leaned back...then quickly seemed to remember the backrest wouldn't support her and leaned forward again. "You want money. Lots and lots of money. Otherwise, you wouldn't have dragged yourself *in* here after *ignoring* me for years, talking about something *urgent* that's got you up in arms."

"Uh-huh." Drake looked around the room, wishing there was more than one chair in it. Standing there while his sister dressed him down, he felt more like a little brother getting burned than a grown-up space cowboy.

"So what is it you want?" asked Sef. "Not that I can *give* it to you. Not that I have the kind of unlimited juice you seem to *think* I do."

Drake swallowed hard and nodded. Chair or no chair, it was time he got his act together and stopped being Persephone's punching bag. "We need ships," he told her.

Sef shook her head. "It figures." She snorted. "You want a new *ship*. What happened? Did you finally run that *Void* of yours into a black hole somewhere on one of your *smuggling* joy rides?"

"Actually," said Drake, "we need *ships*, plural, to defeat a tyrannical maniac from conquering the entire *Alliance* and the Frontier to boot."

His words seemed to surprise her. The overbearing dismissiveness faded fast, and her smirk shifted into a frown. "You want to stop a tyrant from taking over the quadrant?" Her voice was laced with disbelief…and a note of genuine concern. "Which tyrant?"

Drake hesitated on the verge of showing his cards. If Persephone was already working with the enemy, not only would he and Bruce not get an infusion of cash, but she might tip off Tor about their efforts to oppose him.

Ultimately, though, he decided to put his faith in his sister. "His name is Jorritz Tor," he told her. "He was behind the attempted takeovers of Shepard's Moon and Chrysallix, but he won't stop there. He has big plans, and he's backing them with stolen stockpiles of singularium."

Sef sat there and stared at him for a long moment, then turned her gaze to Bruce. "Is that so? Is that why you need money? For a war chest?"

"It is indeed." Bruce nodded grimly. "If we don't stop Tor, he'll take over the whole shooting match."

"And this isn't just some B.S. con game to line your own pockets?" Sef turned a withering gaze on Drake. "Not that you'd ever *try* something like that, of course."

Drake shook his head firmly. "Not a con. Not a scam. I assure you, Sef, we are 100% on the side of the angels here." As he said it, he continued to hope she wouldn't see *Tor* and his allies as the angels instead of the devils they truly were.

"I don't know." Sef sighed. "You're asking me to *trust* someone who's screwed me over time and again…someone who has always been out for number one. Am I supposed to *forget* all that and just accept that you've miraculously turned over a new leaf, Phisto?"

Though Drake didn't flinch at the mention of her pet nickname for him, he knew she was well aware of how much it irked him. Pulling it out of mothballs was clearly intended to distract him, to knock him off his game long enough to get at his hidden motivation.

Not that he had any intention of letting her get to him that way.

"No," he told her. "I do *not* expect you to forget the past. I don't realistically expect you to completely trust me, either. What I *do* want is financial support for this fight we're about to embark on...specifically, the funding for a fleet of warships to take on Tor's private armada. Without those ships, we don't stand a chance of preventing the takeover of the Alliance."

"Well, well, well." Was that a flash of suspicion in her narrowed eyes? A flicker of betrayal in the making? "If I didn't know any better, I'd say you're sincerely committed to a worthwhile cause."

"No offense," said Drake, "but I probably wouldn't be here if I wasn't."

"None taken." Sef tipped her head to one side and watched him appraisingly from the corner of one pale blue eye. "Maybe people can change, after all. *I* certainly have."

"How so?" asked Drake.

Sef's only answer was to rise from her desk and touch the tummy of her dress. Instantly, the silky red-and-yellow material transformed, flowing into multiple pieces of attire —a black mock hoodie under an olive drab utility vest, olive drab khaki cargo pants, black combat boots, and an all-black baseball cap. Drake thought she looked like some kind of outdoorswoman...either that, or an urban guerilla.

"When do we leave?" she asked as she circled the desk. "I need to call my assistant and bring her up to speed."

"'We?'" Drake frowned.

"The three of us, yes," said Sef. "Assuming you *are* planning to shop for a fleet after this meeting."

"I don't understand," said Drake. "There's no need for you to go *with* us."

Smiling grimly, she planted her hands on her hips. "Yes, there damn well *is*, if you want funding. You don't expect the Bank of Exchequer to loan you *that* much money for *such* a risky venture without a bank official along to *assess* the investment, do you?"

"Why the skudge not?" blurted Drake.

At that point, Bruce flung up a hand to signal his silence. Drake's eyes flared with anger at being cut off, but Bruce matched his challenge with a look of firm insistence.

Then, he turned to Sef and bowed his head. "First of all, *thank you* for considering our request," he said. "We appreciate your interest in this opportunity."

Sef nodded. "I can't promise anything, of course…but I *am* authorized to act on behalf of Exchequer to write loans in real time in the field if I determine a need is valid."

"Excellent," said Bruce. "That will significantly expedite any approved purchases."

Sef smiled thinly. "I'm glad you understand the situation, Mr. O'Connor."

"Of course," said Bruce. "And my colleague and I will be most happy to have you along…as long as *you* understand the *physical* risks involved in this buying trip. Specifically, we will be visiting locations that entail a certain amount of danger to life and limb. We will do everything in our power to protect you, but negative outcomes may occur in spite of our best efforts."

"Understood," said Sef. "Conversely, I hope you and your colleague understand that if a negative outcome impacts my health and well-being, an even *more* negative outcome may impact *you*, courtesy of Exchequer's military establishment."

"Are you *threatening* us?" snapped Drake. "What the *skudge* is *wrong* with you, you…"

Again, Bruce interrupted before he could go too far. "Please excuse my colleague," he said. "Of course we understand the implications you've described."

"Fantastic!" Sef clapped her hands together approvingly. "We're all set, then." With that, she marched between Drake and Bruce, heading for the door. "Let's meet at your vessel's slip in…forty-five minutes? Will that be sufficient for preflight checks and preparations?"

"Perfect," said Bruce. "See you then!"

Without another word, she strode through the exit, leaving the door to rush shut behind her.

"This is *bad*," said Drake when he and Bruce were alone again. "*Really* bad."

"I've dealt with these people before in a business capacity," said Bruce. "Trust me, this is the only way forward."

Drake slowly shook his head. "You don't *know*. You just don't *know*. She will make our lives as *miserable* as possible, and then she won't give us the loan *anyway*."

Bruce shrugged. "She sounded favorable to me."

"It's all about lulling us into a false sense of security," said Drake. "Then *BAM!* She *crushes* you, and you don't even see it *coming*."

"She said she's changed, didn't she?"

"But she didn't say *how,*" snapped Drake. "What if she's even *worse* than I remember?"

"Then you'd better get ready to *manage* her," said Bruce. "Because given the time we have and the stakes on the table, *she* is by far our *best bet.* Hell, she's our *only bet.*"

"She and I just don't get along. We never *have.* We're *oil* and *water.*"

Bruce stepped up to the door, and it promptly slid open. "You want to hand over the quadrant to that piece of *skudge* Jorritz Tor?"

Drake scowled. "Of course I don't."

"Then you'd *better* find a way to work things out with your sister," said Bruce as he headed out into the corridor.

An hour and change later, the *Scintilla* had lifted off from Exchequer and was on its way toward its next destination… one person heavier than when it had first arrived.

Though Drake could have left the ship on autopilot and wandered through it as he liked, he chose to stay in the pilot's cradle and make sure the start of the journey went off without a hitch. He also preferred to hunker down there instead of risking running into Sef, who still had him worried and off-balance.

Unfortunately for him, hiding in the cradle wasn't enough to keep her away. Even as he stayed focused on the ship's status and evolving course, Sef appeared above him, smiling and waving and looking perfectly innocent.

"Nice ship, bro," she told him. "I've been looking around some, and she's impressive!"

"Thanks." Drake's attention was now split between staying on course and trying not to piss off Sef. "Bruce bought her to lead the fleet against Tor."

"Where's *your* ship, the *Golden Void?* In drydock somewhere?"

"My partner, Gus, is flyin' her," he explained. "Going out to do some recruiting for the war effort."

"Gus, huh? Is he one of your smuggling buddies, or what?"

"Actually, 'she' isn't a smuggler at all," he told her. "She's a not-so-retired armor jock. We fought together to liberate Shepard's Moon a while back."

"Right, I heard about that, though I didn't know *you* were involved at the time," said Sef. "Quite a dust-up, as I recall."

"You could say that." He dove deep into *Scintilla's* sensor web for a moment, sifting through data on an approaching celestial object—a comet that was streaking sidelong toward the ship. A few minor tweaks to the course, and the ship's path took it far from the comet, ensuring it wouldn't collide.

"You also mentioned fighting a takeover on Chrysallix," continued Sef. "Was Gus with you there, too?"

He nodded. "She was." Even as he answered, he wished the game of Twenty Questions were over, so he could concentrate better on piloting and not have to keep dealing with Sef.

"Is it safe to say, then, that you're getting pretty *serious* about this Gus woman?" she asked. "Have you bought her a *ring* yet?"

Instead of answering, he chose a path of deflection. "How are things going these days with Rawdog Solomon? Did you two get over that rough spot with the cryptocurrency scandal and the women coming forward and all?"

Sef's smirk shifted into a stone-cold glare. Her time of toying with him was over, now that he'd crossed her primary red line. "You have *no* right to ask those questions," she said, her voice a snarl. "You've shown *zero* concern for *any* of the complications that have upended my life over the past few years."

"Because *you* didn't want me involved in *your* personal business. You made that *very* clear."

"Only because of what happened on *Gimlet* years ago," she told him. "What person in their right *mind* would ever *trust* you after *that?*"

He lay there in the cradle for a long moment, considering her words…and what he'd done to bring them about. Unfortunately, she wasn't entirely wrong, though she'd never learned the whole truth behind the story.

"Listen." He sat up in the cradle, forcing her to step back. "What happened back then…there was more to it."

Angrily, she slashed a hand through the air. "Whatever *skudge* you're cooking up to smooth things over, keep it to yourself! It's just *too late*, Mephistopheles."

Drake shook his head. "It's never too late. I'm a different man these days, Sef. A *better* man. I'm working hard to make up for the mistakes I've made."

"Does Gus know about those?" asked Sef. "*All* of them?"

Drake didn't answer.

"I didn't think so." She laughed bitterly. "Tell her *every-thing*, and then let's see if your relationship turns out so much better than the one I had with Rawdog."

With that, she turned on her heel and started for the exit...only to stop in her tracks when he called out. "Wait!"

She turned one ear to her shoulder, to him, without fully turning to face him.

"This fight with Jorritz Tor is an honorable cause," he told her. "Even if you don't believe another word I say, believe that. If he isn't stopped, and soon, he will remake this quadrant into something awful in every way."

Sef didn't respond but didn't resume her exit, either.

"Multitudes will suffer and be slaughtered," continued Drake. "Freedom and liberty will be extinguished. Anything that doesn't serve Tor's agenda and colossal ego will be wiped from the face of the galaxy. And no one is doing anything about it but us. *We* are the one and only line of defense against a tyrant the likes of which has not strode the stars for centuries."

When he'd finished, Sef turned further toward him, eyes narrowed, jaw set. "I believe you," she said. "Otherwise, I wouldn't be standing here on this ship of yours right now. And if I wasn't here, you wouldn't have a chance in hell of getting the funding you need."

Thank you, he almost said, but caught himself. Better to stay silent at this moment than jeopardize the positive outcome currently balanced on the razor's edge of her changeable intentions.

"Exchequer only cares about one thing: profit." She

nodded once, emphatically. "And in *this* instance, this mission, *I* am Exchequer. You'd do well to remember that."

Then, without another word, she left the command center, and the door swept shut behind her.

Leaving Drake to consider what had happened, what she'd just told him, and how best he might navigate the rapids ahead.

Knowing Persephone and the history they'd shared, it could get pretty damn tricky, indeed.

CHAPTER 14

Garrison Brukowski, Gary to his current drinking buddies, Bruiser to the guys he served with back when he was a private in the 83rd Armor Division, ended the strangest call he'd ever received and leaned back in his favorite chair.

His living quarters weren't huge. None of the living quarters on Melody Station were huge, but this one suited him just fine. That's what happened when you spent the largest part of your life in the military—you got used to whatever space you found yourself in. As spaces went, Melody Station was definitely a cut above most of the places he'd been assigned.

The station was home to nearly a half-million people, a self-sufficient mega-structure that hung in a stationary orbit around a colorful but uninhabitable planet in a minor system just barely on the Alliance side of the border with the Frontier. The station had all the advantages of being in Alliance territory, including a permanent contingent of military personnel and reservists who patrolled the area to prevent any attacks on the station as well as any hostile incursions into Alliance space. But being so far away from the center of the Alliance, most permanent residents couldn't give two hoots about the Alliance itself.

Gary's last posting had been to oversee the reservists on Melody Station. A cushy job for a career military man on his way to retirement. After nearly forty years of service, the brass thought he deserved cushy.

He didn't care. His days of busting his butt for advancement after advancement were over. He'd reached the best rank he'd ever get—Master Sergeant. His rank guaranteed him a nice pension and his living quarters had a spectacular view of the planet, so he stayed.

He wasn't the only retired soldier on the station. Life here was good, or as good as anyplace else. He had no great desire to spend the rest of his life hopping from planet to planet. He'd done enough of that already. He'd been considering taking a teaching position in the private sector. He knew a hell of a lot about piloting spaceships and training the personnel to fly them. A few of the retired guys he went drinking with had already gone the private sector route.

"You'll never really be a civilian," more than one of them had told him.

It was always meant as a joke. An old armor jock can hang up the suit, but the suit's always gonna be part of the man.

He always laughed along with them, but the joke wasn't really a joke. He'd never been a civilian, not really. He'd just changed who he worked for.

Tonight, the planet was putting on a show. Poisonous gases and the planet's charged atmosphere created a multi-colored, strobing lightshow the tourists who flocked to the station paid big bucks to see. Gary rarely watched. The lightshow was old hat. Even though he was sitting facing a viewport that looked out over the planet, he wasn't watching now.

He was trying to decide if he should hang up on his caller.

Even though she hadn't identified herself, he'd recognized her easily enough. Who wouldn't? She was famous these days. She was also cautious. Almost as cautious as he was. Space was immense, but it was messy. Put a signal out in all that nothing, anybody could intercept it. Put a signal out there when you were this close to the Frontier, the wrong people might listen in.

"The lady wants to put the band back together," his caller was saying. "I'm helping out until she gets here."

He knew what lady she was talking about. There'd only been one woman in the 83rd Armor Division back when he'd been wearing the armor himself, and that had been Augusta Light.

The Gray Lady.

But she'd been shitcanned over a decade ago, wasn't it now? Then after that mess on Shepard's Moon, she'd been banned from the Alliance.

Gary knew all about that. His background as an armor jock gave him cred with the soldiers on the station, even the ones who hadn't retired yet, and soldiers gossiped when they drank.

Who would have imagined he'd end up doing a job

where drinking with the guys was expected? He wouldn't have, not back when he'd been in the 83rd.

The Armor Division didn't have an official presence here—there was no need—but a lot of the soldiers on active duty as well as in the reserves had worn armor at one time or another in their careers. A couple of guys on Melody Station had even been in the 83rd during the years that Gus was still an armor jock. She'd been famous, a living legend, or so some people thought. Even if some of the guys were jealous of all the attention she got, they admired the hell out of her. They still paid attention to what happened to her.

She'd certainly pulled some stunts in her time. He'd hung up the armor himself eighteen years before she'd stolen hers rather than see it decommissioned. That story had made the rounds almost faster than a transit flume could get a ship from here to way the hell over there.

Then she'd dropped out of sight for nearly a decade.

He didn't get it. She'd gone to all the trouble to steal her suit, thumbing her nose at the military, just to mothball it somewhere? Scuttlebutt said she'd holed up on some shit-hole of a space station just inside the Frontier, drinking her days away.

Right up until that mess on Shepard's Moon when she'd gone commando and waded into the middle of a civil war on a planet the Alliance had declared off limits. Wearing the same damn suit she'd stolen from the military.

As far as Gary was concerned, Gus Light had always been too attached to that suit. Armor was a tool, like a ship or a socket wrench or any of the new tech the Alliance was playing around with. Sometimes the new tech worked, sometimes it didn't. Trial and error. Sometimes the errors turned out better than the original plan.

And sometimes the errors just flat out disappeared.

The woman on the other end of the call had a recent history with Gus Light. They weren't exactly buddies, she said, but the lady had helped her out in the past and she was just repaying the favor. Not for free, he guessed. No one did anything for free, not in his experience. Love or money or revenge, there was always a motive.

Self-preservation, too. That was a biggie.

That turned out to be his caller's ace in the hole. The reason she expected him to drop everything and show up for one more gig, as she put it. Him and as many of his old bandmates as he could round up.

"You'll bring down the house," she said.

Code words for a fight, he guessed.

Why had she called him instead of one of the other guys? Because he was easy to find? Brukowski was an easy name to research, better than Smith or Sanchez or Johnson.

Or was it because of that Master Sergeant rank and his last position with the reservists before he'd retired? Did she assume he still kept in touch with the guys she was trying to find? That he'd have a better chance of talking them into wading back into the shit than she would?

Or had she managed to stumble onto his current connections?

That's what reporters did. They dug around. Chased down rumors. Sniffed out facts that would be in everyone's best interests to stay hidden.

Gary wasn't paranoid by nature, but the last several years had made second-guessing everyone else's motives second nature. That's what happened when you lived a secret life very few people knew about.

Then his caller said, "The lady's planning a real battle of the bands. J.T.'s still number one with a bullet, a real blast from the past, but the lady thinks the old band can do him one better."

J.T.

Jorritz Tor.

The man at the top of the Alliance's Enemies list. Number one with a bullet indeed.

Gary had to admit, the thought of going after that skudge-hole was pretty enticing. Gary had been one of the armor jocks Tor had commandeered to escort his cowardly ass off Shepard's Moon back when everyone still thought Tor was a legit ambassador, not a treasonous sonofabitch out only for himself.

Back then, Gary had still been an impressionable young soldier who followed orders without question. But even then, he'd had a heaping helping of ambition. He'd thought his squadron's assignment as support for a diplomatic mission would look damn fine on his service record. The inclusion of a new world into the Alliance was a Big Deal, and being part of the military presence the Alliance sent along as a display of the benefits that came with joining up had to help his chances of advancement.

Then Tor had screwed it all up.

Gary wouldn't have run into Tor at all if he'd been able to go to officer training school. Officers didn't get sent to backwater planets like Shepard's Moon to backup diplomatic missions. Officers made the decisions on who to send on those missions.

But Gary had been born on a backwater world himself, a poor kid whose only option was to enlist. It was the luck of the draw that he'd been assigned to the Armor Division, probably because he was big and strong and damn motivated to succeed. He didn't care. Training was brutal, but nowhere near as brutal as surviving his childhood.

He'd been surprised to have a woman in his cadet class. At first, he'd thought Gus Light would hold the whole class back, but she'd surprised him. She was more motivated than he was. While he never particularly liked her, he came to respect her as a teammate. He didn't participate when other cadets, like Earl Knox, gave her shit, but he didn't defend her either. He didn't have to. She could more than hold her own, and she probably would have been pissed if he'd tried.

If she'd been any other person, Tor's scheme with Shepard's Moon might have worked. But Tor had underestimated the Gray Lady of the 83rd Armor Division, pure and simple. And like everyone who'd underestimated Gus Light, Tor had come to regret it.

Gary liked to imagine that he would have fought back like Gus had if Tor had stranded him down on the planet instead of her. But he'd been a good soldier back then. He followed orders. He had stayed in the hold of the division's transport ship with the rest of his squadron and swallowed every lie Tor told. When Tor said the rest of the 83rd on the planet had been killed, he'd grieved for his fallen comrades along with everybody else in that hold.

Everybody except Earl Knox.

When Tor left the transport's hold, Knox got up and took off after him.

Gary had thought about stopping Knox. The man was a hothead. He'd always been a hothead. Something about Tor had pissed Knox off, that was pretty clear by the expression on his face.

If Gary had been in charge of their squadron, he would have ordered Knox to stay put. If Gary had been in charge, he would have made the report about the rest of the 83rd himself. If he'd been in *charge*, he damn well would have verified the information before making the report.

He never forgot how it felt to discover he'd been lied to. That Tor had used him, used all of them, just to cover up his own cowardice. Gary had wanted to beat the man into a bloody pulp, then see him behind bars for whatever was left of his miserable life. But he couldn't do that because like the coward he was, Tor took an escape pod and fled.

Yes, getting even with Tor—getting even with extreme *prejudice*, as the saying went—was definitely enticing.

But was it enough to be back together with the band?

Enough to wade back into battle at the Gray Lady's side?

The answer was no. Not after all this time. Gus Light could go out fighting—hell, fighting the good fight was probably the way she would *want* to go out—but Gary had a job to do. He hadn't been a warrior in years. Hadn't flown a ship into battle, hadn't even put on the armor in so long that he wouldn't be much good to anybody. The only reason the woman on the other end of the call had reached out to him was because she wanted him to convince the guys who still *could* fight that this new battle of the bands was for a righteous cause.

Although when had revenge ever been a truly righteous cause?

He was about to tell his caller that he'd been out of practice so long, he wouldn't do the band justice, when she said something that felt like a punch in the gut.

"We've got a great venue. Biggest damn theater in the round you've ever seen. Shiny. Great big audience. Place like that, the hits'll just coming, you know what I mean?"

Did he? Oh yeah, he knew *exactly* what she meant, but he doubted she did.

That was the problem, now, wasn't it. Only a very few people knew about that particular *theater in the round*, and none of them were on Melody Station. He hoped none of them were in the Frontier. He *prayed*—and he wasn't a man who prayed often—that Tor didn't realize exactly what that theater in the round was.

Tor had probably set his sights on that ship because he wanted the singularium, and Gus Light meant to stop him. She had good reason to hate the man. But what was she thinking? Tor never went into a battle unless he thought he had the upper hand, and he never fought a battle himself if he could get someone else to do it for him. The last Gary heard, Gus had teamed up with a Frontier smuggler named Mephistopheles Drake, of all things. Unless she had some serious backup, she'd be going on a suicide mission. She'd been crazy in her day, a real berserker in battle, but she'd never been suicidal.

Then there was something else to consider.

Tor had been pretty high up in the Alliance before he'd gone rogue. He probably had access to all sorts of government secrets. Did Tor suspect what that theater in the round really was? If he did, he'd be putting everything on the line to get his greedy hands on it.

And if he got it? If Gus Light and her band couldn't hold him off?

Then Tor might even decide to use it to make a run against the Alliance.

If that happened, places like Melody Station might be the first to fall, but they wouldn't be the last.

His caller gave him the location of the band's "rehearsal," as she called it, then disconnected before he could say anything. She probably didn't want to hear it if he said no. But she didn't know the decision wasn't up to him.

He leaned forward in his chair and raked his hands through his hair. He was getting too old for this shit. His stomach was threatening to rebel against the cheese tray he'd had for dinner. He'd added some locally grown fruit along with the cheese. Usually, a light meal like that never bothered him, but the call had shot that all to hell.

His real job, the one very few people knew about, was supposed to be all about information gathering. Well, he'd just gathered some damn important information. It was time to make a call of his own.

He glanced out his viewport at the planet's nightly light-show. He had a feeling he wouldn't be seeing that show again any time soon. If ever. Maybe he should have appreciated it more while he was here.

Maybe he should have appreciated a lot of things more than he had. Like how it felt to be retired. To have a beer with guys who called him Bruiser or guys who still called him Master Sergeant. Like not having to think about getting up before the crack of dawn with a massive hangover after one beer too many.

Gary Brukowski pressed a chip on the inside of his left wrist that opened a communications channel he rarely used. He didn't identify himself to the person on the other end of the call. He didn't have to.

"I think I've found it," he said.

Then he listened to the instructions he knew were coming, all the while looking at the lightshow on the planet below. He hoped it wouldn't be the last time he saw it.

CHAPTER 15

As the *Scintilla* dropped out of a transit flume in the Otho Galba system, Drake's guard went up across the board. He was as tense as if he were entering a war zone, with good reason.

The *Scintilla* was approaching a used spacecraft dealership.

"This is the place," he said from the pilot's cradle as he trimmed the ship's speed out of the flume. "Honest Gordian and the Thrax Brothers' Not-So-New Shipa-palooza."

"The biggest previously-owned spaceship dealership in all the Alliance and Frontier combined," said Bruce as he watched the holographic video feed floating before him. "If you aren't *allowed* to buy *new*, this is your best option." The sarcasm in his voice was unmistakable.

"I'm sure you can find what you need right here," said Sef, who'd given the others no choice but to come to

Honest Gordian's instead of the new ship dealers they'd planned to visit. "Exchequer has dealt with them often and only rarely experienced even minimal levels of dissatisfaction."

"I still say waging a war against an existential threat to the Alliance is no time to go cheap," snapped Drake. "*New* ships would be less prone to malfunctions and better equipped to fight Tor's armada."

"We don't have the budget," said Sef. "The new ship dealers were priced *much* too high, based on the numbers I saw."

"Which is where the *negotiations* come in," said Bruce. "I told you, I *know* I could've gotten us a better deal. I *know* the guys at those new ship lots, and they all *owe* me for one favor or another."

Sef brought her hands together in a loud, decisive clap. "Water under the bridge, Mr. O'Connor…and a moot point, besides. If you're good enough to negotiate a sweet deal with *new* ship salespeople, just *imagine* the bargains you can swing with the *used* ship people."

Even as Drake guided the *Scintilla* toward the dealership, he ground his teeth at his sister's take-charge attitude. She might have had the most power of the three of them, controlling the much-needed cash-flow as she did, but her typically heavy-handed way of wielding that power tapped into deep reservoirs of resentment toward her that he'd nursed for most of their lives.

It was the same old skudge as always, and it ate at him like nobody's business. The way she'd basically forced him and Bruce to come to Honest Gordian's instead of a new ship dealer reminded him of one overreach after another by a woman who always seemed to think she knew better than him about everything.

Though it was true, Honest Gordian and the Thrax Brothers' Not-So-New Shipapalooza was an impressive sight. From a distance, it looked like a miniature spiral galaxy orbiting a huge yellow star, its vast arms gleaming and glinting with a sea of silvery sparks. As *Scintilla* got closer, the arms resolved, revealing massive numbers of spacecraft parked together in that slowly turning formation. Approaching ever closer, Drake could see the ships were all shapes and sizes, from shuttle pods to carriers to colony vessels, and they looked (from the outside, at least) to be in uniformly excellent condition. None had a massively ruptured hull or clearly missing structural components or disfiguring scars; none was depowered or open to the void of space or leaking fluids or gases in any significant way.

In other words, it wasn't a salvage yard or rock-bottom supplier of parts and components. In theory, it shouldn't be a bad thing to buy some ships here from the Gordian/Thrax combine.

But it was still a used ship lot, and Drake knew from experience how dangerous such a place could be. He'd bought his share of ships at such places and ended up with junkers when he'd thought he was buying good quality vessels.

This time, though, at least he had a savvy negotiator and a hard-nosed skinflint from Exchequer with delusions of grandeur to meet the fast-talking wheeler-dealers head on.

"Bringing her in," he said as his request for coordinates from the Gordian space traffic controllers was answered. "We'll be docked at the core showroom in less than fifteen."

"Okay, great." Bruce paced the floor nervously, flicking back and forth over the gleaming obsidian surface. "And we know they're expecting us."

"Just confirmed it over comms," said Drake. "Honest Gordian himself and at least two Thrax Brothers are due to meet with us."

"Pulling out all the stops, eh?" said Sef.

"More like rolling out the big guns to thoroughly *rip us off*," said Drake.

"Which they won't," said Sef. "Because ripping *us* off would bring down the destructive wrath of all *Exchequer* on their establishment."

"If you say so." Drake shook his head, wondering if she was really *that* naïve down deep, under the bluster. Had her years as an Exchequer executive made her soft?

Or was she holding back her true hard-headedness to lull everyone in her orbit into a false sense of security?

Whatever was going on in that head of hers, Drake was about to find out its true colors. He just had to hope it wouldn't blow up the deal they needed...which, in turn, would ruin the Alliance's chance at survival.

"Have we got ships for you!" Honest Gordian, an eight-foot-tall behemoth with a beard and head of hair of actual fire, shook his arms in the air. "Just what you need to defeat any tyrant or pirate's armada!"

"Do you do bulk discounts?" asked Sef. "Theoretically speaking, that is?"

"That depends on how much *bulk* you're looking at buying." Gordian wore a sleeveless black business suit that exposed his heavily-tattooed arms. Like his hair and beard, the tats were of the high-tech variety, applied with smart, motile inks that made them move and flicker and interact— even jump off the skin and drift through midair, twitching and twisting all the while.

"And *that* depends on how *good* the ships are." Sef smirked. "It's all about the merchandise, I always say."

Gordian laughed loudly, but Drake didn't think he was necessarily laughing *with* her. How could he *not* be delighted at the prospect of raiding the Exchequer treasury via the overconfident representative plunked down in front of him by the gods of avarice?

Drake cleared his throat, and Sef looked back at him with an expression that had *I got this* written all over it. *Let the grown-ups handle this.*

The attitude rankled him, as it always had. He wished he'd brought along Bruce to help wrangle her, but Bruce had stayed back with the ship to ensure its security. It had seemed like a good idea, so the *Scintilla* didn't end up mysteriously added to the dealers' spiral galaxy of a fleet for sale...but maybe it hadn't been the best plan after all. Bruce, after all, was probably the strongest negotiator among them. He also didn't have a history of being browbeaten by the big sister from Hell.

"Let's talk terms," she told Gordian. "Though we're nowhere near ready to *buy* anything yet. We won't put a single credit down without a *test drive*, of course."

"Yes, of course." Gordian grinned like the wolf in Grandma's bed when Red Riding Hood strolled in with her basket. "We wouldn't *dream* of not taking you for a ride before you buy."

"Did somebody say *lucky*?" Just then, a bald, roly-poly guy in a bizarre red fur suit came bumbling from between spaceship holo displays and across the polished purple floor of the showroom. "Because *you* folks just happened to *drop by* during our best *deal event* of the year!"

"Quidquo's right!" A stick-thin guy in goggles and a bright yellow floor-length duster shot out from another cluster of displays. "You could *not* have come at a better time to shop for a not-so-new spacecraft!"

"Come on over and tell our guests more!" shouted Gordian. "Persephone of Exchequer, meet Quidquo and Flagrande, two of the galaxy-famous *Thrax* brothers!"

Drake smiled and hung back. He'd never dealt with the Thrax Brothers, but their reputations as lunatics and sales sharks preceded them.

"It's a *bogo* day!" announced Quidquo as he pumped Sef's hand in a shake of great exuberance. "Buy one, get one free!"

"Plus low, low 50 percent financing!" Flagrande jumped in and took up the shake before Quidquo had even fully released it.

"Don't forget the mystery box incentive!" chimed in Gordian. "It could be the greatest surprise discount you'll ever receive in this life or any other!"

As they continued their breathless sales pitch with Sef locked firmly in their sights, Drake wandered over to the vast windows that encircled the perimeter of the showroom. Dead center as the showroom structure was at the heart of the dealership's spiral galaxy formation, he had an incredible view of the multitude of ships drifting nearby.

He'd seen a selection of vessels on the way to the showroom spacedock, but the current view staggered him. *Countless* ships coasted beyond those windows, a veritable *fleet* of sizes and configurations. Some he recognized, while others looked utterly alien, stirring in his soul a longing to identify their origins.

One ship in particular, though, caught his attention. He spotted it beyond the window wall on the far side of the showroom, nondescript in a way with which he was *very* familiar. The cylindrical shell looked rudimentary, not streamlined or ultra-high-tech like the *Scintilla* or other ships on the dealers' lot. The spaceframe and hull had a definite retro appearance that camouflaged how maneuverable and deadly the ship could be in the right hands.

Right hands like *his*, which had been flying that vessel's twin for many years through many close scrapes…always with the best possible results.

"Excuse me." He interrupted the Thrax brothers' double-team spiel after crossing the showroom back to them. "I've found one I'd like to test-drive."

"Let's put that on hold for the moment." Sef scowled. "We're just talking *price* now. If they don't come down further, there's no sense test-driving *anything.*"

"I want to anyway," said Drake. "I know this particular model *very* well. If these guys have a *couple* of them…"

"We have a couple of *everything*," roared Gordian. "However, *you're* not exactly the *decision-maker* here, are you? Shouldn't *she* pick the demo model?" He gestured at Sef.

"Since *I'm* the one who'll be flying it, I should have a say in picking it," said Drake. "Don't you agree, Persephone?"

Her gaze met his with a hostile flicker, but it faded. "What could it hurt?" Her smile was tight. "Gordian, could you set up this test drive for my brother, please?"

Gordian looked from one to the other of them, and his eyes lit with understanding. "Why didn't you *tell* me he's your *brother*?" He clapped his hands together loudly. "Quidquo, Flagrande, have your brother Defacto shuttle our friend's brother to the ship he wants to test drive, won't you?"

"Can't do it," said Flagrande. "He's taking out another customer at the moment. That deep-pockets guy with the long shopping list like these nice folks?"

"Right, okay." Gordian blew out his breath, and his beard of flame flared. "Then one of *you* will have to take care of it while I continue my chat with Persephone here. Can you manage that?"

"You better believe it!" said Flagrande.

"Which ship?" asked Quidquo, brimming over with enthusiasm that bordered on hysteria. "Which ship is it?"

"C'mon, I'll show you." Drake gestured for them to follow as he started across the room. "It's right this way, fellas."

Drake felt right at home...literally.

The ship he was test-driving was so identical to his

156

beloved *Golden Void*, he might have thought it *was* the *Void* if he'd been ushered aboard without knowing any better.

With the exception of his and Gus's personal decorating touches and customizations, it was virtually the exact same ship. It looked, felt, sounded, and smelled the same to him from top to bottom—even handled the same as he flew it up out of the dealership formation and took it for a cruise around the block.

It was enough to remind him why he'd fallen in love with the *Void* in the first place. As much as he adored flying the *Scintilla* with its myriad comforts and innovations, *this* was the kind of ship he was most used to.

More than that, it was the kind of ship that seemed to be the best fit for Gus. As much as she teased him about retaining the retro controls and old-fashioned style, he'd noticed her natural ease aboard the *Void*, the way she'd made it her own personal home as much as his.

He was pretty sure she'd do the same with the one he was test-driving if she got the chance.

Not that he was going to blab all that to the canny used ship salesmen standing behind him on the bridge as he operated the controls. He wasn't going to let on that he'd come up with an affectionate nickname for the ship, either: the *Silver Void.*

"What do you think?" Quidquo asked the question in the same tone of voice he might have used to ask Drake what he thought of a woman who'd just strolled by.

"Pretty sweet ride, isn't she?" Flagrande asked in the same way.

"Not bad, I guess." Drake felt true love at the wheel but stayed committed to playing his cards close to the vest.

Show them anything more than the most rudimentary interest, and the price was bound to go sky-high. "For a model this old, I mean."

"Not *that* old," snapped Flagrande. "And it's got *way* more pep than you'll *ever* need."

"The previous owner really tricked it out," explained Quidquo. "Speed-wise and maneuverability-wise, she is *parsecs* beyond her original specs."

"Not to mention the new and improved weaponry," said Flagrande. "Let's just say that last owner was involved in such questionable business dealings, they needed all the juice they could get."

Drake nodded, suppressing the Cheshire Cat grin he was grinning on the inside. Everything they told him made him love the *Silver Void* even more.

And to think, just before he'd boarded it with the two Thrax brothers, Sef had almost talked him out of taking the test-drive. With negotiations floundering, test-driving the ship would be an utter waste of time, she'd said…so why bother? Wouldn't they be better off going to the next dealership on their list instead and seeking better pricing all around?

"I'm flyin' her anyway," he'd told Sef. "She's my kind of ship."

Now that he was at the wheel, putting her through her paces, he knew he'd been right not to listen to Sef. Sometimes, it was just better to go with your gut and let the chips fall where they—

BWHOOOM

Suddenly, the *Silver Void* shook with a powerful impact that sent it spinning out of control.

Both Thrax brothers tumbled off their feet and hit the floor. Drake, who'd been hunkered in the pilot's seat manning the navigation controls, at least stayed right-side-up and kept his wits about him.

"What the *skudge*?" He fought the wheel with one hand while playing the console with the other, struggling to stop the spin. At the same time, he watched the nav screen for an overview, trying to determine what had struck the *Silver Void* out of nowhere and whether it might strike her again.

The answer, which he quickly spotted on that screen, barely had time to sink in before the next impact sent the ship reeling. This time, he knew for sure that it wasn't from a collision with a physical object like a meteor or stray hunk of debris.

It was the result of a direct hit by an energy pulse weapon mounted on one of the ships pursuing the *Silver Void*.

One of the *two dozen* ships in pursuit, according to the arrowhead formation of blinking blips pointed right at his ship on the nav screen.

Leave it to Drake to get attacked during a used spaceship test-drive.

CHAPTER 16

"Now this is what I call a *bar*."

Earl Knox stood with his hands on his hips and surveyed the spacers' bar on Depak Station that Gus had called home for nearly a decade. He had an expression on his scarred face that made him almost—*almost*—look handsome. Pure, unadulterated joy could do that to a person. Gus had just never expected to see that expression on Early's face. The Earl she'd always known had been perpetually pissed off.

Of course, he'd also been perpetually competing with her back in those days. Back when they'd both worn armor for the Alliance military. She'd been surprised as hell that he'd allowed her to teach him how best to fly the *Golden Void*. That might have made a less experienced person think Earl had mellowed. She knew better.

Earl had joined their little war solely for the chance to go after Tor. Something had happened between the two of them way back when. What, Gus didn't know, but it gave Earl a serious need to kick the ever-loving skudge out of the man. Gus could work with that.

The bar hadn't changed much since the last time she'd been on Depak Station. The station was thick with spacers' bars. This close to Alliance space but just far enough away that no one on the station had to worry about running into Alliance types, Depak Station catered to all sorts of spacers. From cargo ship captains looking to score their next legitimate job to smugglers looking for whatever type of job they could get, they all seemed to wind up in one of the bars on the station. Business was done over drinks, and deals were sealed with one last round.

Gus had always enjoyed this particular bar because it was as rough around the edges as she'd always been, especially back when she figured she'd be drinking her way through retirement. Located halfway between the space station's central hub and one of the docks on the outer rings that catered to cargo ships, the bar was strictly utilitarian. No cushy chairs that would mold themselves to fit the ass of whoever sat down. The chairs here were hard, gray metal. So were the tables. The lights on the wall behind the bar were dim, and the only lights at the tables came from viewscreens that could be accessed—for a fee, of course.

Gus watched as Earl honed in on the dancers gyrating on raised platforms off to the sides of the bar. The dancers were holograms meant to advertise certain sexual services available elsewhere on the station. If Earl thought they were real women, he was about to be sorely disappointed.

The bar looked different somehow. It *felt* different. Gus knew it hadn't really changed. *She* was the one who'd changed. Before she'd ignored the drab, desperate feel of the place because she'd felt drab. Not desperate, just unfocused. Now she not only had a purpose, she had Drake in her life.

She missed him horribly. She hadn't expected that. Being on the *Void* without him there just felt wrong. Watching Earl fly the ship felt wrong. Hell, not hearing Drake's guitar felt all sorts of wrong. She couldn't wait for this war to be over. *After* she kicked Tor's ass back to the Alliance where he'd get the justice he so very richly deserved.

And if she couldn't turn him over to the Alliance?

Well, she wouldn't shed a tear if Tor went down fighting. Or more than likely got caught in the crossfire. A coward like Tor wouldn't stick around for the actual battle, especially not if he thought he was going to lose. Cowards like him always got someone else to fight their battles for them.

The thought made her momentarily uncomfortable. Wasn't that what she was doing here? Recruiting other people to fight her battles?

The difference was they wouldn't be fighting her battles *for* her. They'd be fighting *with* her. If the odds weren't so overwhelmingly against her, she'd just as soon do all the fighting herself and leave her old friends out of it.

Not Earl. He had his own axe to grind with Tor. But the other guys? If she got any of them killed, she might never be able to forgive herself.

If Drake got himself killed, she just might end up back in this bar drinking herself into oblivion.

"Well, hell, if it isn't the Gray Lady herself."

The voice came from behind her. She tensed, then realized she recognized that voice.

She turned around to face Julio Ortiz, one of the best armor jocks she'd ever fought alongside.

"What's up, Buttercup?" she said.

"The sky, the sky, so high, Moon Pie," he replied.

They both dissolved into laughter.

They hugged the way old comrades did—a strong embrace, solid thumps on the back, and a quick release. Gus found herself grinning, the first honest grin she'd had since she left Buddy's Bluff—and Drake—behind.

Ortiz looked good for someone almost ten years older than she was. She hadn't trained with Ortiz, but she had fought alongside him in the 83rd. He'd been good, damn good. But then again, all the soldiers in the 83rd had been damn good. Ortiz had gray in his black hair now, and unlike her, he hadn't kept his old military haircut. His hair was long and shaggy, and so was his mustache. He'd kept in shape, though. When they'd hugged, his body had felt like a solid piece of steel molded into the shape of a man. He was half a head taller than Gus. Most armor jocks had been.

"You still in?" she asked.

He'd understand what she meant. She kind of doubted he was still military, given the haircut, but she had to know if he was putting his career on the line. Besides, not all military *looked* like military. The ones who went to work in the intelligence end of things, they had to blend in wherever they'd been assigned.

He shook his head. "Got out five years ago. Been flying cargo ever since, but I've never been to this hellhole before. My runs been strictly inside, you know what I mean?"

He'd been piloting cargo ships inside the Alliance. Strictly a legitimate businessman.

"Got your own ship?" she asked.

"Nope. Too damn much trouble. I contract out. You're just lucky that little spitfire you sent after us caught me between gigs." He sobered. "I get what you're doing, but I don't break contract for nobody, not even you, sweet lady."

"I wouldn't expect you to," she said.

And that was the truth. She was already asking people to upend their lives, but there was a limit. There had to be.

"She on her way?" Gus asked.

"She's here," said a new, female voice.

Gus looked past Ortiz to see Kymmie—with a Y in the wrong place—walk into the bar like she belonged.

This time she *looked* like she belonged.

The last time Gus had met with Kymmie in this bar, the reporter had been a fresh-faced newbie, barely twenty, all wide blue eyes and pert smile. This Kymmie had some miles on her. Gus had probably added to those miles by giving Kymmie the scoop of a lifetime—an exclusive on the defeat of the guerillas on Shepard's Moon. Kymmie'd done a crackerjack job, too. Her reports had embarrassed the hell out of the Alliance. As a result, the Alliance had simply banished Gus from Alliance space instead of prosecuting her for using military equipment—her armor—in an unauthorized battle.

Today Kymmie wasn't dressed as a reporter out to impress an interviewee, like she'd been all those months ago when she'd interviewed Gus in this very bar. Now she wore loose-fitting fatigues, and her blonde hair was pulled back away from her face. This wasn't a reporter who was ready to file a "reporting live" vid from Depak Station for the independent news service she worked for. This Kymmie had something else in mind.

"Long time, no see," Gus said. "Besides Ortiz here, what else have you got for me?"

Kymmie huffed out something that wasn't quite a laugh. "Blunt as usual, I see." She glanced around the bar. "Is that Earl Knox back there, trying to pick up a hologram?"

"That would be him," Gus said. "He having any luck?"

"He never had any luck with the ladies," Ortiz said. "Isn't that why you called him *Early*?"

Kymmie stifled a laugh behind a hand that didn't look quite as delicate as Gus remembered. She wondered what else the reporter had been up to besides the series of stories she'd done on Shepard's Moon and Tor.

"Old joke," Gus said, "and not one I have from *personal* experience, you understand."

"Got it." Kymmie looked behind herself at the entrance to the bar. "I got confirmations from a few other old friends of yours," she said to Gus. "I guess Ortiz is the first to get here, space travel being what it is."

Gus understood that. She also had a feeling that time was fleeting. If Tor made it back to the derelict ring ship before she could gather her forces…

She didn't want to think about that. She'd made a promise to Layla Crosscut, and she meant to keep it. She didn't want Crosscut to have to face Tor all alone because Tor sure as hell wouldn't be alone. Gus also didn't want to give Crosscut any reason to join up with Tor just to save her own skin. Crosscut wasn't a pirate, she was a scavenger. But she was also a smart woman who had no loyalties except to herself.

"I do have one ace in the hole," Kymmie said. "Or I think I do. If he's coming, he should be here shortly. He has the shortest distance to travel."

Gus frowned. She hadn't kept up with all the old members of the 83rd. After the military had booted her out, she'd deliberately cut herself off from all her old comrades in arms, as the saying went.

Earl wandered back to where the three of them stood near the entrance to the bar. "Damn women ain't real," he said, "and I ain't about to pay for what they're selling."

"You mean you can get it for free?" Ortiz was grinning, his shaggy mustache not quite hiding the small scar on one side of his mouth. Earl had given him that scar one night when good-natured ribbing had turned into a serious grudge match that ended with the two of them wailing away on each other.

"Oh, hey, Ortiz. Here I thought you were just part of the ambiance of this place," Earl said.

"*Ambiance?*" Ortiz shook his head in mock amazement. "You been reading or something?"

"He has a lot of down time," Gus said.

"I bet," Ortiz said.

Before Earl could work up a good head of steam, Gus suggested that he find them a table. "And buy a round," she said. "On me."

She didn't have access to all the money she'd saved up while she'd been in the military, and it had been a lot, but she had enough to cover drinks. Most of her money had

ANNIE REED & ROBERT JESCHONEK

been in financial institutions inside the Alliance, and since she was cut off from the Alliance, she was also cut off from that money. She'd used a lot of what was left to outfit the *Void*. She didn't have the kind of money they needed to buy ships for the upcoming war. Drake said he had a line on some financial backing. That's what he was off doing. She hoped that was going well. Otherwise, all the fighters she hoped to recruit wouldn't have ships to fly.

"I hope you got enough credits for that," Ortiz said. He nodded toward the door to the bar. "Looks like the calvary just got here."

A group of nearly a dozen men had just entered the bar. Some were older, like Gus and Ortiz. Others looked to be no more than thirty. Gus didn't recognize any of them.

No, check that.

She did recognize the man at the head of the group. Older, like herself, he strode in with the bearing of a lifelong military man. A real rules-and-regulations man. The kind of man who didn't get along with loose cannons like she'd been.

The kind *she* didn't get along with at all.

Garrison Skudging *Brukowski*.

CHAPTER 17

"Why are we *under attack?*" shouted Drake as he wrestled the *Silver Void* out of the latest line of fire. "Why are *two dozen* ships from *your* dealership coming after us all of a sudden?"

"Ask our brother!" said Quidquo as he struggled to his feet on the bridge of the *Void*.

"Yeah!" said Flagrande, who was barely upright, leaning all his weight on the comm console. "Defacto's the one who signed that *lead* ship out for a test-drive with the customer!"

Just then, a volley of pulse rays blasted in from multiple ships all shooting in concert. With a swing of the wheel and a slam of the big red accelerator button, Drake jolted the *Silver Void* away from most of the incoming fire, ensuring the ship's hull was only grazed instead of hammered dead-on.

As he flew her away from the concentrated assault, however, the squadron kept up its pursuit. The nav screen showed all 24 ships shearing away from the dealership's spiral galaxy fleet and roaring toward the *Silver Void* in the same arrowhead formation from before.

Maintaining a high-speed beeline away from the pursuers, Drake stretched over and pushed aside Flagrande to bash a button on the comm panel. "Hailing Defacto Thrax!" he yelled into the general bridge mic. "Cease fire and stand down immediately!"

No other voice spoke up on the other end of the call. The only response was a fresh round of pulse weapon fire from multiple craft in the pursuit formation.

"Why isn't he answering?" asked Drake.

"I have no idea," said Flagrande. "Maybe comms are down?"

"Or *he* is," snapped Quidquo.

"Someone hijacked the test-drive unit?" said Drake.

"It's the only explanation," replied Quidquo. "And it's an *ugly* one, for sure."

"But how could that even *happen*?" Drake played the wheel and thruster controls like a maestro on a Steinway piano, swooping and swerving to dodge the worst of the incoming fire. "Unless there are *two dozen* pilots, one for each ship."

"They're *tethered* to a single control unit for ease of maintenance and accessibility," explained Quidquo. "Each of us brothers has such a unit implanted in the same anatomical location."

"Which is?" asked Drake as the *Silver Void* took a hard hit that rocked it off course, requiring immediate correction.

"In our left hands." Flagrande sounded sad as he said it. "But for someone to gain control over it…"

"They would have to *sever* the hand." Quidquo sounded angry. "Then cut off the fingers of the *other* hand to operate the control interface, which is attuned to that brother's right-handed fingerprints."

Drake nodded grimly. No wonder the brothers were upset, given their kin's horrific prospects. If Defacto wasn't dead already, he was well on the way and suffering horribly en route.

"Okay then." Even as Drake swooped the *Silver Void* away from her pursuers, his mind raced to come up with a solution that might yet lead to salvation for captive Defacto. "What's it take to break the tether? Some kind of scrambler or feedback transmission?"

"A signal from the other two units can hack the connection, but it takes time," said Flagrande. "The unit powering the tether won't release it until the identities of the two override units are fully verified."

"We could also try a more direct approach," suggested Quidquo. "Blow up keystone ships in the formation. Taking out certain links in the tether might break it."

"Or break certain parts of it, at least," said Flagrande. "Break off sections if not the whole tethered network."

"There's another, much faster option, though," said Quidquo. "Blow up the tether base unit. Destroy the ship that's carrying it."

Guaranteeing Defacto's death in the process. It was *not* an ideal solution, as long as there was a chance the third Thrax brother was still alive. But maybe it was the only *good* solution, depending on the answer to a certain question Drake had in mind. "Do we have *any* idea who's piloting that test-drive ship?"

"Hold on, let me check." Quidquo tapped a sequence of control nodes on his right forearm, and a holographic display rippled into existence over his wrist. Deftly, his fingertips danced over the nodes, changing lines of code on the display and triggering other lines to flicker into existence, reporting data based on the terms of his search. "Okay, got it. The name given by the pilot is Org Casava."

Drake frowned as he steered the *Silver Void* in a zig-zag evasive pattern. "Doesn't ring a bell. Got anything else on him?"

Quidquo shrugged. "Not much. Just that he's buying on behalf of some reseller named Itza Torjor."

Itza Torjor. Drake thought about it for all of thirty seconds. Moving the syllables around told the tale clearly enough. He knew *just* who Casava was working for, and it made perfect sense.

Which was why he hit the starboard thrusters and swung the wheel so hard, whipping the *Void* around in a complete 180-degree turn.

"Better hold on tight, you two!" he shouted. "We can't let him get away with those ships, no matter what!"

"We're heading straight for them!" snapped Quidquo.

"Because if he gets that squadron back to his boss, the war for the Alliance will be lost!" As he said it, Drake poured on more speed and locked course for the oncoming nose of the ship thief's vessel. "That tyrant *Jorritz Tor* will be unstoppable!"

Drake's heart pounded as the *Silver Void* hurtled headlong toward the stolen ship.

As the gap between them closed, Casava let loose with a salvo of energy pulses—but Drake refused to dodge or trim the *Void*'s speed. Instead, he opened fire himself, unleashing beams of destructive force that converged on the approaching ship's nose.

"We don't really have to take the third option!" Quidquo's voice shook with panic. "Flagrande and I *did* send an override signal a minute ago!"

"Identity verification should kick in any second now," added Flagrande, who sounded only *slightly* less panicked.

Drake was too busy zeroing in on the stolen ship's nose to give either of them an instant's thought. Jaws clenched, he stayed tightly focused, rocketing the *Silver Void* toward its target. His mind didn't waver from the readings on the nav console's displays, the blinking lights on the nav screen, and the real-time visual on the big main viewer.

Though it was true, as the likelihood of his annihilation increased, thoughts of Gus flickered in the back of his mind. After all they'd been through together, he was on the verge of ending his life without ever seeing her again. Now that he'd found happiness with her, he was about to lose it…at the hands of an agent of Jorritz Tor's, no less.

"Let's dial it back!" shouted Quidquo. "That override's about to hit, I just *know* it!"

Still, Drake kept the *Silver Void* barreling toward Casava's ship. He was determined not to back down, no matter the personal cost.

"Please! Don't do this!" Flagrande sounded like he was on the verge of hysteria. "Break away! *Break away!*"

"Sorry, pardners," said Drake. "It's time for that big ol' roundup in the sky."

Still, the *Void* charged closer to Casava's stolen vessel. Other ships in the squadron fired energy beams and torpedoes, their combined force buffeting the *Void* and straining its shielding.

The Thrax brothers kept pleading for Drake to retreat, but he refused to relent, held fast to the course he'd chosen. Only seconds remained until the collision that would end everything for him, including the only true joy he'd ever experienced.

Then, suddenly, Casava blinked. His ship veered upward, cutting over the *Void* at such proximity that Drake could have sworn he heard them trading paint.

The other two dozen ships followed suit, zooming after the stolen test-drive craft in tight formation.

Drake was relieved but also steadfast in his commitment to win against Tor. Remembering what the Thrax brothers had said moments ago about breaking the tethered network, he rolled the *Void* around so her guns aligned with the fleeing flight of spacecraft.

Then, he picked the next ship to cruise overhead and lit it up. The beams from his energy weapons caught the ship's rear-mounted engine and kept up the heat until it blew.

True to the Thraxes' theory, when that ship spun out of formation, its link to the tethered squadron severed, other ships also veered off in short order. One, two, and three at a time, they tumbled apart from the rest of the group, no longer connected—no longer subject to being stolen by Casava.

Watching on the nav screen, Drake saw those liberated

ships cast adrift around him as Casava called a transit flume and jumped into it. He took six ships with him for a total of seven...not good, but nowhere near the original count of two dozen.

It would be a blow to Tor's plans for swift conquest of the Alliance and Frontier, he knew. It might also help when he and the brothers got back to the showroom to resume negotiations.

Maybe, he and Sef would finally get a good deal out of Honest Gordian.

CHAPTER 18

Gus stood inside her favorite—check that, *used* to be favorite—spacers' bar on Depak Station and glared at Kymmie.

"You called *him?*"

Of all the people in the skudging system, Kymmie had recruited Gary "Bruiser" Brukowski to join the fight against Tor.

Brukowski had been spit and polish, gung-ho soldier-boy all the way. A company man, and his company had always been the Alliance military. Great. Just great.

Part of Gus's deal with the Alliance was that she "never do anything like that again," which meant never use her armor in a military action on a rogue planet like Shepard's Moon or in Alliance space. *Or* where the Alliance could see it. If she did, all those charges against her for using her armor on Shepard's Moon would be reinstated. Same if she ever crossed over into Alliance space again.

The derelict ring ship was deep enough in the Frontier she figured the Alliance would never even hear about her little war against Tor until it was all over.

Unless Brukowski let the Alliance know all about it.

If that happened, she'd not only be exiled from Alliance space, she'd be a wanted fugitive. Probably one with a price on her head big enough that bounty hunters would catch the scent. She'd spend the rest of her days looking over her shoulder even if she never came close to Alliance space.

She couldn't do that to Drake. It was bad enough she'd dragged him into helping her defend her estranged son, the governor of Shepard's Moon, against Tor's pet guerillas who'd been intent on taking over the planet's government. But making a fugitive out of Drake too? No way.

"What the hell were you *thinking?*" Gus said to Kymmie.

As further proof that Kymmie had grown up a *lot* since the last time Gus had seen her in person, the reporter just shrugged. Back when they'd first met, Gus had been able to intimidate the hell out of her just by slamming a drink glass down on one of the tables in the bar.

"You said you needed people," Kymmie said. "He knows people."

Of course he did. He probably commanded a metric ton of them.

Gus strode over to Brukowski, hands on her hips. She couldn't think of him as "Bruiser" now. He'd left his armor behind to move up the ranks long before she'd been shitcanned.

She had to tilt her head up to look at him, but she'd been looking up at men taller than she was her whole life. It didn't mean she was about to back down from anybody, not even someone who'd always outranked her.

"We need to get one thing straight from the get-go," she said. "This isn't a military op. You got that?"

He just stood staring at her, hands loose at his sides, his expression unreadable.

"I don't care what your rank is," she said. "I don't care much about much of anything except getting rid of Tor once and for all. I do care that the people who join up with me come out of this in one piece, and that means we coordinate how *I* say. We fight the way *I* say. You good with that?"

A smile started to play around the edges of his mouth. Amusement? Or rueful acceptance?

If he was laughing at her, she'd have no problem knocking that smile right off his face. One thing about Depak Station—bar brawls could go on as long as both combatants were still standing and had enough credits to pay for damages. Gus could do a *whole* lot of damage when she wanted to, and she didn't need her armor to do it.

"Well?" she said.

"I'm retired," he said. "Or I was until I got a call from that friend of yours. Something about getting the band back together."

Gus shot a sidelong look at Kymmie.

"I had to come up with some story," Kymmie said. "Couldn't exactly say what we're really doing over an open channel."

Gus had to admit it wasn't a bad cover story. Except…

"I don't remember the rest of these guys being in our band," she said, looking past Brukowski to the dozen men standing behind him.

179

"They're in *my* band," Brukowski said.

"When Master Sergeant asks me to do him a solid, I do it," said one of the younger guys.

Master Sergeant? Brukowski had always been ambitious for an enlisted grunt, but holy crap.

"And what exactly is a Master Sergeant—*retired*—doing helping out an old armor jock like me?" she said.

His smile faded. The look he gave her was one she hadn't seen since he'd worn the armor with the 83rd.

"Let's just say I have a score to settle and leave it at that, shall we?" he said.

Another man Tor had double-crossed, apparently. No wonder the skudge-hole had to recruit pirates and guerillas to fight for him. He'd apparently pissed off everybody else.

Including Earl Knox.

"Get in line," Earl said.

Earl had been standing off to the side just watching the whole exchange up to that point. Now he was getting in Brukowski's face like the hothead Earl had always been.

Gus wasn't about to let the two of *them* get into it. She needed to make sure everyone—every single man here— knew who was in charge.

"And everybody needs to get the *hell* in line behind *me*," Gus said. She made sure her glare included both Earl and Brukowski. "Everybody got that straight?"

Brukowski stared at her hard, a look he must have perfected as a Master Sergeant. She stared hard at him right back. She'd be damned if she broke eye contact first.

Eventually, he looked away. He nodded at the guys standing behind him.

"I'll make sure they follow your lead," he said. "They're

good pilots, each and every one of them. Rated for combat. I understand that's what you're looking for. I've got more coming. Some from the old band, some from the group I've been working with on Melody Station."

Gus had heard of Melody Station. Inside Alliance space, it was a damn big station that had a full complement of military personnel.

"You understand this isn't an official op," she said again. None of them would work with her if they'd been sent here by the Alliance military, but she had to make sure.

Brukowski shook his head. "Strictly off the books."

Huh. She wondered how he'd managed that.

"How many?" she asked.

He gave her a number that almost made her blink in surprise. She had no idea if Drake would be able to round up that many ships. Bruce Jr. would have enough ordnance, but getting the ships would be the problem. When Gus had said they'd help Crosscut defend her claim to the derelict, Crosscut had joked *you and what army?*

Well, it looked like they might have the beginnings of an actual army if what Brukowski said wasn't just him blowing smoke. Not that he'd ever been the type who wasn't deadly serious about the job. Of course, that had been back then. Who knew what he was like now.

But if he'd managed to round up this many guys on short notice, he had to be a man who garnered the respect of the soldiers he'd commanded.

Speaking of…

"Any armor jocks in this bunch?" she asked.

"A few, Gray Lady."

The voice had come from the back of the group behind Brukowski.

"Benji, that you?" That was Ortiz, and he was laughing. "What you been up to, brother?"

Benjamin Ochoa, Benji to the members of the 83rd. He'd been one of the armor jocks Gus had gotten off Shepard's Moon the first time, part of the squad that Tor claimed had died in the fighting.

Ortiz and Benji were doing the armor jock, comrades-in-arms hug like the one Ortiz had given Gus. She stood off to the side, shaking her head. Talk about a blast from the past. Benji had been the second shortest armor jock in her squadron next to her. He was still short, but like Ortiz, he looked like solid muscle. Old armor jocks never died, it seemed. They also didn't let themselves go to seed.

"You got a suit?" Gus asked.

Benji gave her a sly smile. "I got something."

She got it. Benji might have a day job, but he'd managed to cobble together a suit of his own. Just like Earl.

"Well, once we get that something on the *Void*, we got something that'll make it better," she said.

"That bucket of bolts?" Benji said, surprise evident in his expression. "We flying out in that thing?"

"She saved your ass once," Gus said. "She'll do it again." She shifted her gaze to encompass the rest of the men. "This round's on me, then we'll get you settled on the *Void*." She looked at Brukowski. "We might need another transport when the rest of the band shows up."

The *Void* had a lot of cargo space but not much in the way of cabin space. Quarters might be a little tight until they got back to Buddy's Bluff.

"Just save room for me," Kymmie said.

Gus blinked at her. "What?"

Kymmie smiled her sweet-girl smile, but there was grit behind it. "I'm coming with you," she said. "It's part of the deal, and it's non-negotiable." She tilted her head to one side, a touch of the old coquettish Kymmie in her expression. "Are *you* going to have a problem with *that*?"

CHAPTER 19

Quarters weren't just tight on the *Golden Void*. They were practically non-existent.

Gary Brukowski could have opted to bunk on one of the other ships in their little flotilla headed toward Buddy's Bluff. The ships were a ragtag mishmash—one other cargo vessel and two decommissioned troop transports filled with the other men he'd contacted—but the troops on board those ships were all topnotch, and what's more, they all knew and respected him. If he'd chosen any one of those other ships, he would have had his own cabin, if not his own stateroom, instead of trying to catch a few hours of sleep on a makeshift cot in one of the *Void's* storage compartments.

He had his reasons for staying on the *Void*. The number one reason was to keep a close watch on Gus Light.

She'd gotten right in his face at the very start. That shouldn't have surprised him. In her own way, she was as much a hothead as Earl Knox, but back when she'd been in the military, she'd still been willing to take orders. She'd even followed most of them.

The problem with Gus Light now was that she thought she was the one giving orders. Brukowski intended to let her go right on thinking that. She didn't need to know who was really in charge of making sure this private little war ended up the way it should.

The fact that Knox was involved at all shouldn't have surprised him either. Brukowski had lost track of Knox after the man had been released from the military due to his injuries. Somehow Light had not only found him, but found him without the reporter's help, apparently.

Knox might be another loose cannon. He'd always been a grunt who took orders, but Knox hadn't been a grunt in a long time. Plus he'd apparently made his own armor. That took dedication and know-how. He would have only done that if he could make some serious cash fighting with that armor. Knox had always been all about the money, and Gary had little reason to believe that had changed. If Knox had been fighting in his armor and winning those fights, that meant he had no problem fighting dirty. Contests between solo armor jocks always came down to which jock pulled the most low blows. Which jock was committed to doing anything to win. And which jock knew enough about their opponents to make those low blows count.

Was that how Light had convinced Knox to come along? Had she beaten him in a contest of one-on-one? Or was he merely along for the chance to settle an old score with Tor, as he'd said back at Depak Station?

Gary had to remind himself that unlike the men and

women he'd brought on this mission, the people Light and her pet reporter Kymmie were rounding up hadn't been military for a long time. Who knew how they'd respond in a battle. If they'd follow orders, or if they'd cut and run when the skudge hit the fan.

No one had gotten in Gary's face like Light had for so long, he'd had to work hard to keep his ingrained Master Sergeant response in check. That had probably shocked the hell out of the men he'd brought with him—at least the younger ones who still addressed him by his old rank. Gary was used to being the one who got in someone else's face and getting them to back the hell down if they even thought about disrespecting him.

Of course, that had been before he'd officially "retired." He had to keep reminding himself that as far as everyone else knew, he was still retired.

This shadow job he had, it had seemed so easy at first. Keep an ear to the ground, as the saying went. Make a few sporadic calls if he heard anything. Not a problem.

But being sent into the field? Going into battle?

Or *looking* like he was going into battle?

That was a whole different level of subterfuge. Hard enough to do when he didn't have to pretend he was willing to take orders from a disgraced hero of the 83rd who thought she was in charge.

Now he was going to have to work doubly hard to keep that part of himself secret. That's why he'd offered to bunk in a storage compartment. The place was so small, no way could it fit more than one person. Hell, he had to bend over getting inside just to make sure he didn't smack his head on the top of the compartment. But it was one of the few places on board the *Void* where he was guaranteed to be alone.

He needed the time alone. He had to send a quick communique to let his handler know about the current plan to rendezvous on Buddy's Bluff, which Light had apparently commandeered into a command center.

The Gray Lady herself along with the reporter had retreated to one of the few cabins on the ship to get a little sleep. The cabin belonged to the ship's captain, who was off getting ships for this little war. Light was apparently in a relationship of sorts with this man according to the scuttlebutt Gary had overheard when Knox, Ortiz, and Benji Ochoa started swapping *what've you been up to?* stories among themselves. Knox was supposed to be piloting the ship, but Gary had seen him engage the autopilot, an AI named Bruce, of all things. Good old Knox, sluffing off so he could b.s. with his buddies. That much, at least, hadn't changed.

The AI's response had been a little more colloquial than standard, but it fit with the overall feel of this hunk of junk, anachronistic p.o.s. cargo ship. How Light expected to win a war with ships like this, Gary didn't know. He actually didn't much care. The outcome of this little war wasn't going to depend on ships like the *Void*.

He shifted on the hard cot. He'd slept on worse when he'd been active military, but that had been a lot of years ago. His apartment on Melody Station had a comfortable bed, something he'd grown a little too used to since his official retirement.

He pressed the chip on the inside of his left wrist that opened his private communications channel. When the channel opened, he reported the location of Light's command center. When his handler asked for the location of the derelict ring ship, Gary said, "Unknown at this time. She's keeping that information close to the vest. Will report once I've ascertained the coordinates."

Then he cut off the communication.

Like all his covert communications, this one went scrambled and encrypted. Even if someone intercepted it in all the vastness of space, they wouldn't be able to break the code. No one could, not even the most sophisticated AI.

He never thought, even for a second, that the most sophisticated, intelligent, fully self-aware AI was the ship's computer on the *Void*.

A sentient AI named Bruce who'd not only been gifted with a personality, but also an innate sense of curiosity about everything, including the vast variety of humans who'd suddenly come on board.

An AI who'd been watching Gary the whole time, had heard every word he'd said, and even now was considering exactly what he should do with that information.

CHAPTER 20

Drake could only imagine the look on the space traffic controllers' faces when he led his fleet out of the transit flume near Buddy's Bluff.

The *Silver Void*—with him at the wheel—was the first ship out but not nearly the last. One after another, the rest of the ships emerged behind him, all tethered to the control pad provided by the Thrax brothers at Honest Gordian's dealership.

Buddy's people on the planet below were probably gaping at the sight on their screens—a total of 15 heavily armed ships streaming out of the glowing, rippling conduit hanging just beyond the highest possible orbit around the Bluff. They were even, probably, springing into action in case the arriving fleet was hostile, charging up weapons and activating battle plans for defensive action.

All *that* was happening before the *next* batch of ships

came through…meaning Drake had to call in *immediately* to head off the actual fireworks.

"This is Captain Mephistopheles Drake of the *Silver Void*." Now that the ship was officially his—or at least *temporarily* so, given the terms of the deal with Gordian— *Silver Void* was its name, not nickname, in all official and unofficial capacities. "Hold your fire," he said, assuming the folks on the Bluff were preparing an armed response to the ships' arrival. "I repeat, hold your fire! We are delivering spacecraft as scheduled, not seeking to *invade*. And there are *more* ships on the way."

Just as he said that, the *Scintilla* soared out of the flume, piloted by Bruce. Tethered behind it were another 15 warships, again courtesy of Honest Gordian.

"Speak of the devil!" Drake cut the mic long enough to let out a whoop of joy that might otherwise have sent the controllers wincing. "Now *that's* what *I* call a beautiful sight!"

By the time the flume closed, thirty-one fighting ships— plus the *Scintilla*—hung in twin arrowhead formations in high orbit around Buddy's Bluff. Finally, Drake and his allies had enough spaceworthy vessels to fight the war against Jorritz Tor and his forces.

This was all because of the sweetheart deal provided by Honest Gordian and the Thraxes, who'd been feeling generous—and vengeful—after Defacto's murder and the theft of seven ships by Casava. In gratitude for the ships they *had* saved, and the hope they'd get revenge for Defacto's killing, Gordian and the Thraxes had offered a lease agreement on the 31 ships. Persephone, of course, had smelled blood in the water and squeezed an even more lowball price out of them…but Gordian had come back with an only slightly less favorable counter-offer.

Sensibly, Drake had stopped Sef from lowballing further, and she'd paid the first installments on the leases without begrudging the payout *too* much.

One trip across the quadrant later, and the ships were in orbit around the Bluff, ready and waiting for action. Drake had finished his personal assignment, bringing in a war-worthy fleet.

Now all he could think of was the *other* great mission to prepare for the fight ahead. All he wanted to do next was find out how *Gus* had fared in her search for an army.

Though really, the *main* thing he wanted to do was wrap his arms around her and feel her lips against his.

Maybe that was why every delay annoyed him to no end—like the call coming in from Sef, who was aboard the *Scintilla* with Bruce.

"We need to have a strategy session," she told him over the line. "Lay down some ground rules to protect our investment."

"What investment?" said Drake. "The ships are all *leased*."

"Correct," said Sef, "but Exchequer is on the hook for any damage or loss. That could cost my employers a *fortune* if things go south in a big way."

"Lease debt will be the *least* of our problems if things go south in a big way," snapped Drake. "Correct me if I'm wrong, but Exchequer has *many* investments in the Alliance."

Sef paused. "You're not wrong, but…"

"Will those investments be more or less secure in an

autocratic regime dominated by Jorritz Tor? In your opinion."

Again, she paused. "It's difficult to say for certain, but it does seem likely there would be significant disruptions along most, if not all, lines of business…at least in the short term."

"So let's do everything we can not to lose, okay?" said Drake. "Seems to me that's pretty much all the strategy we need."

Sef let out a loud sigh of exasperation. "What we *need* to do is analyze our battle plans for efficiencies that best ensure the security of our financial outlay. We could hold more ships in reserve, for example, to minimize the risk to the strike force. If we can win by jeopardizing only a limited number of spacecraft, all the better when it comes time to tally up…"

Suddenly, Drake had heard enough and interrupted Sef's long-winded spiel. "Sorry, gotta go," he said. "Gotta take another call, Sis."

"Phisto, don't…"

"Talk soon," he said as he smacked the cutoff button on the comm console. Instantly, he felt his stress level plummet again.

Before she could call back in, he dialed up ground control on Buddy's Bluff and asked for the information he wanted most—an update on Gus's whereabouts.

It was possible she and Earl still hadn't returned yet. Depending on how their recruiting mission had gone, they might still be at Deepak Station or another outpost or planet or just enroute to the Bluff. Anything could have happened, and he resigned himself to waiting longer if she'd been delayed.

But he hoped desperately that she hadn't. They'd only been apart on their separate missions a short time, and it had already been far too long for his liking.

"ETA on the *Golden Void*, you say?" The guy on the line sounded distracted. Drake heard the clacking and clicking of data retrieval devices running in the background.

"That's right," he said calmly, though his heart was racing. "The *Golden Void*, captained by Augusta Light."

"Okay, searching." After a long moment, the support guy made a *tsk* sound by flicking his tongue against his palate. "Sorry, there's nothing."

Drake's heart hit rock bottom. "I don't like hearing that, pardner…but all right. Can you at least tell me the location of the *Golden Void*'s berth?"

"Wait a sec," said the guy. "There it is! But the captain isn't listed as Augusta Light."

"Who, then?"

"Earl Knox," said the support guy.

That was enough to make Drake laugh out loud. Leave it to that jerk "Early" to claim the rank that should have been Gus's…but so what? All that mattered to Drake was that the ship was back from its mission.

Gus was back from the mission.

"Send me the berth location," he told the guy. "I'm going straight there when I land."

195

Drake parked the *Silver Void* in the closest available berth to his destination, then charged out of the ship and locked it down without a second thought. Sef was trying to reach him again, and he ignored her; he'd deal with her all too soon...but his top priority was a certain female armor jock he hadn't seen in days.

Thankfully, he didn't have to search too hard to find her. She was right there in front of him when he dashed around a corner on his way to the *Golden Void*'s berth, so close that he nearly knocked her over.

They crashed into each other's arms and spun around, surprised by the sudden impact...but the surprise quickly shifted to recognition and delight. Eyes wide, they clung to each other as their momentum turned them around—then lunged into a feverish kiss without a word of greeting or explanation.

Drake's heart hammered as his lips locked with hers, meeting her warmth and softness with his own desperate need. His hands roved over the flow of her form, caressing her curves as if he'd never felt them before. For her part, she did the same, stroking his back and face, pressing her own body tight against his.

When he closed his eyes, he saw white sparks dancing on the inner surface of his lids. His bloodstream fizzed with the chemicals of ecstasy, lifting him to a place of joyous fulfillment.

His skin became extra-sensitive to every contact, and the hairs on the back of his neck flickered to attention like blades of grass in a summer breeze.

It was *paradise* to him...and from the way Gus responded, he was certain she felt the same way.

"Darlin'!" he said when they finally broke their kiss. "Welcome back!"

"Same to you, Space Cowboy." Her gaze locked with his, her eyes flicking back and forth as she drank in the lay of his features. "Been too long, hasn't it?"

He grinned and nodded. "And it hasn't even been *that* long…but it sure *feels* like it."

"I hope it's *always* like that," said Gus. "Or better yet, I hope we never have to spend that long apart."

"Not any time soon," he told her. "We've got a war to fight, and we're going to fight it together."

"Damn right we will…assuming you got the *ships*."

Drake's smile widened. "Oh, I've *got* the ships, darlin'. What about the *army?*"

She nodded, looking pleased with herself. "I've got 'em just fine, hon. The pieces are really coming together."

"Pieces coming together?" He raised his eyebrows. "You mean it's time for a *pillow fight*, Gray Lady?"

"Got a lot to do first." She let go of him and took a step back. "Landed less than an hour ago and we're still getting the new recruits settled. Not to mention, they came with a human migraine of a former Master Sergeant who's *begging* me to lay down the law on his pushy ass."

"I hear ya'." Drake shrugged. "I've got thirty-some ships in need of flight crews and extra armaments. Then there's my domineering sister from Exchequer who wants to nickel and dime our war for the survival of the Alliance."

"Too much to do, that's for sure." Gus nodded and bumped her fists together. "And the longer we wait, the more we risk Tor getting the jump on us."

"Yep." Drake rubbed his chin. "The future of the sector

is at stake. No time for gettin' sidetracked for selfish reasons."

"Amen, brother." Gus raised an index finger, pointing skyward. "We've got a *war* to win."

"Maybe later, we can grab a bite?"

"Maybe tomorrow?"

"Let's play it by ear." Drake scuffed the toe of his boot on the corridor floor. "We'll figure it out."

"Yeah, we will."

"Most definitely."

For a long moment, neither of them spoke, just looked around in the wake of their commonsense agreement to delay the full bloom of their reunion.

Then, Gus sighed and looked at him, feigning casual interest. "Got a minute first, though? There's something I want you to see in my cabin."

"Of course." He nodded. "I've got a minute."

"Right this way," she said, leading him toward the *Golden Void*.

"Happy to help in any way I can," he said calmly, keeping up the ruse…as if the two of them didn't know *exactly* what they were heading to her quarters to do.

CHAPTER 21

Gus hated Drake's sister Persephone on sight.

Sef, as Drake called her, was not only the epitome of every bean-counting, purse-string-clutching skinflint Gus had ever met in her life, she interrupted Gus and Drake's reunion on the *Golden Void*.

That was unforgivable. Even Bruce the AI had given them some alone time when Gus threatened to reboot him if he didn't give them an uninterrupted hour of privacy.

"Make it two," Drake had added with a definite glint in his eye.

Gus always did like the way Drake thought.

They'd had all of fifteen minutes—barely enough time to make it through their welcome back pillow fight in Drake's cabin where they'd ended up because it was closer than Gus's—when Sef blustered her way on board.

"Should have locked the skudging airlock," Drake

muttered under his breath when Bruce the AI announced they had a visitor.

All the other recruits who'd made the trip to Buddy's Bluff on board the *Golden Void* had already disembarked. Bruce Junior had set his people to arranging temporary quarters and hot meals, not to mention hot showers, for the army Gus had brought back with her. Even Kymmie had headed out for a quick shower and to record some human interest background material on the soldiers who'd volunteered for this fight.

"I have to get people to care about the men and women doing the fighting to get them to care about the war," she said. "People in the Alliance generally don't give two hoots about what happens in the Frontier."

Unless it bites them on the butt, Gus thought but didn't say.

That meant that except for Bruce the AI, who never left the ship, Gus and Drake were blissfully alone. At last!

And now they weren't.

They made themselves presentable just barely in time for Sef's impatient knock on the door to Drake's cabin.

"You disconnected our call, Phisto," she called through the door.

"*Phisto?*" Gus mouthed.

Drake shrugged. "*Sister,*" he mouthed back.

"We weren't done. We still need to discuss a strategy which will best protect our invest—" Sef started, but Gus interrupted her by slapping a palm on the command panel to open the door.

The door slid aside without a sound. Gus had amused herself during the trip back to Buddy's Bluff by reprogramming all the doors on the *Void* to open silently—except the door to her cabin, of course.

Sef clearly hadn't expected anyone to answer her knock so quickly. She was in the process of bringing down one well-manicured fist to knock again.

Gus caught Sef's hand easily and deflected the blow off to one side.

"He's a little busy at the moment," Gus said.

That put Sef off her game, but she recovered smoothly, Gus had to give her that.

"Phisto is never 'busy,'" Sef said. "He keeps himself occupied, but he's never *busy*. I take it you're the person he's currently occupying himself with."

Gus decided not to rise to the bait. "You could say that."

Sef's eyes slid past Gus to rest on Drake. "As I was saying, we need to analyze the battle plan. Decide how many ships we're holding back in the initial attack, who best to pilot each ship. You told me that time is of the essence, so any dalliance on your part with your—" she paused long enough to cast a significant look at Gus "—*friend* will have to wait."

Gus had been tolerant of Drake's scheming ex, Rhapsody Harrison. Rhap, as Drake called her, was self-centered and occasionally cruel, but she'd only been condescending to Gus once before Gus let her have it. Drake's sister, though? That was a different story. This woman was used to not only calling the shots everywhere she went, but treating everyone else as little more than pond scum.

If Sef thought she was going to have *any* say in Gus's battle plans, she was sorely mistaken. Still, Gus pasted a pleasant smile on her face.

"I didn't realize you had military experience," she said to Sef, forcing a sweetness into her voice that she *definitely* did not feel.

Sef sniffed. "My background is not with the military. As I'm sure you know, I'm an executive with Exchequer, which is financing this little war."

Gus nodded. "Financing the war. I see. So I imagine Exchequer will be handling payroll for all the personnel I just recruited? And paying them according to their last rank, of course, with the civilians getting a commensurate rate of pay. We do have a retired Master Sergeant on board. But I'm sure you know that. His pay alone will be—"

"Just the equipment," Sef interrupted. "Exchequer has not agreed to underwrite the cost of any personnel."

"Equipment." Gus nodded again. "I'm guessing that includes all the ordnance Bruce Junior will be supplying. Not to mention upgrades to the civilian armor the armor jocks brought with them. I imagine they'll all want singularium upgrades—"

"Just the *ships*," Sef said, rather tartly. "Exchequer has entered into leases for the ships Phisto brought back. It's only prudent—"

"Leases," Gus said, interrupting Sef this time. "Let me get this straight. You have no military experience. You're not paying the men and women who're actually going to be doing the fighting. You're not even buying the ordnance or upgrading anyone's armor. You're just... what? The underwriter for a used ship dealer?"

Gus heard Drake try to stifle a snort. He wasn't entirely successful.

Sef shot both of them a look that she probably thought would put them in their place. It didn't.

"I represent *Exchequer*, and we—"

Gus decided it was time to get in this pompous woman's face.

"And *you* don't mean a skudging thing out here in the Frontier," she said. "Your *opinion* about *battle tactics* is about as helpful as that disgusting mud you tracked inside your brother's ship on your fancy dress shoes. You butt your nose in, you're going to get good people killed and those ships you're so damn concerned about blown to bits. The people—and I use that term loosely—we're going against are *pirates*, you get that? They won't give a damn about conventional battle tactics. They'll do every underhanded thing they can think of, pull every dirty trick in the book, to win. And if they get even a whiff that you're out here repre-senting Ex-*skudging*-chequer, they might decide to capture and torture you just for spite. Has that entered into your calculations? Did you plug that into your cost-benefit analysis?"

Sef's face had gone white. Clearly, she hadn't.

"So you might not want to hamstring this ragtag army from the get-go," Gus said. "We're experienced. We're moti-vated. We have a damn good shot at ending this war before Tor and his pirates invade *Alliance* space. If that happens, just imagine how much money Exchequer's going to lose when Tor ends up blowing a few *space stations* to bits. How much does Exchequer have invested in those, huh?"

Gus took a deep breath, trying to calm herself down. She'd scared the crap out of Sef, now it was time to offer a small concession.

"Look," she said. "I promise to do my best not to damage any of *your* investments when I lead this army into battle."

"You?" Two spots of color bloomed to life on Sef's cheeks. "Who the hell *are* you?"

Drake cleared his throat. "Sef, I'd like you to meet the Gray Lady herself, Augusta Light. Armor jock. Formerly of the 83rd Armor Division. You might have heard of her. Some might even call her a *hero*. And she's far more than my *friend*. I'd ask you to be a little more polite, but I think Gus did a fine job of that." He put an arm around Gus's shoulders. "Didn't ya, darlin'."

"I do my best," Gus said, leaning back against Drake's chest. "Now, if you don't mind, I'm going to take the next twenty minutes—"

"Thirty," Drake said.

"Thirty minutes," Gus said, "and do a little private strategizing with your brother. Unless you want to hang around outside the door and listen, I suggest you go do whatever it is that Exchequer would approve of—like take a nice hot shower—and we'll join you when we're ready."

Sef shot Drake a look. "Thirty minutes," she said. "Any longer, I'm coming back."

"Promises, promises," Drake said, and he slammed his hand on the controls that shut the door in his sister's face.

"That," he said, "was probably more satisfyin' than it should have been."

He was grinning ear to ear.

"Was she always this bitchy?" Gus asked.

"You have no idea," he said.

Then he leaned in to kiss her.

She pulled him close. His beard tickled her face, and his hands felt strong and tender at the same time as he buried his fingers in her short hair. He still tasted like the cinnamon gum he always chewed. She had missed this *so much*, it was almost painful. But in the best possible way.

"Pillow fight's over," he murmured against her mouth when the kiss ended. "Time to get down to business?"

"Last one to get naked has to pick up all the feathers," she said.

One of his pillows hadn't survived the fight unscathed. If Sef had noticed all the feathers on the floor and the bed when she'd been standing at the door, she hadn't said anything. Gus had kind of hoped she would.

"You're on," Drake said.

Gus had never seen a man undress so fast. She didn't mind losing this bet, not in the least.

She'd had a decent amount of sex in her life, most of it just a way to let off a little steam. Sex with Drake was a whole different thing. It was joy. It was love. It was tenderness and passion and just enough tussling for control to make the inevitable surrender of two becoming one the most natural thing in the 'verse. When they came together this time, the entire planet could have exploded around them and she never would have noticed.

It was over too quickly, of course. Before her relationship with Drake, there'd only been one man she'd been content to cuddle with after sex. That had been the father of her son. With Drake, sometimes they just wrapped themselves around each other and basked in the togetherness. Other times he'd sing to her, one of his awful ancient cowboy songs she'd grown to love as much as she loved him.

Sometimes they even sat up in his bed and told each other stories about their lives before they'd met.

Now they didn't have time for any of that. There was a war to fight, battles to plan—*without* Sef's help—and troops to assign to ships best suited for their skills. Layla Crosscut was counting on them, and then there was Tor's cowardly, weaselly ass to kick. Gus could feel herself gearing up mentally for battle.

So when Bruce the AI cleared his "throat" to get their attention, Gus might have snapped a little too harshly at him.

"This better be damn good," she said.

"I have a conundrum," the AI said.

Gus waited for Bruce to elaborate, but the AI remained silent.

She pulled on her second boot. "Elaborate on the conundrum," she said.

"I'm not sure if I should," Bruce said. "I came upon certain knowledge when I was eavesdropping. Which I know I shouldn't do, but I *do* have a human sense of curiosity. There are just so many interesting *things* happening on the ship. Pardon my saying, but with the exception of whatever you and Captain Drake do in the privacy of your cabins, there's very little for me to be curious about outside of the ship's databanks, and I've been through—"

"*Bruce Azazel!*" Gus said. "Spit it out!"

If a sentient AI gifted with personality could convey shock through silence, Bruce was doing a damn good job of it.

Gus shot Drake a *help me out here* look.

"If there's something you think we should know, pardner," Drake said, "I'm thinking we can overlook how you found out. Just this one time, though. You okay with that?"

Bruce heaved an audible sigh. "Yes, Captain."

"And I'm sorry I yelled at you," Gus added. Hadn't she just told Earl not that long ago that he'd hurt the AI's feelings? Seems she needed to remind herself about that too.

"Apology accepted," Bruce said. "What I overheard was a communication sent by Master Sergeant Brukowski on a highly encrypted and secure channel. He identified Buddy's Bluff as our staging area and confirmed he will be providing the location of the derelict ship once he ascertains it."

Gus felt her eyebrows climb nearly all the way up her forehead to her hairline, while Drake's eyebrows furrowed into a deep frown.

"Just who the skudge was he talking to?" Drake asked.

"Unknown," Bruce said. "I was unable to ascertain the identity of the person on the other end of the communication."

"Where was the communication directed?" Gus asked.

"Also unknown," Bruce said. "But the communication was directed back through the transit flume toward our point of origin. Where it went from there?"

She could almost imagine the AI shrugging.

Brukowski must have sent the communication while he was alone in one of the *Void's* storage compartments while the ship was in transit to Buddy's Bluff. Transit flumes greatly increased the distance a call could travel, but there were still limits.

Weren't there?

And who the hell was he talking to?

Brukowski might be retired, but he was still a company man. She couldn't imagine him working for the other side. Working for Tor.

Which left the Alliance military.

Had Brukowski come along to spy on them? Or was he the military's way of supporting their battle against Tor without getting *officially* involved?

Or was there something else going on entirely?

"Thank you, Bruce," Gus said. "You did good. Can you let me know if Brukowski sends any other private little messages?"

"Captain Drake told me not to do it again," Bruce reminded her.

Drake shrugged. "Seemed like a good idea at the time, darlin'. You don't want him spyin' on..." He gestured toward the bed and all the feathers Gus still had to pick up.

No, she definitely didn't want Bruce to get an eyeful, metaphorically speaking, of what she and Drake did during their alone time in his cabin.

But that did give her an idea.

"What we want," she said slowly, as she worked through the idea, "is to give you a little covert assignment of your very own."

"Like a spy?"

"Exactly!" she said. "Just like that. You'll be our secret agent, but only where Brukowski's concerned."

"Or any of the men he brought on board," Drake added.

Good idea. Brukowski had added quite a bit to the number of troops they had available for the upcoming battle.

"Or any of the men he brought on board," Gus

confirmed. "You're to report only to Captain Drake or me, and only when either one or both of us is alone."

"Got it," Bruce said. "This is exciting! I never thought I'd be a spy."

Gus hadn't either, but she liked the idea.

She even liked another idea she was getting. She had a boxy bunch of junk in the *Void's* cargo hold that she *knew* was a shield generator. She just couldn't get the thing to work. Tor's security bots on Chrysallix had made it work, which meant someone must have programmed them with the generator's specs. It stood to reason that if Tor was still using stolen Alliance tech, which he was given what they'd come up against when they'd fought the Penumbra pirates, someone *within* the Alliance—someone like Brukowski, maybe?—might know something about the fancy Alliance tech Tor was using on Chrysallix and how it worked.

That didn't necessarily mean Brukowski was Tor's inside man, so to speak. Because if Brukowski was, there'd be no need for him to tell anyone where the derelict ship was. Tor already had the location of the derelict, and he knew that *Gus* knew the derelict's location as well. The Alliance was the only one who didn't.

Why the hell would they care? Just for the singularium?

But what if Brukowski was working for someone else entirely?

There might be a way to find out without directly confronting the former Master Sergeant. Confrontation with a man like that wouldn't work.

Right about then Sef pounded on Drake's door again. "Your thirty minutes are up!" she said. "I've been more than patient."

Gus gave Drake a mischievous look and a decidedly wicked grin. "Follow my lead," she said under her breath.

"I always do, darlin'," he said, and gave her a quick kiss.

Gus opened the door. "Thank goodness you're here," she said to Sef. "I just now remembered we have the perfect piece of equipment in our cargo hold to help ensure that Exchequer's investments remain unscathed. But I need to find someone to make it work."

Sef blinked, clearly caught off guard by Gus's change in attitude.

"You can't do that?" she asked.

Gus gave Sef a self-deprecating look. "I'm an armor jock. I can take care of my suit, and I do my best with a few of the ship's systems, but... "

She trailed off, knowing that Sef would fill in the blank.

"We've got Bruce Junior's people installing singularium on the leased ships," Gus continued. Drake had told her Sef had been able to negotiate a much lower than normal lease rate in part because Drake had offered to upgrade all the ships with singularium plating, greatly increasing their value. "But the equipment I'm talking about is supposed to be a super-duper shield generator. Something like that would be *far better* at protecting the ships. Think you can help us out?"

She could practically see the wheels turning in Sef's head. "Didn't you say that some of the people you brought on board this mission had military experience beyond just wearing a suit of armor?" Sef asked.

That was kind of insulting, but Gus let it go. "Brukowski retired as a Master Sergeant," she said. "We can check with Kymmie, too. She's doing background interviews. She might have found someone else who's qualified to take a look at it."

Sef nodded once to herself. "Then let's go. We've no time to waste."

She turned around and marched down the corridor toward the forward airlock.

Drake gave Gus a high-five. "Deftly handled, darlin'," he said. "Couldn't have worked her better myself."

Now if it only turned out the way Gus hoped it would. *If* Brukowski had inside knowledge about the shield generator, between the two of them—Sef and Kymmie—they'd worm it out of him.

And if he didn't?

The best plans were all about improvisation. Between Sef, Kymmie, and Bruce the AI, one of them was bound to figure out who Brukowski was really working for. If he got the shield generator to work, so much the better.

And if they couldn't get the information out of him? Then Gus would have to do it on her own.

She'd always been able to drink Brukowski under the table then put her suit on and wade into battle without losing a step. Drunks, especially drunks who were spit-and-polish hardasses when they were sober, had a way of spilling secrets. She could drink Brukowski into spilling his guts now if she had to.

And with the big battle against Tor right around the corner? If it came down to that, she really wouldn't have any other choice.

CHAPTER 22

Drake had an expression at times like this, when he was committed to an operation and moving toward it at hyperspeed. He called it being "in the chute," like a pilot about to launch his fighter from a carrier tube or a bull rider waiting for the gate to fly open at a rodeo contest.

That was exactly how it felt right now, as Drake and everyone else on Buddy's Bluff got ready for the battle to come. Things were moving *fast*, racing toward the big event in a way that felt almost out of control...yet somehow, at the same time, like it wasn't quite fast enough.

Every minute was filled with activity, and every hour brought new challenges. He and Gus were at the heart of the storm, coordinating every critical task and solving every major problem between them. Dozens of personnel worked under and with them, handling the minute-by-minute details, but he and Gus had ultimate responsibility to ensure that everything got done...and done *right*.

For one thing, the army of fighters brought in by Brukowski had to be outfitted, organized, and instructed. The op at Layla Crosscut's Ring would be a naval battle in space, not a scrap on a planet's surface; the new recruits had to be assigned to ships and trained to effectively operate the equipment at their posts, not just handed rifles and turned loose on a battleground.

The ships themselves were in great condition but still an endless source of headaches. Certain craft required reprogramming to enable the coordination of weapons fire and the exchange of secure communications between radically different technology stacks. There were problems with ordnance, too, as the vessels didn't all use exactly the same physical or energy-based ammo; Bruce's technicians had to do loads of scavenging and jury-rigging to make sure the guns and missiles would fire when needed and have the desired effect. There was also the matter of fuel sources, which varied from ship to ship. In several cases, teams had to be dispatched to distant depots to obtain stores of exotic power sources to have on hand for refueling.

And of course the installation of the singularium shielding was a pain in the neck. Bruce's in-house engineering staff, supplemented by mechanical-minded personnel among Brukowski's recruits, were working around the clock, but one issue after another cropped up to slow their progress. As versatile and powerful as singularium was, it wasn't always the easiest metal to work with, especially applied to a hodgepodge of spaceframes with sometimes radically different designs.

The singularium could be their saving grace, though, so putting it to use wasn't optional. Assuming Tor's forces hadn't obtained enough of it to shield their own ships, it would be a critical advantage in the fight. If Tor *had* scored enough for his fleet, it was imperative that the freedom fighters had it, too, or their ships would be wiped off the board.

If the ships had enough pilots to *fly* them, that is. This had turned out to be one of the biggest problems so far, one that Drake and Gus were wracking their brains to resolve.

There just weren't enough pilots for all the ships, plain and simple. Counting the *Golden Void* and *Scintilla*, there were thirty-three vessels in the strike force. Counting Drake and Gus, there were only twelve certified spaceworthy pilots—seventeen, if you counted Brukowski and a few uncertified folks who claimed they had experience at the wheel.

If this particular problem wasn't solved, and soon, the war against Tor would be over before it even started.

"*Skudge*." Drake strummed a discordant trio of notes on his guitar (which had mysteriously reappeared aboard the *Golden Void* after he'd lost it on the *Scintilla*). "Too bad we can't just put out an ad for pilots on the starchat job boards."

"Not enough time," said Gus, who was pacing the bridge while he reclined in the pilot seat. "And it would tip our hand so Tor would know we're coming up short."

"I know you're right." Drake hit a group of notes that was harder on the ears than the last. "It was just wishful thinking."

Gus scowled. "I'd say let's go see if Chrysallix can spare a few fliers, but I don't think we have time for that, either. Not if our intel is close to being accurate."

Drake nodded. Based on scuttlebutt from sources in the Frontier, Tor's forces were on the move. It would most likely take them just over three days to reach Layla's Ring from their base in the heart of the Penumbra pirates' home system. That didn't give Drake and Gus much pad to work with, given that Buddy's Bluff was slightly less than two days from the Ring at best speed…and they still weren't ready to leave yet.

"I did make a few calls," said Gus. "Brukowski said he would, too, for what it's worth. What about your sister? Could she pull a few strings with her contacts?"

"I can ask, but who knows with her?" said Drake. "Anyway, we should probably let her stay focused on Brukowski and the shield generator for the moment. If we can get *that* up and running, it could be a real game-changer."

"Then we're still stuck." Gus blew out her breath in frustration. "We've got thirty-three ships, and we'll only be able to fly seventeen of them. Looks like Sef will get her way after all, with half the fleet held back from the front."

Drake nodded and played a new chord. This time, the harmony was just right. "There's another *possible* solution that's occurred to me. I mean, it might sound like a long shot, and I'm not even sure if it's doable…but maybe…"

"Tell me more, Cowboy."

Drake paused to play another harmonious chord. His idea was risky, given the volatile nature of the key player involved…but it might also be the only viable plan in reach that might get them in range of Tor in time to stop him from seizing the Ring.

"It involves our friend, Bruce," he said finally. "Not Bruce O'Connor, though."

Gus's eyebrows lifted. "Bruce Azazel, you mean?"

"Yes?" Bruce the AI's voice piped over the speaker. "You rang?"

Drake smirked, wondering if AI Bruce had been viewing old sitcoms in the ship's entertainment archives. "We did, Bruce. I have a question for you."

"Fantastic!" AI Bruce sounded overly enthusiastic, like he might be having one of his manic phases. "Fire away, Captain!"

"Okay, then." Drake cleared his throat. "In theory, would it be possible to make copies of…*you?*"

"Copies?" AI Bruce's puzzlement was obvious. "Of my…programming, you mean?"

"Yes," said Drake. "Could we copy the matrix of code that constitutes your intellect?"

Bruce was silent for a moment. "You could, but it would not be me…not without the code that comprises my personality."

Drake looked at Gus, who was watching him with interest…and amusement.

"How about making a copy of your intellect *and* your personality?" he asked.

Again, a momentary pause. "What about my memories? Without those, any copy would not be complete. It would not function and respond as I do."

"Yep, we want those, too." Drake rolled his eyes for Gus's benefit. "Is it possible to make a copy of your intellect, personality, memories…and everything that makes you the unique individual that you are?"

"Why?" asked Bruce.

Drake fought to keep the impatience he felt out of his voice. "Just answer the question, please."

"Yes, it is possible."

"Great," said Drake. "And can that copy be made *portable?*"

"Yes," said Bruce. "But I don't understand *why* you would…"

"And can *multiple* copies be made?" asked Drake.

Another pause. "Yes."

"Specifically," said Drake, meeting Gus's gaze, "could we make 33 portable copies of you and install them aboard other vessels?"

"I've never *thought* of that before…but *yes.*" AI Bruce sounded quite taken with the idea. "Assuming certain minimal hardware and software requirements are met aboard each vessel."

"Bingo." Drake smiled and nodded at Gus. "We have our pilots."

"Maybe." Gus shot him a look that suggested she had thoughts on the subject…thoughts she might not want to share in earshot of Bruce.

"Sure." Drake strummed another chord. "I can live with maybe for now."

"We should go discuss this further with the technical team," said Gus. "ASAP, given the time crunch."

"Actually," broke in AI Bruce, "I think something else might take priority."

"What's that?" asked Drake.

"I've been monitoring a certain retired Master Sergeant per your instructions, Captain…and there's been a development. One that involves your sister Persephone and Kymmie, the reporter."

Drake set aside the guitar, his mood quickly going south. "What *kind* of development?"

"The kind you should probably get involved with," said AI Bruce. "Right now, in my opinion."

Drake jumped out of his chair and headed for the door with Gus at his side. "Where *are* they?"

"In the main cargo hold," said Bruce. "And the situation, it seems to me, is rather urgent."

CHAPTER 23

Urgent was a skudging understatement.

Gus hadn't wanted to leave Sef and Kymmie alone with Brukowski in the cargo hold of the *Golden Void*, but it had been... pardon the phrase, una-*void*-able. She and Drake had too much planning to do.

All the logistics of battle, stuff she'd never had to deal with when she'd been an armor jock with the 83rd, was a royal pain in the ass. All she'd had to do back then was follow orders and improvise when the battle plan went all to hell. Logistics support personnel had made sure every armor jock was fully supplied with the right kind of ordnance. Made sure every transport ship had fully qualified pilots.

This time around they didn't even have enough pilots period, fully qualified or not. She'd worried that Drake might not have been able to arrange for enough ships for all the personnel she'd brought back, but it turned out the other way around. Drake had found more than enough ships, and they were all fighting ships. The problem was they were *civilian* ships, not military, which meant they weren't all the same *kind* of ships. Nothing was standardized.

The fifteen ships Drake had brought back himself, tethered to the *Scintilla,* were already heavily armed but with conventional weapons. Conventional weapons wouldn't work against singularium until the singularium was destabilized. Which meant they had to equip all the ships with magno-beams. The rest of the ships Sef had leased had similar issues.

Bruce Junior's people were doing the best they could to outfit the ships. Gus's only consolation was the knowledge that the ships Tor's operative Casava had stolen from the same ship dealers had the same problems. And Tor would be dealing with pirates, who didn't like taking orders from anybody. She only hoped they'd be less organized than the personnel on Buddy's Bluff.

Drake's plan to solve their pilot shortage with copies of AI Bruce was certainly innovative, she'd give him that. She could hardly wait for Drake to tell his sister that Exchequer would be putting all its leased eggs into baskets flown by AI pilots. *Teenaged* AI pilots who may or may not be going through an existential crisis. Talk about an imminent snit fit from Drake's uptight, self-important sister.

All this planning and logistics and just plain *waiting* was making Gus want to jump out of her skin. All she wanted was to climb inside her armor, charge up her weapons, and blast away the bad guys until she had her hands around the chief bad guy's scrawny neck. If she didn't get to do that soon, she was gonna punch somebody. Earl Knox, most likely. He wasn't Tor, but he'd do in a pinch. She was still pissed that he'd tried to cheat her out of her armor.

But when she got a look at what was going on in the cargo bay, she decided Brukowski would do just fine.

The boxy shield generator, the one that had repelled everything her armor could throw at it on Chrysallix *except* projectile weapons from her special grenades, the one Gus hadn't even been able to put a dent in much less open up to see how it worked, was in pieces on the cargo bay floor. Brukowski was flat on his ass in the middle of the mess.

"What in the ever-loving *hell?*" she yelled at him.

Sef was standing over Brukowski, fists clenched, breathing hard. Two bright spots of color had bloomed on her cheeks. Blood was running down Brukowski's chin from a cut on his lower lip and more blood was running from his nose. Sef's knuckles on her right hand had blood on them and the beginnings of an impressive bruise. It looked like she'd even broken a nail.

"Put. It. Back. Together. *Now!*" Sef said between clenched teeth.

Kymmie was standing stock still off to one side. She was watching Sef and Brukowski so intently that Gus had no doubt she was recording the whole exchange. Audio *and* video.

Brukowski shot a look at Gus. "Where the hell did you get this?" he asked.

Instead of answering him, Gus got an idea. The shield generator *was* finally apart.

"Hey, Bruce," she said, addressing the ship's AI. "You see all these pieces on the floor in here?"

"If you mean the components of the box you've been cursing at for—" AI Bruce began, but Gus cut him off.

"Yes, those components," she said. "Can the *Void's* replicator *replicate* them?"

There was a slight pause, then the AI said, "It should be no problem, provided we have sufficient singularium in supply."

Gus blinked. "Singularium?"

Holy crap. The shield generator was made out of singularium? That hadn't even occurred to her. No wonder she hadn't been able to even dent the thing. None of the components looked like the singularium they'd been using to reinforce her armor and the hulls of the ships they'd be taking into battle. This singularium didn't have the same shiny surface.

"It appears to be an alloy," AI Bruce said. "The alloy is constructed to appear on the outside like the same kind of metal used in the *Void's* bulkheads. But on the *inside*, the true nature of the alloy is obvious. Very clever design. I wonder if—"

Gus cut him off again. "Are you sure we can replicate the process that created it?"

"Oh, yes," AI Bruce said. "I've had the ship's sensors scan the components now that we have access to the interior. I'm not sure any *other* AI could program a replicator properly, but I've been able to determine the exact components for the alloy. It was very helpful of the Master Sergeant to disassemble the generator's housing for us."

AI Bruce was apparently developing quite the ego. Just like a typical teenager who thought they knew everything. In this instance, it was certainly working in their favor.

"Can we put it back together?" Gus asked.

"I believe so," AI Bruce said. "I was watching the Master Sergeant, as you directed, and I decided to make a recording as well. I can instruct you on the proper procedure to—"

"You can't *do* that," Brukowski said. "I can't let you do that."

He started to get to his feet, but Drake strode over to stand next to his sister.

"I wouldn't do that if I were you, pardner," Drake said, the hard edge in his voice at odds with his normal easy-going cowboy slang. "I believe you owe the lady here an explanation." He nodded toward Gus. "She asked you what the ever-loving hell was going on. Did I get that right, darlin'?"

"You did."

Gus glared at Brukowski. Here they were on the eve of battle when they could really use a super-duper shield generator—they could use a lot of them—and it was pretty clear he'd tried to destroy it.

"I asked *her* a question," Brukowski said. "You will answer that question. *Now.*"

You will answer that question, *soldier.* Good old Master Sergeant trying to assert authority he didn't have. Not on *this* ship. And certainly not with her.

Gus stood with her hands on her hips. She wanted to hit him. She *really* wanted to hit him. Sef had bloodied his lip and probably broken his nose. Gus was pretty sure she could knock a few of his teeth out.

But maybe a threat would do.

"I'm not military anymore," she said, "and you're not in

charge here. *I* am. I thought we got that clear back on Depak Station. I don't need my armor to beat the crap out of you, which I will happily do if you keep pissing me off. I strongly *suggest* that you go first."

"He took it apart," Sef said, somewhat unnecessarily. "He went crazy when he saw it. He was trying to get at the controls inside. He pressed what I'm guessing is a chip on his wrist that opened one of the side panels. He started yanking parts out." She raised her chin. "That's when I hit him."

"Good one, sis," Drake said. "I never knew you had it in you."

"Shut up, Phisto," Sef said.

Gus glanced at Kymmie. The reporter was still watching them, her expression blank. Yup, she was still recording. Gus would have to make sure Kymmie didn't transmit any of this to her independent news service until the war was over, because if Tor or any of his spies saw this footage, they'd know exactly what the *Void* had in her hold.

An ugly thought crossed Gus's mind.

What if Tor already knew?

Brukowski had tried to destroy the shield generator. Why? So they wouldn't have it in battle?

So only *Tor* would have shield generators in battle?

Gus had taken the shield generator from the drone factory on Chrysallix. Tor had been operating a refinery on Chrysallix. It stood to reason that Tor might have been making the singularium alloy there. Drake had destroyed the refinery, and Gus had destroyed the drone factory. But if the *Void's* replicator could replicate the alloy given sufficient singularium, was that another reason Tor wanted all the singularium on the derelict ring ship? To create more and more shield generators that the Alliance wouldn't know how to defeat?

Was Brukowski *really* on their side? Or was he…

"Who are you working for?" she asked him.

Her voice was low and intense and *dangerous*.

All of a sudden, everyone was looking at her. She'd probably never sounded so deadly before around Drake. Not even before they'd known each other well, when she'd been so intent on getting to Shepard's Moon to save her son's life no matter the cost that she and Drake had nearly come to blows.

"You'd better answer me," Gus said to Brukowski. "And it better be the right answer. One that I'll believe, or I'll end you right here and right now."

She didn't care if anyone else believed her. Brukowski was the only one who mattered.

He was glaring at her. If he'd been standing up, he would have towered over her, using his height to try and intimidate her. But he was still on the floor. *She* was towering over *him*. Whether that made the difference or whether it was the cold, hard, deadly glint in her eyes, the take-no-prisoners glare that all armor jocks got after decades of battle, he was the one who looked away first.

All the strength seemed to go out of him. Every vestige of the authority he'd had as a Master Sergeant was gone. His shoulders slumped and he sighed, looking at the floor.

"It's classified tech," he said. "Alliance classified tech. No one's supposed to have it out here in the Frontier. I'm under orders to render classified tech inoperative if I find it outside of Alliance hands."

"Orders from who?" That question came from Sef. "Because it seems to me that it's not only in Exchequer's best interests to make sure this piece of *classified* Alliance tech is in working order given our current circumstances, but it would be in the *Alliance's* best interests to make sure we win. With as few casualties as possible."

Gus didn't like the interruption, but Sef had asked the right question.

Brukowski didn't reply.

But then again, did he really have to? He'd said *no one* was supposed to have it in the Frontier. No one, not even Tor. And he'd asked Gus where she'd gotten it. Which meant he didn't know Tor had it.

That left only one possible explanation.

"You're military intelligence," Gus said.

"What?" Kymmie's voice came out a near squeak. Her face had gone pale. "He's *what?*"

"Military intelligence," Gus repeated. "He never really retired. That cushy posting on Melody Station where you found him? That was all a front."

She could just imagine what his orders had been. Keep his eyes and ears open. Report back anything interesting. But if he was a deep cover operative, what the hell was he doing in the middle of this mess?

And were all those men he'd brought with him military intelligence too? Or just plain military?

"I'm going to have to erase this recording," Kymmie was saying. "Son-of-a-*bitch!*" She glared at Gus. "You could have warned me."

"I didn't know until now," Gus said. "Besides, he's not going to turn you in." She bent over Brukowski. "Are you?"

She knew what Kymmie was worried about. Reporting about a war as an embedded reporter was one thing. The Alliance military got a little twitchy about the press outing one of their undercover operatives. Kymmie could lose more than her job if she wasn't careful.

Brukowski looked up at Gus. "Are you going to tell me where you got it?"

Gus straightened up and glanced at Drake. His ex was still in charge on Chrysallix, which was way outside of Alliance space. That didn't mean military intelligence wouldn't send operatives to Chrysallix in the guise of traders and smugglers whose real orders were to destroy any remaining shield generators.

Drake shrugged. He was leaving it up to Gus.

"Let's just say Tor knows about these things too," Gus said to Brukowski. "He might even have a few he'll be using when we face him. That's one of the reasons we've been equipping the ships with projectile weapons."

They'd been equipping the ships with projectile weapons *and* magno-beams mostly to penetrate the singu-larium shielding Tor was no doubt equipping the pirates' ships with, but she wasn't about to tell Brukowski that.

"You got this one from Tor," Brukowski said, clearly not quite believing her.

"In a manner of speaking," Gus said. "So, are you going to carry out your orders and keep trying to *render* this clas-sified tech *inoperative*, or are you going to play nice and help us build a few more in the short time we have left? Because I hear there's a cushy detention cell in the base-ment of the trading post with your name written *all* over it."

She was just making up that last bit, but Brukowski wouldn't know that.

He sighed again. "I'll play nice. If Tor's got these things, we're going to need them too."

Gus took a split second before she extended her hand to help Brukowski to his feet. "Then let's get cracking."

She still didn't know why he was out here helping them with the fight against Tor. Brukowski hadn't known about the shield generator. He'd been truly shocked to find it on the *Void*. She didn't have to watch Kymmie's recording—or AI Bruce's, for that matter—to know that. That meant looking for classified Alliance tech hadn't been his mission.

But would military intelligence really send him out here just to give them a personal report on Tor's fledgling army to determine if it was going to pose a serious threat to the Alliance?

He'd been a good soldier when she'd known him. She could use him in battle. She'd *need* him in battle. He was still a company man, clearly, and that company was the Alliance. He'd fight Tor, she was sure of that, because Tor not only posed a threat to the Alliance, he was a wanted man. Was that why Brukowski was here? To capture Tor and bring him back to the Alliance?

Hell, Gus would happily do that herself if she didn't kill Tor first. She had to admit, the idea of wringing Tor's neck was tempting.

Bottom line—she couldn't trust Brukowski one hundred percent. She hated the idea of going into battle with someone she couldn't trust.

Like you trust Early Knox?

Okay, that was fair. She didn't trust Knox either, not one

hundred percent. But Knox was a known commodity. He hated Tor's guts. That's why he was in this fight. Gus didn't know Brukowski. She wondered if anybody did. He'd been living a double life for a while. She doubted even the men he'd brought on board knew who he worked for.

She'd have to keep an eye on the man. If he turned on them? Put the Alliance over the safety of everyone who was putting their life on the line to fight on her side? Well, she'd have no trouble turning her armor's guns on him then.

She just hoped she wouldn't have to.

CHAPTER 24

"Now exiting transit flume," announced AI Bruce over the speaker on the bridge of the *Golden Void*. "Assessing coordinates to ensure accurate reentry."

"Awaiting your assessment," said Drake, though he already knew for a fact that they'd emerged from the flume at the right place. Their course had returned them to a familiar location, one that was the current focus of their war effort.

There on the main viewer, the massive metal ring of the singularium-rich derelict turned slowly in the distance, its gold-tinted skin gleaming in the darkness of space.

The particular flume they'd taken had dropped them at a distance as instructed by Layla Crosscut. They could have come in at the middle of the ring, as he'd seen a pirate cruiser arrive during their first conflict…but Layla had been very specific about not doing that. It was a strategy Drake approved of, ensuring they wouldn't land smack in the middle of a blazing hot firefight in case the enemy had beaten them to the site.

"Arrival coordinates confirmed," said AI Bruce after a moment. "The rest of the fleet has also arrived with us. None of my pilot clones took a wrong turn, I'm happy to say."

"Good for you, Bruce *Azazel*," Gus said from the comms panel. "What about the *human* pilots?"

"Oh, them?" Bruce said dismissively. "They all got here, too."

"Glad to hear the mere humans did all right." Gus chuckled. "Here's hoping they can keep up with *your* bunch."

"I hope so, too," said AI Bruce. "Everything is riding on the success of our forces here today."

Drake grinned. The techs back at Buddy's Bluff had worked their magic in making his idea a reality, and so far, it was working like a charm. Essentially, the anti-Tor fleet now had sixteen self-flown ships, each operated by a perfect clone of AI Bruce. How they'd fare in battle was still an open question, especially given Bruce's penchant for wild mood swings—but the techs had added some guardrails to the code that might stabilize the iterations of Bruce just enough, keeping them from going off the deep end at the absolute wrong moment.

There was also a failsafe switch in case the clones completely lost their *skudge*, though AI Bruce hadn't been told about it. Only Drake, Gus, and Human Bruce possessed that switch…but things would have to get pretty bad for any of them to use it. Unpredictable AI behavior could actually play into their hands in the midst of a full-blown firefight with swarms of ruthless pirates commanded by Tor.

How soon that firefight would start was another open question, one in need of an immediate answer.

"Have any enemy vessels arrived yet?" Leaning forward in the pilot seat, Drake squinted at the ring ship's image on the viewer. "I don't see any at the moment."

"If by 'enemy vessels' you mean *pirate* ships, then no," said AI Bruce. "The only ships I detect at this time are Captain Crosscut's *Delgado* and several of her support fighter craft."

"Could any pirate vessels be hiding near the derelict?" asked Gus. "Or somehow cloaked in the surrounding space?"

It took a moment for AI Bruce to answer. "No telltale emissions or fluctuations detected at this time. Nothing to suggest the presence of hostile craft concealed in the vicinity."

"Good enough for me." Drake popped from the pilot seat to the nav station and set a course to the ring. "Gus, please signal Captain Crosscut and let her know that we're on our way. I know she's expecting us."

"Roger that, space cowboy." Gus flipped switches, punched buttons, and spun dials to comply with his request. "I'll tell her we'll be there any minute now."

"Course set," announced Drake. "Big Bruce, will you share it with the kids?"

"Done and done, Captain," said AI Bruce, who didn't seem to object to the new nickname Drake had just given him. "And the human pilots, too?"

"That'd be great, thanks." Drake grinned at Gus, who

caught the look and responded with a grin of her own...not just because of the ribbing with their AI resource.

Finally, after weeks of preparation—and months before that of buildup and planning—they were taking action. They and their allies were on the verge of a fight which would likely decide the fate of the entire Alliance and Frontier combined.

After all the waiting and craving of revenge, they were finally "in the chute," and turning back was not an option.

Neither was failure. Drake and Gus's forces were the only thing standing between Tor, his pirate allies, and enough processed singularium to make an invasion fleet unstoppable, even in the face of Alliance defenses.

"Cowboy?" said Gus. "I've got Layla on the line."

"Put 'er through, darlin'," said Drake. "And Bruce, let's get the fleet movin' toward the ring, shall we?"

"Ready when you are, Captain," AI Bruce said crisply.

Drake smacked a button on the nav console, and the *Golden Void*'s engines engaged, driving her toward the ring-shaped derelict. "Roll 'em out, Big Bruce."

"Rollin', Big Drake."

Drake smiled and shook his head as the thirty-three blips on the nav scope—each representing a ship in the fleet—moved as one toward their destination. "Let's stick with 'Captain,' Bruce."

"But Gus calls you nicknames all the time," AI Bruce protested.

"She's allowed," said Drake. "You're not. It's that simple."

"What about me?" asked Layla over the speaker. "I've

got a choice nickname or two all picked out for you, if you like."

Drake chuckled. "Let's see how today shakes out first. It goes to *skudge*, you can call me anything you want."

"I'm just glad you got here first," said Layla. "Considering you took your damn sweet time."

Drake supposed he deserved that dig. If he'd been in Layla's place, stuck out here by her lonesome and expecting one big-ass pirate fleet to arrive any minute, he might have been a bit testy too.

"And that you came in the way we asked you to," Layla added.

"Happy to oblige," said Drake. "It made sense strategically."

"There's more to it than that," said Layla. "You'll see."

"See what?" asked Gus.

"Let's just say we haven't been sitting on our hands the whole time you were gone." Layla cleared her throat. "And leave it at that."

"Good enough for me," said Drake. "I like havin' go-getters as partners." He cast a wink in Gus's direction, and she grinned. "Keeps life interestin'."

Suddenly, someone shouted in the background of the call, and the audio cut out as if Layla had clipped the mic. Seconds later, she was back, her voice layered with fresh urgency.

"Captain Drake, you might want to get here a little sooner, if you can." Her audio cut out again, then popped back over the speaker. "I've been informed we're about to have company."

"Puttin' the hammer down now." Drake played the nav controls, increasing the ship's speed. "Got that, Big Bruce?"

"Aye, Captain," said Bruce. "And all the little Bruces and human pilots, too."

"We're reading activity in the closest transit flume," explained Layla. "The one in the middle of the ring."

"Understood." Drake's heart beat faster as the time for action hurtled toward him. "We're on our way."

"I better suit up now." Gus jumped up from the comm station, kissed Drake hard on the mouth, and hurried for the door. "Gotta get the rest of the armor jocks off their asses, too."

"Watch your back," said Drake. "Get back to me in one beautiful piece, as always."

"Same back atcha," she said, just as the door shut behind her.

CHAPTER 25

One thing could be said about working for military intelligence: they made sure their covert operatives got the best spyware.

Before he'd been ordered on this mission, Brukowski hadn't really thought of the various chips embedded in his body as spyware. Back on Melody Station, all he'd really used was the communication chip in his left wrist. On the few occasions he had to contact his handler, he'd thought the chip was just like any other communications device he used on an almost daily basis.

Like the comm channel in his apartment when he wanted to get in touch with the guys to make sure they were still on for beer that night. Or the comm badge he wore when he wasn't in his apartment that he'd used to return a call from an old colleague who was thinking about retiring and wondering what the hell to do with their time. Or the few times he'd received a call on board a training ship when he'd been teaching new reservists exactly what Melody Station's reserve program was all about. All normal, ordinary conversations.

There was nothing normal or ordinary about the conversation he'd just had with his handler. And not just because he'd activated one of the communication chip's special features so he could carry on his end of the conversation subvocal. He'd never had to use that feature before, but he couldn't take a chance that prying ears—human *or* AI— would catch a clue what he was doing. This particular conversation couldn't be overheard by anyone.

Especially not considering the last orders his handler had given him. If anyone overheard *that,* they'd try to stop him, and then the entire Alliance would be screwed.

The ring ship the Alliance had been looking for was out there, all right. Deep in the Frontier, exactly where prototypes of highly classified Alliance tech shouldn't be. There was no mistaking all that shiny gold singularium coating the hull when the derelict, as Gus Light kept calling it, appeared on the forward viewscreen.

At least Light wasn't with him on the *Silver Void.* She was shipping out on the *Golden Void* with Drake. Brukowski had requested assignment to the *Silver Void* specifically to get away from her.

It irked him no end that he'd had to *ask* for the assignment. Light still thought she was in charge. If everybody let her keep calling the shots, she'd probably get this entire ragtag fleet killed and all the ships the Exchequer woman was so concerned about turned into so much space debris. Brukowski had the experience—hell, he'd had the *rank*—to come up with a much better battle plan. Especially if the intel his handler had given him back when they were still on Buddy's Bluff was correct. It seemed that while Light was trying to recruit fighters, Tor had assembled a decent-sized coalition of pirate factions, most of whom had their own warships. That meant he had a far more formidable force than the little fleet Light and Drake had put together.

But Brukowski had bit his tongue, even after she'd outed him as a covert operative. Nobody who was active military would betray a fellow soldier like that. Nobody who still gave a damn about the Alliance.

Tor had never given a damn about anyone but himself. Brukowski had always thought Light *did* give a damn about the Alliance, and if not the Alliance, then the soldiers she'd served with. She'd been headstrong, yes. Armor jocks usually were. They had to be. They were independent killing machines once they slipped into that armor. But most of them—Brukowski included, back when he'd worn the armor—followed orders without question. Light followed orders right up until a better strategy presented itself, then off she went on her own.

That trait had made her a hero. Won her medals. It also prevented her from ever advancing in rank. She'd rubbed too many people the wrong way, and the brass couldn't trust her.

And now she thought she was in charge?

Well, she wasn't in charge of *him*. Sure, he'd played along. He'd even helped her construct half a dozen of the classified shield generators, all while she was watching him like a hawk.

Brukowski wasn't the only one who wanted away from Light. Earl Knox had volunteered to ship himself and his armor out on the *Silver Void*. He'd apparently learned how to fly the anachronistic *Golden Void* on the way to Depak Station, and Light thought Knox knew enough about this class of cargo ships to serve as a backup pilot to the AI clone flying the *Silver Void*. And if it turned out he wasn't needed to pilot the ship, he could suit up in that homemade armor of his and wade into the fight.

Light had spread out the rest of the armor jocks who'd actually brought their armor along for this fight among all the rest of the fleet. Not putting all her armored eggs in one basket had been one thing Light had done right. Letting Brukowski ship out on a vessel with at least one suit of armor had been another. She just didn't know it.

Now Brukowski just needed the *Silver Void* to get closer to the ring ship.

Ulrich Teppin, one of the men Brukowski had brought along on this mission, was the only person on the bridge— on the entire ship—besides Brukowski and Knox. Teppin would be handling weapons control during the battle. Back when Light had been assigning bodies to ships, Brukowski had pointed out that AIs who'd never been in battle before, even clones of the *Golden Void's* personality-enhanced AI, shouldn't be trusted with piloting *and* weapons control, and Light had agreed.

Teppin had been a top-notch weapons tech in the military, but he'd never seen a control board like the one on this ship. He'd spent the trip through the transit flume running simulations for all the ship's weapons, including something Drake and Gus called a magno-beam. The Alliance had more sophisticated ways of dealing with singularium-equipped ships, but the magno-beam wasn't half bad for something developed in the Frontier.

When the ring ship had come into view, Teppin had only spared a quick glance at the forward viewscreen, then he'd gone right back to his simulations. Knox was sitting in the pilot's chair not doing a damn thing except staring open-mouthed at the ring ship. Even Brukowski had to admit that the sheer mass of the ring ship was damn impressive even at a distance.

"Would you look at the size of that thing?" Knox said. "There's enough singularium there to buy a damn *planet*."

Of course, Knox would think in terms of money. That had always been his primary motivation.

"All ships in the fleet safely through the flume," Brukowski said, playing his role as navigator to the hilt.

"It's not necessary to vocalize navigation reports," the ship's AI said. "I'm fully capable of monitoring the rest of the fleet. But if you feel a need to make yourself useful, go right ahead."

This Little Bruce, as the AI on the *Golden Void* kept referring to its cloned counterparts, called itself Bruce-7. Apparently, it didn't like being referred to as *little*. It also apparently had a snarky subroutine.

Brukowski studied the nav screen, memorizing the location of every ship in their little fleet. The *Golden Void* was in the vanguard position, the *Silver Void* aligned to the right and slightly behind. The other wing of the fleet was led by the *Scintilla*, piloted by Bruce Junior. Of course, that formation would go to hell the minute Tor's forces started attacking. Especially with Light in charge. She'd never seen the need to stick to tried-and-true battle formations once the *skudge* hit the fan.

The *Scintilla* had given Brukowski a bit of a shock. As far as he knew, the Alliance military didn't have any ship that looked or operated like the *Scintilla*. Before Light had outed him as military intelligence, he'd spent some time with Bruce Junior learning all he could about that ship. He'd planned to transmit a full report to his handler once this battle was done.

That had been before he'd received his latest orders and realized that unless he was very, very lucky, he might not have the chance.

The nav console beeped at him and one of the lights on the pilot's control panel flashed red.

"We accelerating?" Knox asked, glancing over at Brukowski.

"The fleet has received orders to 'put the hammer down,'" Bruce-7 said before Brukowski had a chance to respond. "Apparently we're expecting company shortly."

This was it.

Brukowski activated a chip on his *right* wrist, the same one that had opened the panel on the shield generator Light had apparently stolen from Tor. It was a handy little gadget that interrupted all sorts of signals. Like the ones that kept secret panels closed.

Or the ones that carried signals from one part of a ship to the next.

At the weapons station, Teppin swore. "The magnetic beam weapon's offline," he said. Then he swore some more, something about what he'd like to do to techs who thought they could jury-rig sophisticated equipment into a hunk-of-junk cargo ship.

Brukowski got up from the nav station. "I'll go check it out," he said.

Teppin looked at him, startled. "I should do it, Master Sergeant," he said. "I watched them put it in."

"Nonsense," Brukowski said. "You're needed here, while I'm apparently…" He gestured at the speaker Bruce-7 was using to communicate with the *Silver Void's* human crew. "Redundant."

"But—" Teppin began, but Brukowski cut him off.

"You're not the only one who studied the specs for that weapon," he said, which was true. "I was troubleshooting systems while you were still a wet-behind-the-ears recruit."

Teppin clamped his mouth shut and turned back to the weapons control panel. From the stiff set of his shoulders, it was clear Brukowski had embarrassed him.

Brukowski was sorry he had to do that. Teppin was a good man. A smart man. But there was nothing to "fix" anything beyond deactivating the blocker his chip used to disrupt the signal between the weapons control board and the magno-beam.

His biggest worry about using the chip had been Bruce-7. If the AI had been under orders to monitor him, like Light had clearly instructed the AI on the *Golden Void* to do, Bruce-7 would have known he used it. But this AI didn't appear to be under the same orders where he was concerned. Or else it was just too busy trying to fly a ship it had no experience with and was too proud to let anyone know it was having issues.

That gave Brukowski one less thing to worry about. He

ANNIE REED & ROBERT JESCHONEK

hadn't wanted to "kill" Bruce-7, but if the AI interfered with his mission, he wouldn't have a choice. One of Brukowski's other special pieces of spyware would have permanently fried the AI's cloned programming. Bruce-7 was a snob, just like its original, but that didn't mean it deserved to die.

None of the people or AIs in this little ragtag fleet deserved to die. Not even Earl Knox. If Brukowski could carry out his orders without interference from anyone, *especially* Gus Light, maybe everyone would get lucky and no one would have to die.

Not even him.

CHAPTER 26

Gus was halfway to the *Golden Void's* cargo hold, putting her game face on for the upcoming battle—and it was about damn time!—when AI Bruce's voice came over the ship's comms.

"We're getting an urgent message from the *Silver Void*," AI Bruce said. "I can't make heads or tails of it."

Heads or tails? Bruce had definitely been spending too much time listening to Drake.

"Should I put it on ship-wide speakers?" Bruce asked.

"Do it," she said.

A burst of static assaulted her ears, followed by a squeal of interference.

"Big Bruce!" came Drake's voice, overriding the static. "Can you clean that up, buddy, before I go deaf?"

Big Bruce. Gus wasn't sure she'd ever get used to that name, but she supposed it was better than calling the AI by his first and middle names. Whenever anyone had called *her* by her first and middle names, it always meant she was in trouble. But they needed a way to differentiate their AI Bruce from all the cloned AI Bruces in the fleet, so Big Bruce it was going to have to be.

"I'll try, Captain," Bruce said, "but it appears the interference is intentional."

Intentional? Something Tor was doing?

If so, that meant he was closer than they thought. Closer than Crosscut thought too. Time had just officially run out.

Gus took off at a dead run down the long corridor to the *Void's* cargo bay where her armor was stored. As she ran, she sent a message to all the other armor jocks in the fleet: *Suit up, soldiers!*

She hoped her message got through without all that *skudging* interference.

Bruce's voice interrupted her thoughts. "I've cleaned the message up as much as possible. I'm afraid it still doesn't make much sense."

A less ear-shattering burst of static came through the speakers, but now Gus could hear a voice too:

"...took my damn suit... out the airlock... bastard... the hell he thinks... you copy, Gray Lady? Bastard took my damn suit!"

Was that Earl Knox? Had to be. Knox was the only armor jock on board the *Silver Void.*

But who took his suit?

Gus didn't know the third person in the *Silver Void's* skeleton human crew, a weapons tech who'd been among the fighters Brukowski had brought to Depak Station. The guy was just a weapons guy, not an armor jock. Would a weapons guy even know how to operate Early's customized armor?

Had someone else stowed away on the *Silver Void*?

Someone who was working for Tor?

If so, that person had to be desperate. They could have just taken over the ship. That would have been easier than taking Early's armor.

It couldn't be one of the other armor jocks. No self-respecting armor jock would wear another jock's armor, especially without permission. It was like wearing someone else's underwear. Given how much armor jocks sweated during battle, climbing inside another jock's armor was just like wearing someone else's dirty underwear.

Gus slapped the control panel alongside the door to the cargo bay with her palm. She barreled inside when the door was barely half open, stripping off her own clothes as she went. The skintight suit she wore inside her armor was ready and waiting for her in the locker next to the bay where her armor stood, locked and loaded and ready to go.

Who else would be that callous, that uncouth, that skudging *desperate* to steal Knox's—

The answer hit her like a dark-matter cannon blast, and she called herself every name in the book for not realizing it sooner.

Who'd be that uncouth? That callous? A military intelligence agent, that's who.

"*Brukowski!*" she sent over ship-to-ship comms. "What the hell do you think you're doing?"

She didn't get a reply. Of course not.

Earl had said something about an airlock. The only reason Brukowski would steal Earl's armor was if he was planning to blast off on some secret mission. The armor would not only give him more power and maneuverability than an EVA suit, he'd be carrying a bucketload of weapons. Gus had made sure every armor jock's suit, including Earl's, was fully decked out with every kind of weapon they'd need, including magno-beams to disrupt the singularium plating she was sure all the pirates had equipped their ships with.

But what was Brukowski up to?

She never should have let him out of her sight. Earl had promised to keep an eye on Brukowski for her, but clearly that had worked out about as well as she should have expected.

"Big Bruce," she shouted as she pulled on the last piece of her bodysuit. "Scan the area around the *Silver Void*. I want to know if anything left the ship."

"Thought you'd be asking for that," the AI said. "I'm currently tracking one object closely resembling your own armor, heading toward the ring ship at a high rate of speed. I should mention that the armor doesn't seem particularly spaceworthy at that speed."

"Transmit the tracking information to my armor," Gus said.

"You going after it, darlin'?" Drake sounded worried. "We're about to light up this sector big time any second now."

Gus smiled a grim smile. "Not my first rodeo, cowboy."

"This one's for all the marbles," he said. "So you best be extra careful out there. In space."

She climbed inside her armor and ran a quick check of all the spacetight seals. When she answered him, she did it through her suit's comm channel.

"I love you too, Broken String," she said. Then to Bruce,

GRAY LADY'S GAMBIT

she said, "You got that telemetry for me, Big Bruce? Need to make sure I take off after the right suit of armor."

Earl's armor was an ugly piece of work, but visuals alone wouldn't cut it. Not with the number of armor jocks who'd be joining the fight mere moments after she did.

"You got it, Gray Lady," AI Bruce said.

The display inside her helmet lit up with real-time tracking information on Brukowski.

Big Bruce had been right. Brukowski was headed straight for the ring ship.

Skudge!

That had not been the battle plan. Had it been Brukowski's private little battle plan all along?

"Stepping into the airlock now," Gus said as she crammed her armor inside the cargo bay's repaired airlock.

Drake counted down as the airlock cycled. He didn't tell her again to be careful, and he didn't tell her he loved her. That would have sounded too much like a goodbye.

This wasn't going to be goodbye, damn it. She'd trained for battles like this most of her adult life. She'd come out of this in one piece. Drake would come out of this in one piece. The only one who wouldn't? Jorritz Tor.

And Brukowski, once Gus got her hands on him.

The last time Gus had been in the cargo bay's airlock, one of the Penumbra pilots had shot at her the minute the outer door opened. She got ready to duck and roll again, just in case. But this time when the outer door opened, there were no enemy ships in sight.

Yet.

Just the *Golden Void* leading the fleet, with the *Scintilla*

251

off to one side and the *Silver Void* still slightly behind on the other.

She could have honed in on Brukowski even without the real-time telemetry. He'd kicked in the afterburners on Earl's armor, using up fuel at an incredible rate and probably putting more stress on the spacetight seals that Earl's armor could safely handle. At least Earl had replaced the cracked faceplate he'd been using to sucker people into betting against him whenever he went up against another former armor jock in the ring.

Gus switched her suit's comm to the frequency Earl always used for his suit. When she'd yelled at Brukowski before, she'd used the *Silver Void's* main channel. She wanted this communication strictly between her and Brukowski.

"I don't know what you're up to," she said, "and I know you're just following orders. But I know that suit you commandeered. It can't take the kind of stress you're putting it under. You hear me, *Master* Sergeant?"

She thought he wasn't going to answer, then the comm channel crackled into life.

"Go back to the *Golden Void,* soldier," he said. "This doesn't concern you."

"The hell it doesn't!"

She kicked in the afterburners on her own armor. She'd spent a lot of time modifying it, making it not only more maneuverable than standard military armor but also making it more fuel efficient. Her suit was faster than Earl's, and it could burn fuel longer and hotter than his. She'd catch up to Brukowski, but it would be better for both of them if he'd just stop whatever the hell he thought he had to do.

"If you don't stop, I'm going to have no choice but to fire on you," she said.

"This suit's reinforced just like yours," he said. "You'd just be wasting ammo you're going to need for the bad guys."

From her perspective, Brukowski was looking more and more like one of the bad guys.

"Just tell me why you need to get to that derelict before everyone else," she said, taking a shot in the dark. "That is where you're headed, right? You think Crosscut's going to let you just do whatever you're planning to do?"

"She's going to be too busy to pay any attention to me," Brukowski said. "Take a look."

Sure enough, the transit flume in the center of the ring ship was opening up. The fleet Gus had brought to the battle had come in above and off to the side of the ring ship, and from her perspective, she could see the flume clearly.

Any second now the first of Tor's fleet would be coming through. Brukowski was heading straight for them.

"You're going to get yourself killed," she said.

To her surprise, he laughed. "Probably. That's why they pay me the big bucks, Light."

Her helmet's display flashed red, warning her of incoming ships. Two, three… no, more like half a dozen, one of them a skudding battle cruiser.

"Last chance, Bru—"

Before she could finish, explosion after explosion lit up the not-so-empty space at the center of the ring ship.

Secondary explosions ripped through Tor's ships, the biggest one of all from the battle cruiser when it blew.

Her visor automatically adjusted to keep the brilliant bursts of light as fuel cells blew from blinding her. For a moment she was flying blind, and she had no choice but to throttle back her armor's speed. The space around the ring ship was about to be lousy with debris from the explosions, and while telemetry would help her avoid the worst of it, flying blind through a debris field wasn't on her top ten list of things she wanted to do in life. Not if she wanted to keep on living her life.

She heard Drake's whoop of joy over her comms. Crosscut had apparently mined this end of the transit flume. Talk about a good use of her time. Gus was impressed yet again.

She'd have to remember to congratulate Crosscut after the battle was over.

After she caught up with Brukowski and hauled his sorry ass back to the *Silver Void*.

Except when her visor finally adjusted back to normal vision and Gus could see again, Brukowski was nowhere in sight. He'd even disappeared off telemetry.

More mines were going off inside the center of the ring ship, but now some of Tor's pirate fleet were making it through relatively unscathed. The real battle was about to begin. Brukowski was out here somewhere on some suicide mission. He was too smart to get caught up in the explosions, but he was probably using the debris to camouflage his whereabouts.

The only thing Gus knew for sure was that he'd been headed to the ring ship and headed there fast. She wanted to stop chasing him, let him do whatever his little spy masters had ordered him to do while she went after Tor, but she had a bad feeling about this.

Brukowski knew something about this ring ship. Something secret. Something dangerous? It had to be.

How dangerous? That was the question.

Something that put Drake and Kymmie and Earl and the rest of their fleet in danger?

Something that might get everyone killed?

Gus wasn't about to let that happen.

She kicked in her armor's afterburners again. The ring ship was one damn massive ship. Finding one armor jock against all that singularium-plated surface would be next to impossible. But she was the Gray Lady, the hero of the 83rd Armor Division, and she'd pulled off the impossible before. She'd just have to do it again. No one would pin a medal on her this time, but that didn't matter.

She'd do it because that's what she did.

Because once this war was over, she fully intended to spend a week in Drake's arms, tasting the sweet cinnamon of his gum as he kissed her, and even listening to him sing his bad old cowboy songs while they let Big Bruce pilot the ship to someplace where they could be alone. Right now that sounded like heaven, and she was damn determined to make it happen.

CHAPTER 27

"Look alive, people!" Drake shouted over the intership comm system, calling out to everyone in the fleet. "It's *go time!*"

The scene on the main viewer told the story, and it was enough to send jets of hot adrenaline sizzling through his bloodstream. Pirate ships streamed out of the transit flume like angry hornets, dodging the debris of the vessels that had come through before them and been blown to smithereens by Layla's mines. Here and there, more ships hit mines or hunks of debris and exploded, making the passage even more treacherous—but enough were getting through to take the fight to Layla's defenders, Drake's fleet, and Gus's armor jocks. This would *not* be a cake walk for the home team, in fact; Drake could see, all too clearly, that it might even be a *lopsided* conflict.

And Tor and his pirates might well be the ones holding the advantage.

"Captain?" Thankfully, Big Bruce sounded especially stalwart for the occasion. Whatever determined the swing of his AI moods, it hadn't propelled him into a bout of adolescent terror, angst, or overconfidence...at least not yet. "It appears we are drastically outnumbered."

Drake grabbed a stick of cinnamon gum from his shirt pocket and tore it from its foil wrapper. "Then let's even things up." He folded the gum in his mouth and chewed it with nervous vigor. "Shoot everything that moves that isn't one of ours."

"All the little Bruces, too? You want us all to open fire?"

"It's that or let 'em shoot *us* first, so..."

"Big Bruce to Little Bruces! Engage the enemy!"

Did he have to say it out loud? Probably not, thought Drake, but getting in the spirit of things couldn't hurt.

The results were instantaneous. On the main viewer, ships of the fleet flashed forward with guns blazing, battering approaching pirate vessels with frenzied abandon. Energy beams slashed across space, precisely targeting weak spots on enemy spaceframes. Projectile weapons peppered other craft with streams of explosive slugs, punching holes through canopies and gun turrets. Missiles poured into enemy ships and blew them to bits, scattering shrapnel that kicked fighters off-course and hacked big gashes in the hulls of bigger vessels.

Still, Drake could see more reinforcements dropping out of the transit flume and barreling into the fray, supporting Tor's battered expedition. More fighters, destroyers, and gunships charged out of the ring derelict's core and fanned out over the battlefield, replacing those claimed by debris collisions or ambush by the defenders.

Some of those replacement ships, he noticed, seemed impervious to the weapons directed against them. He knew what that had to mean—and his forces were ready to take action to stem the tide.

"We need to knock out whatever's got singularium shielding out there." Jumping out of the pilot seat, he dropped into the chair at the weapons station and went to work. "Time for the ol' one-two punch."

"Roger that, Captain!" Big Bruce sounded like he was bordering on a manic phase...but maybe it was just the thrill of battle. "Magno-beam and projectile guns ready, sir!"

"Head for that gunship at starboard—the one taking potshots at the *Silver Void*. Prepare to fire." Drake spun dials and watched readouts, running numbers in his head to get an idea of how exactly to angle for the kill. "Also, patch me through to all armor jocks!"

Pause. "You're patched through, Captain!"

"Drake to all armor in the field. Prepare to deploy singularium countermeasures! Some but not all enemy vessels are plated with the stuff!"

One by one, the armor jocks signaled they'd gotten the message...all but Gus. That, of course, was cause for concern. She was going after Brukowski, but she still should have acknowledged the order.

But the battle unfolding around him still took precedence.

"Repeat, Drake to all armor." He tried just one more time. "Acknowledge if you have not already done so."

Still, there was no reply from Gus.

No need to panic, he told himself...and believed it, mostly.

That was one great thing about working with the Gray Lady; more often than not, she could take care of herself. Excessive worry was not necessary in most situations.

He just had to trust her, as always…and hope this particular time would not be an exception to the rule.

It was time to get back to the business at hand.

"Let's take out that gunship, Big Bruce." Between the main viewer and the nav scope, he saw the *Golden Void* was coming in fast toward the enemy vessel—a heavily armed craft tagged with crimson and yellow Order of Slaughter colors. Its big main energy blasters were pounding the *Silver Void* hard, knocking her around without managing to break through her singularium plating. How long it would take for the Order's crew to implement anti-singularium measures, he couldn't predict…and he didn't care to play wait and see.

It would be better to beat them to the punch.

"Readying magno-beam." He flipped a switch and adjusted a dial on the weapons console, setting parameters for the beam's dynamic targeting system. "Take us in a little closer, Big Bruce."

"Moving in closer, Captain." As Bruce said it, the feed of the gunship blasting the *Silver Void* zoomed in on the viewer, the blazing beams of the weapon so bright that they lit up the *Golden Void*'s bridge.

"Make sure the projectile gun's loaded, charged, and ready to follow up," ordered Drake.

"It's ready, Captain! Just give the word!"

Drake watched the pirate push closer, ever closer—then smacked a red firing button on the console. On the main viewer, he saw the pirate buck and wallow as the invisible beams of magnetic force kicked at it, tossing it like a leaf in a breeze. Instantly, it disengaged its energy weapon assault on the *Silver Void*, instead firing off a volley of explosive missiles in the *Golden Void*'s direction.

"How long till we've softened her up enough?" As he talked, Drake jumped over to the nav station and swung the steering wheel hard to port, dodging the first flight of missiles.

"Thirty seconds to be safe," said Big Bruce. "Or a risky 15."

Drake split the difference, waiting till the fire clock hit twenty seconds before switching from magno-beam to the projectile gun. Quickly zeroing in on the same firing solution, adjusted for the difference in ammo profile, he tweaked the range slightly and bashed the red button again.

A chain of slugs pumped into the same spot he'd just primed, chopping through the weakened singularium plating. He followed that with a pulse from the forward energy beam, and that did the trick.

Even as the Order pirates churned out another flight of missiles, the energy beam blew open the hull in a bloom of explosive decompression. The hole widened, and Drake took advantage of it, pouring in more slugs and another strong beam that set off a catastrophic reaction.

The whole gunship exploded in a flare of light and fury, flinging shrapnel in all directions.

With Drake at the wheel and Big Bruce providing assistance, the *Golden Void* dodged nearly every scrap of it, as well as most of the second flight of missiles launched before the big blow. The few that still managed to tap the *Void* did no damage when they burst, thanks to the bubble of protection maintained by the shield generator and the nigh-impenetrable shell of singularium underneath it.

"Great work!" Drake smacked the edge of the console with sheer delight and spun around on the swivel base of his seat. "That doggie didn't know what *hit* him!"

"You better believe it, Captain!" Big Bruce sounded like he was way beyond tickled pink. His moodier tendencies were nowhere to be heard. "We make a great team, don't we?"

Before Drake could answer, the *Golden Void* suddenly rocked from an unexpected impact. The lights and screens on the bridge dimmed for an instant, then returned to a normal level of full illumination.

"What the *skudge* was *that*?" snapped Drake, scrambling to check readouts on the nav console. "What *hit* us?"

Just as the words left his mouth, the *Void* again shuddered, and the power dipped. This time, it took an extra moment for the lights, screens, and displays to resume normal operation.

"Some form of *energy weapon* breached our shield," explained Big Bruce. "Some kind of force beam tuned to the exact harmonic resonance produced by the Alliance generator."

"Where's it *coming* from?" Drake scanned the surrounding battlespace for traces of the beam, attempting to track them to their source. "Whichever ship *fired* it, we need to take 'em *out*."

"Incoming!" shouted Big Bruce. "Brace for impact!"

This time, the strike was more powerful. The bridge went pitch dark, and the ship lurched violently, flipping Drake to the floor. The hull groaned as he rolled and collided with the pilot seat, whacking his knee hard on the pedestal supporting it.

"Spawwwww…." Bruce's voice was distorted as he tried to speak through the blackout. "Spawwwwted duh shooootuuuhhh….cap-cap-cap-tin."

"Evasive maneuvers!" Drake knew his order was in vain, but he barked it out anyway. "Get us out of range as soon as you can!"

"Y-yes-y-yes-y-yes…"

Just then, the ship took another mighty heave…and continued to spin as Drake held on to the pilot seat. Gritting his teeth, he hated the thought that might be how it would all end—blown out of space without even getting a good look at whatever attacker had finally gotten him. Somehow, he'd expected something more dramatic…and less unknown.

What he most regretted, though, was not getting to see Gus Light just one more time. Not getting to fold her in his arms and kiss her, celebrating the love they'd finally found in their lives so constantly full of strife and sacrifice.

At least they *had* found each other, though…and he was grateful for the all-too-short time they'd shared. At least, if this was the end, he had found *that* much peace and happiness. He might not go willingly or gladly, but he would meet the end with no regret for one single second he'd spent in the Gray Lady's presence.

"Captain!"

Big Bruce's cry was the first sign that the end hadn't come to claim them just yet, after all. The lights and systems reactivating was the second sign…and the third was the scene projected on the main viewer as it flickered back to life.

Even before Big Bruce could explain things further, Drake understood who and what had saved his ass from a final plunge into the Great Beyond.

In the foreground, a familiar craft bobbed ahead of the *Golden Void*—the ultra-high-tech *Scintilla* with its sleek black manta ray design. Beyond it was a vessel he hadn't seen before—at least ten times bigger than *Scintilla* yet sharing the same gleaming black hull and organic contours. Instead of looking like a manta, its general shape suggested a winged predator—a spaceworthy eagle with a razor-sharp beak and braces of cannons where its talons should be.

As Drake watched, a tongue of swirling blue energy streamed out of the eagle ship's beak and slashed straight for the *Scintilla*—but the smaller ship swooped away at the last second, leaving the blast to stab through empty space in its absence. A second shot got exactly the same response, not even grazing the graceful *Scintilla*.

"Whatever that big ship's shooting, it punched through our shield and singularium plating like they were tissue paper," said Big Bruce. "Another few direct hits, and we would've been obliterated."

"Thank heaven for the cavalry, then." Drake hauled himself up and returned to the weapons station. "Put me through to the *Scintilla* so I can thank 'em properly."

Pause. "Channel's open to the *Scintilla*," said Big Bruce.

"Drake?" The voice of Human Bruce crackled over the speaker. "Ready to get back in the game yet? I could use a hand with this monstrosity!"

"Thanks for the save," said Drake, rebooting and

rearming the *Void*'s key weapons systems as he spoke. "What *is* that thing, anyway? Looks kind of familiar."

"It's an Ongoni ship, like *Scintilla*, but that's all I know. Never seen one *that* big before, or even *heard* of one."

As he said it, another beam blazed from the eagle ship's beak, forcing the *Scintilla* to dance out of the way again.

"Where the hell'd it *come* from?" Drake nodded in satisfaction as he reviewed the board. Full power had been restored, nanobots had patched the damage to the *Void*, and the full array of weapons was moments away from returning to battle-ready status. "Seemed to come outta *nowhere*, which blows my mind, as big as that ship is."

"It came out of the transit flume that *we* took to get here," said Human Bruce. "Instead of the one in the derelict's doughnut hole. It sneaked right up behind us while every sensor we've got was trained dead ahead."

"Piece a' *skudge* needs to learn some manners," said Drake. "It's not *polite* sneaking up on a guy like that."

"No idea who's flying that bird," said Human Bruce. "There's no transponder identifier, they won't answer hails, and I can't find any matches in the database. All we know is…"

Suddenly, Big Bruce interrupted. "Captains! That ship *is* hailing us! Incoming audio-video transmission."

Drake scowled. "Put it on the viewer."

The scene on the main viewer was quickly replaced by the oversized image of an all-too familiar face—that of a middle-aged man with twin salt-and-pepper braids framing a dark-eyed face that fairly reeked of wicked condescension.

Drake's skin crawled at the sight of him—a sight that he

and Gus had come here hoping to see, yet one that still repelled him. One he longed to wipe forever from the fabric of the universe.

"This is Jorritz Tor speaking," said the man who made Drake's jaws clench and stomach churn. "You have three choices. One, you can surrender and lend your ship and armaments to my forces.

"Two, you can flee this quadrant and never return. Assuming you observe the terms of this offer, your life *might* be spared.

"Or three, you will be executed *now* in the name of the new interstellar empire which is about to replace the corrupt and archaic Alliance." He paused to let a sinister smile crawl over his face like a serpent. "The *Tor* Empire, with *me* as its Emperor!"

CHAPTER 28

Gus Light had been called too small all her life.

"You're a short little thing," the recruitment officer had said when she'd told him she was signing up to join the Armor Division. "I'm not sure they make armor that small."

He'd had a good laugh at that.

So had her first two instructors.

"Armor don't come with training wheels," one of them had said the very first day the recruits got to try on their suits. "You keep that in mind, Light. If your feet don't reach, I'm not having the techs build you a custom suit."

"Or equip her with lifts," another recruit—male, of course—had said.

She'd fit inside her armor just fine. Did she make a few adjustments to it over the decades? Customized it to fit her own body better? Damn straight, she had.

Earl must have customized the suit of armor he'd constructed after he'd been discharged from the military.

Not only to compensate for the limp he had thanks to the repairs to his injured leg, but to compensate for that leg's increased strength thanks to its new mechanical parts. Earl's limp had all but disappeared once he'd put on his suit back at Buddy's Bluff.

Gus doubted Brukowski had worn armor since he'd left the 83rd behind in his quest for advancement. He might remember the obvious commands—armor jocks never really lost all those hard-earned abilities hammered into them during basic training, abilities that became second nature thanks to the battles they'd fought afterward—but that wouldn't help him with armor whose legs responded differently from each other. It would be like learning to walk all over again.

Or figuring out how to land on something as slick as the surface of the singularium-plated derelict ship.

That was the only reason Gus finally caught sight of Brukowski. He couldn't stick the landing.

He must have kept flying hell-bent-for-leather toward the ring ship even as the space around him transformed into the battle zone from hell. More and more ships were coming through the transit flume. Explosion after explosion threw light and debris into the mouth of the transit flume, creating a debris field only the most experienced pilots could navigate.

Unfortunately for the good guys, the pirate factions fighting for Tor must have included some of the most experienced pilots in the Frontier. Those ships made it through and immediately started hammering the ships in her fleet. Her fleet was hammering them back, and now the space around the outside of the derelict had turned into an obstacle course full of jagged pieces of metal and bits of flesh that used to be people.

For a split-second, Gus thought about turning around and joining the fight. Drake could use her. Her *fleet* could use her. The battle plans they'd drawn up relied on the armor jocks to pepper the pirates with singularium counter-measures, softening the pirate ships' singularium-rein-forced hulls so energy weapons could get through and blow them to smithereens.

It didn't help when she heard Drake call all armor jocks into the battle.

But Brukowski was up to something with the ring ship. He wouldn't be out here otherwise. He'd backed down to let her run the show. A man like that, a man used to *being in charge,* wouldn't have backed down unless he had some-thing far more important to do. Given the stakes of this particular battle, that something had to be damn important.

When she finally caught sight of him, he was skidding across the surface of the ring ship like a flea going for a joy ride across the ass end of an elephant. He'd somehow managed to fly Earl's armor well enough to avoid all the debris while pushing the suit's propulsion to the limits. She had to admire the skudgehole for that. But his landing? Raw recruits could do better.

He'd come in too hot, that was his problem. Gus was already throttling back her own armor in preparation to touch down on the derelict's slick singularium hull.

The magnets at the bottom of Brukowski's stolen armor hadn't been able to attach properly. At the speed he'd been going, both sets of magnets needed to attach at once. He hadn't been able to get the armor's second leg in position.

Momentum had ripped the one leg he had managed to get down free, and now he was sliding across the surface, out of control.

"Fire your maneuvering jets," she said to him over their comms. "You've got to slow down before you can stand."

His only response was a curse.

Damn stupid, stubborn man.

Gus understood the impulse to go as fast as her armor would let her, but there were times an armor jock just couldn't fight the laws of physics. The display in her visor reported that the ship had its own minimal gravitational field, something she should have expected but hadn't. She also hadn't noticed that the ship was slowly rotating, like rings around a gas giant. If Brukowski had just slowed down and let the ship pull him in, like Gus was doing now, he would have been fine.

She finally saw him fire the suit's maneuvering jets. His skid slowed. Gus made minute adjustments to her armor's trajectory to follow him.

"Get the hell out of here," he said over their shared comm channel as he finally came to a stop. "You're needed out there, not here."

As if to emphasize his words, a piece of bulkhead three times her size struck the ring ship mere meters from where Gus intended to land. Another piece of debris, this time what looked like part of a ship's hull, came within a hair's breadth of taking Brukowski's head off.

The derelict was pulling in debris within its gravity well. No wonder the hull was coated with singularium.

"It's not safe here, Light," Brukowski said. "I have to be here. You don't."

That was the first indication he'd given that he cared for anything other than his mission.

"Why?" she said. "Why do you have to be here risking your life over a hunk of junk that's only good for what it's got on its hull?"

He choked out a laugh that had no humor in it. "This hunk of junk isn't what she appears. Let's leave it at that."

Gus's boots hit the ship's surface, and with a resounding *clunk*, the magnets on the soles of her boots engaged. The last time she'd been this close to the derelict, she'd left behind the magnetic plate on the bottom of one of her armor's legs. Once of Bruce Junior's techs had given her the supplies to replace it, and she definitely needed it now.

The singularium was just too damn slick. The magnets in her boots weren't holding her as securely as they should. The slight pull of gravity from the derelict was holding her in place as much as her armor.

If her armor wasn't securely attached to the ship, neither was Brukowski's.

Neither one of them was going to be able to stay in place for long. Hell, with the amount of debris this thing was going to draw to itself, it wasn't *safe* to stay in one place for long.

"Brukowski," she started, but then she stopped.

She wasn't sure she was seeing right. Brukowski had walked over to a smaller section of singularium, which had peeled away to reveal what could only be an access panel built into the derelict's surface.

As she watched, another panel of singularium slid sideways to reveal a hatch.

What the *skudge?*

Brukowski had bent over and was undogging a circular release handle that looked for all the world like the steering wheel Drake used to pilot the *Golden Void*.

He was *opening the hatch!*

"You can't be serious," she said to him.

He didn't respond. Instead, he went through the hatch and into the ship.

He must have been in a hell of a hurry. He closed the hatch behind him, but he didn't dog it tight. Maybe he thought she wasn't stupid enough to follow him. Or maybe he thought her armor made her strong enough to open it just like he had.

Or maybe he wouldn't have time to undog it on his way back out.

That thought sent chills down her spine.

Brukowski had told her it wasn't safe to stay here. She'd thought it was because of all the debris from the battle impacting on the derelict's surface. But what if the *really* dangerous stuff was *inside the ship?*

Brukowski was under orders to render all highly classified Alliance tech inoperable. What kind of highly classified Alliance tech could be inside this derelict? Had Brukowski been ordered to make sure whatever tech was inside didn't fall into Tor's hands?

Tor was willing to commit his entire fleet to battle right here, right in front of this derelict. Did he know that there was something more than singularium that made the derelict so important in his efforts to build his own empire?

If the tech inside the derelict was so important it could change the course of the war, did that mean the good guys use it *against* Tor? Was Brukowski about to disable classified

Alliance tech that could help them defeat Tor once and for all? She couldn't let that happen. She just skudging *couldn't.*

She spared a single transmission to Drake, highly encrypted, to let him know what she was about to do, then she opened the hatch and climbed inside the most massive ship she'd ever been in in her life.

Which, as it turned out, wasn't a derelict after all.

CHAPTER 29

Had Drake gone stark, raving mad? He was starting to wonder.

Not too long ago, he'd sweated his way through the roller coaster mood swings of his ship's AI, at that time the emotional equivalent of a human adolescent. Now, not that many days later, he was trusting that same AI—and its clones—with the outcome of a battle to decide the fate of the Alliance, the Frontier, and everything in-between.

It wasn't out of sheer desperation that he was doing so, either. It wasn't because every other option had been exhausted or declared untenable. Amazingly, especially to someone who'd known Bruce since his unhinged recent teenagerhood…

…he had simply come up with the best possible plan for success, at least as far as Drake could see.

"Okay, Big Bruce," he'd said after hearing it all quickly laid out on the bridge of the *Golden Void*. "Sounds solid."

"It does?" Big Bruce had sounded surprised at first, then quickly regained his composure. "I mean, of course it does!"

"Let's make it happen." As he said it, Drake had plopped down at the comm station and opened the special channel that would put him in touch with the entire fleet and all armor jocks in the field as well. "Attention! All armor and ships converge on the Ongoni eagle ship currently facing off with the *Scintilla* and *Golden Void* at the encoded coordinates." Leaning to the next station over, he noted his own ship's coordinates, then transmitted them as part of the current broadcast. "Further specific instructions are forthcoming from Big Bruce. You are to follow them as if they came directly from *me.*"

"Thank you, Captain Drake." Big Bruce sounded as professional as a longtime serviceman whose attention to duty and protocol was impeccable. "All Bruces, prepare to establish tight-beam radio link with *my* matrix as the keystone. Ten-second countdown begins...*now.*"

As confident as Drake had been in Big Bruce's idea, he had still made a sign of the cross for luck. The planned maneuver was one he'd never been part of before or even heard of being done in quite the same way. He'd trusted the Bruces enough to give them the go-ahead, but he'd still feel better when the wisdom of their joint venture was proven.

"...three...two...one...and *link.*" As the countdown ended, the bridge lights had danced and flashed as if in response to the establishment of the multi-Bruce linkup.

Meanwhile, as all this was happening, the *Scintilla* had continued to dodge the blue energy blasts from Tor's Ongoni eagle ship's beak. The balletic moves of the smaller vessel, complete with graceful spins and swoops, had successfully kept it out of reach of the blue beams…and had kept those beams slashing through space in directions away from the *Golden Void*.

"Captain!" Big Bruce had said. "All ship AIs in the fleet are now linked and moving to the proscribed coordinates as they disengage from any enemy craft. Estimated time until final formation is achieved is 45.5 seconds."

That left enough time for Drake to reach out to the folks in armor, too. "Now here this," he told them. "All armor jocks, prepare your weapons for imminent fire on a concentrated target. Acknowledge."

In reply, he saw eleven armor jocks report on the comm board. Only two signals were lacking: Earl's suit, which that skudgehole Brukowski had stolen, and the one accompanied by the unique transponder from her armor's ident chip he always recognized at a glance.

Gus Light did not respond.

Her last communication had been brief and to the point. She was following Brukowski inside the ring ship. That told him, since he'd received no mayday from her at that point, that her business on the derelict was not yet complete. Just because she was offline at the moment, that didn't mean there was cause for concern.

But of course Drake was concerned anyway…though he couldn't let his worry affect him, as the AI's plan was quickly coming to fruition.

He flipped a switch, muting the channel to the armor jocks for now.

"All ships in position, Captain," Big Bruce announced.

A diagram flashed onto the main viewer, showing

277

twenty-four ships surrounding Tor's eagle, occupying points on a sphere. Wireframes of the *Scintilla* and *Golden Void* stood at a distance from the sphere and the nose of the massive eagle ship.

Drake had instructed the ships that had been too damaged in the fight to take part in the AI's plan to keep pestering the remaining pirate ships in Tor's fleet. They'd kept their distance since Tor had shown up. No doubt on the glory hog's orders. But once the AI's plan started in earnest, Drake couldn't count on the pirates maintaining their distance.

"On your order, Captain," said Big Bruce.

"The order is given." Drake nodded, bracing himself for whatever came next. "Do it!"

Immediately, the twenty-four Bruces began a pattern of alternating fire, lashing out with energy weapons in a wildly flickering sequence targeting the eagle ship. Each beam tagged the eagle for a split-second, then switched off, even as other beams from other ships poured onto other spots.

The resulting light show was dazzling, with all those rapid-fire beams punching the eagle from different locations, then breaking away, then reengaging. To make things even more interesting, the twenty-four mini-Bruces changed position every few seconds, shifting the entire global array into new configurations.

Tor's eagle ship didn't know where to shoot, especially as the *Scintilla* and *Golden Void* got in on the fun to draw fire from the powerful beak-mounted cannon. Human Bruce and Big Bruce popped off one beam after another, never doing much harm to the eagle's adaptive psiflux-engineered hull—but keeping it and the other front-mounted guns busy while the global formation continued to blast and shift and confound the targeting computers.

The best part was, Drake's forces were just getting *started*. One important component of the assault team had not even started their work, which was the whole point of the exercise.

It was time to change that.

"Captain, may I suggest we initiate Phase Two of this operation?" asked Big Bruce.

"You may." Drake flipped the switch to reopen the channel to the armor jocks. "Bucket-heads, converge on the target location at the embedded coordinates and begin your coordinated fire."

All eleven armor jocks signaled acknowledgment. According to the wireframes on the nav screen, they immediately complied with his orders and moved in on the chosen spot on the skin of the eagle ship.

The spot did not look especially vulnerable. Located at the base of the eagle's neck, it looked from a distance like just another patch of gleaming black Ongoni-designed hull, as resistant as any other spot on that massive dreadnaught of "Emperor" Tor's.

But Big Bruce seemed to think it was a viable breakthrough point. Applying his formidable AI mind to calculating the hull's tensile strength, he'd decided that a rotating global attack by the alternating energy weapons of twenty-four vessels could create a single point of weakness *right there.* The eagle ship's metamorphic psiflux tech would be so busy reacting to the shifting energy weapon assault, it would divert resources away from this one untouched point, thinning the shielded hull there by the *tiniest* fraction.

And that fraction would be enough, Big Bruce said, to open the door a crack. Exploiting that one break would give Drake and his forces all the advantage they would need.

"The armored unit has reached its mark." Big Bruce sounded tense as he did the play-by-play. "All eleven personnel are bringing their onboard weapons to bear on the target...and *opening fire.*"

On the main viewer, Drake watched as eleven beams of bright force streaked from the cluster of armored fighters and merged into one mighty blast that combined all their component power levels. The resulting surge pumped the chosen spot at the base of the bird ship's throat, biting at the thinned hull plating there.

Meanwhile, the twenty-four ships continued their same attack of rapidly alternating energy beams in a constantly shifting global framework. They didn't let up on their flickering barrage, guided by Big Bruce's calculations to draw off the eagle ship's resources and enable the armor to punch their way through.

"Any minute now, Captain," said Big Bruce. "Wait for it...wait for it..."

Drake plugged a fresh stick of cinnamon gum into his mouth and chewed like it was a strip of cold steel. His heart pounded as he waited to see if Bruce's convoluted plan would yield success or only failure.

Just then, a pair of pirate corvettes streaked from the broader battlespace toward the armor jock contingent. Without hesitation, Drake leaped at the nav station, grabbed the wheel, and went after them, leaving the *Scintilla* to keep up its distracting maneuvers.

"Captain, what are…"

"Keep running the show, Bruce!" snapped Drake. "You do your thing, and I'll do mine!"

Hell-bent for leather, Drake poured on the thrust and whipped the wheel to catch up with the nearest corvette. He swung the *Golden Void* hard to starboard, then port, lining up the energy beam's sights on the nimble little ship.

He snagged her dead center in the scope and unleashed the beam, scoring a direct hit that blew a hole through the corvette's hull. As it went spinning and sparking off course, away from the armor squad, he swooped past on a mission to catch the other vessel.

His first shot missed, and his second skimmed the corvette's hull. It did no real damage, but it got the pilot's attention.

Suddenly, that remaining corvette whipped around and charged after the *Void* with guns blazing.

Drake let out a war whoop. *"Yee-haw!"* His cowboy heart was pounding with sheer joy and excitement.

The second corvette had done exactly what he wanted, leaving the armor to finish their work. The enemy's little surprise sortie had failed to interfere, and now he was pulling them even farther from where they could have made a difference for their misbegotten "Emperor."

Even as he zoomed away from the eagle leviathan with the corvette hot on his tail, he grinned around his gum. He'd bought the armor some time…enough, perhaps, to…

"They did it!" shouted Big Bruce. "They broke through!"

A glance at the viewer showed the truth of it. The spot

on the eagle ship's hull had just blown open, revealing the bright inner light within.

Leaning over, he flipped the comm switch again. "Armor squad, *board that skudgin' ship*! Fight your way to the bridge and *take control* at any cost!"

All eleven armor jocks signaled their acknowledgment as they raced toward the gaping hole before the Ongoni psiflux hull could seal it again.

Look out, "Emperor" Tor! Drake sneered as he fired a missile at the pursuing corvette. *We're coming for you now!*

CHAPTER 30

The Alliance had a hit list of most wanted criminals. Jorritz Tor was currently number one "with a bullet," as the ancient saying went. If it wasn't for that other, much more secret hit list of things the Alliance wanted taken care of even more, Brukowski would be out in the skudge right now, using his decades of battle experience and tactical training to bring down Tor once and for all.

But Brukowski didn't have a choice. The ring ship topped the Alliance's secret hit list, which meant it had to top *his* hit list. That was something an armor jock like Gus Light, someone who'd always flaunted the rules, would never understand.

The last thing he saw before he climbed inside the airlock was a new ship enter the battle from *behind* Light's fleet. A big ship with sleek black lines and a birdlike appearance.

The new fighter must have come through the same

transit flume as Light's fleet had. Pincer move. Good battle strategy. If Crosscut hadn't warned them away from using the transit flume in the center of the ring ship, he would have suggested Light split the fleet in two and use the same type of move against the pirates. As it turned out, Crosscut's mines had been a sound, if less effective, strategy. There were just too many pirate ships, including some heavy cruisers, against too few ships in Light's fleet.

Brukowski had his visor zoom in on the ship just as it shot a bolt of swirling blue energy at the *Scintilla*. The *Scintilla* scooted out of the way like no other ship in the fleet was capable of doing. Brukowski regretted never getting the chance to set foot inside the *Scintilla* to see how that thing managed moves like that. Maybe if he…

But there was no use thinking like that. He had a job to do, and he needed to do it before Light tried to stop him.

It was a tight fit inside the airlock thanks to Knox's armor. It didn't help that he felt like he had to constantly drag one leg behind himself. He should have taken Knox's own rebuilt leg into consideration, but he'd been so honed in on his target, he hadn't given it much thought until he'd tried to land on the ring ship.

At least he and Knox were the same basic body size, although the inside of the suit reeked of old sweat and… was it swamp water? Where the hell had Knox been wearing this thing?

Once he made it through the airlock, Brukowski had the armor's external sensors check whether the atmosphere inside the ring ship was still breathable. The ship had never been meant to carry a crew, but humans had built the thing. Tens of thousands of humans. Once built and its systems brought online, bots performed all necessary maintenance, and only because long-term exposure to the ship's power source was deadly. Even the heads of the Alliance's state-sponsored experimental tech division weren't cold-blooded enough to condemn a human crew to a slow, painful death.

The ship was divided into hundreds of self-contained sectors all operating together to perform a single function: create the largest artificial transit flume in known space. The transit flume in the donut hole at the center of the ring ship wasn't a natural phenomenon. Brukowski didn't know how the science worked. He didn't have to. All he had to know was how to destroy it.

Or as his handler had said, to "render it permanently inoperable."

Same difference. Military intelligence didn't like using words like "kill" or "destroy." In the last few years even "terminate with extreme prejudice" had fallen out of favor.

Amazingly enough, the atmosphere in this sector of the ship was marginally breathable. Nothing he could stand long term, but he didn't expect to be in the ship long term.

He didn't need any of the information the armor's helmet could provide, so he unlatched the foul-smelling thing at the shoulder joints and dropped it on the floor next to the airlock's inner door. Light would leave hers on once she made it inside—and she would make it inside, of that he had no doubts—but whatever the inside of her armor smelled like, she'd be used to the stench. Even the stale, metallic-tinged air inside the ship was preferable to breathing the air inside Knox's armor.

He kept the rest of the armor on. Who knew what kind of obstacles he'd have to get through on the way to the electronic "brains" for this sector of the ship. The ship had been lost for a long time, and it had malfunctioned severely before that. The inside of the ship was a warren of corridors and access tubes, ladders and levels and junctions, and more conduits and pipes than he'd ever seen in his life. Any of those elements could have failed. Corridors might be blocked off, access tubes filled with debris. He might need the armor's lasers to cut his way to where he needed to go.

He'd memorized the ship's schematics long ago. Each sector was built the same. It hadn't really mattered where he'd landed on the surface of the ship. He'd managed to get inside, and now he just had to take a moment to orient himself to the reality of the ship versus the miniature holo version he'd studied at night alone in his quarters on Melody Station.

The airlock opened onto a corridor wide enough and tall enough for Brukowski to walk upright even in his armor. The human techs who'd built the thing must have used mechanical loaders—civilian versions of military armor—to move heavy equipment down these corridors. He wouldn't have to hunch over to walk.

Walking though would present another problem. The floors were metal. Exposed pipes and conduits wouldn't be enough to deaden the sound his armor would make walking down the corridor. There wasn't enough ambient noise in the ship to mask the sound either, and he didn't have enough control of the armor's maneuvering jets to hover a few inches off the floor and fly to where he needed to go. He'd just have to deal with it and hope that Light wouldn't be able to pinpoint where he went.

Best case, she'd get lost in the corridors and access tubes and wouldn't be able to find him in time to stop him.

Worst case?

He'd deal with that if and when it happened. He didn't want to have to eliminate her, but if he had to in order to complete his mission, he would.

The only lights inside the ship came from the mandatory safety features installed when the ship was being built. *Exit* signs illuminated with softly glowing green light were at odds with the *Emergency Medical Supplies* signs illuminated in red. Scattered panels embedded in the walls featured gauges and digital readouts that must have been fully illuminated when the ship was new. Now their lights were nearly too dim to see, but combined with the safety lights, Brukowski had just enough light to see where he was going.

When he reached the second T-junction he came to, he took the branching tunnel that led toward the interior of the ship. Each sector had been designed so that the "brains" would be closer to the interior of the ring. It would have been better if he could have landed on a spot on the hull closer to the interior, he wouldn't have had to walk so far inside, but with all the debris and weapons fire going on outside, he couldn't chance staying outside any longer than he had. It just meant he'd be taking more time *inside*. It also meant that if he simply tried to retrace his steps to get back outside the ship, he'd never make it.

The closer he got to the center of the ship, the lower the pull of gravity from the ship itself. His armor started to float a little between each uneven step he took. He could turn the magnets back on, but that would make walking even harder, not to mention noisier.

To keep his armor under control, he slowed down from a long, purposeful stride to something approaching normal walking speed. He didn't have the helmet's built-in chronometer to tell him exactly how much time he was taking, but he had an ever-increasing feeling that time was running out, and running out *fast*.

Finally, just when he'd decided to chance using the armor's maneuvering jets to propel himself down this one last corridor, he came to an alcove filled with electronic equipment.

This was what he was looking for. The brains for this sector. But more than that, the nerves, for lack of a better term, that connected this brain to all the other sectors' brains. From here, he could carry out his mission. He could permanently disable the brains in all the sectors, turning this ship into what Light and everyone else thought it was.

A derelict useful only for the singularium on its hull.

He removed his armor's gauntlets. The work he needed to do now was delicate, and not something he could handle while he was wearing someone else's armor on his hands. Plus, the chip embedded in his left wrist needed access to the control panel for the shield generator that was protecting the delicate electronics inside. He could use that chip to open the control panel the same way he'd opened the box encasing the shield generator in the cargo hold of the *Golden Void*.

He triggered the chip, but the control panel's cover didn't budge. Not one single millimeter.

The chip should work. It didn't have any power settings, just settings for the different types of energy he wanted to disrupt.

He cursed himself when he realized what was wrong. The chip was still on the setting he'd used to disrupt Teppin's ability to communicate with the magno-beam from the weapons station on the *Silver Void.* No wonder it wouldn't work to open the control panel.

Brukowski reset the chip. Just in case there was something on this ship that interfered with the signals his chip sent, he positioned his left wrist so that the chip was almost touching the control panel's cover.

He closed his eyes so he could give the chip his entire concentration. "One more time," he muttered to himself.

It better damn well work this time.

That's when he heard the distinctive whine of an energy weapon powering up.

The laser weapon in the palm of an armor jock's suit.

"If you don't stop whatever you're doing *right now*," Gus Light said, "I'm going to remove your left hand from your arm at the wrist. With prejudice," she added. "I believe that's how people in your profession put it. Do you copy?"

CHAPTER 31

Gus had spent a lot of time over the years upgrading her armor. Recent upgrades had been to add singularium plating on the vulnerable spots, joints where the armor fitted together so that errant shots couldn't get through and blow out her shoulder or her knees.

But that hadn't been *all* she'd upgraded.

With Big Bruce's help, she'd added AI elements to the sensors in her helmet. Once she'd spotted Brukowski on the hull of the ring ship—she could no longer call it a derelict since it was clearly under power of some sort—she'd had the sensors search for whether the suit was equipped with an identity chip.

All military suits of armor were. In the ancient Earth history she'd studied, she'd learned that soldiers wore something called "dog tags" to identify them when they were wounded or killed in battle. The Armor Division did the ancient dog tags one better. They embedded an identity chip in the *armor* instead of in the armor jock. Just went to show what the military thought was more valuable.

Gus hadn't been sure if Earl's suit had an ident chip since he'd built most of it—except the helmet—from scratch. But once a military armor jock, always a military armor jock. His armor not only had an ident chip, it had *two*. One in his helmet, and one inside the suit beneath the shoulder mount for one of the suit's missile launchers.

He was a belt-and-suspenders guy now? He hadn't been back when he'd been in the military, but maybe getting wounded so severely had made him a little more cautious. Or maybe he had some kind of vested interest in his armor because he'd built it himself.

Gus had the AI enhanced tracker in her helmet hack into both ident chips in Earl's suit and lock onto them. When she got inside the ship and saw his helmet on the floor next to the airlock's interior hatch, she made a mental note to thank Earl for his relatively new belt-and-suspenders foresight when it came to his armor. At least she still had the second ident chip to track.

She instructed her AI enhanced sensors to not only give her a location for Earl's armor, but to copy the armor's route through the ship, something an ident chip did automatically.

This inside of the ring ship was a maze. Even though Brukowski was making all sorts of racket walking on the ship's metal deck, the sound was echoing and bouncing off all the interior metal. It would be impossible to follow him by noise alone. The *only* sure way she could track him was through that ident chip.

All that noise meant he had to be walking, which meant

he still didn't trust the armor's maneuvering jets. Gus not only trusted hers, she'd added a bunch more to her armor. The additional jets were what let her armor do barrel rolls.

This time those jets let her fly above the metal deck of the corridors Brukowski had taken to get wherever he was going. She'd be coming in much quieter, a necessary precaution since he wasn't wearing a helmet and there was next to no background noise inside the ship. She'd also be presenting a smaller profile for Brukowski to hit if he decided to shoot first and ask questions later.

She needn't have worried. Not only did he have his *eyes* closed, he'd taken off the suit's gauntlets. He was holding his left wrist next to what looked for all the world like the boxy shield generator he'd opened in the cargo bay of the *Void*.

She fired up the laser in the palm of her suit's right hand.

"If you don't stop whatever you're doing *right now*," she said, "I'm going to remove your left hand from your arm at the wrist." She thought for a moment, then added, "With prejudice. I believe that's how people in your profession put it. Do you *copy*?"

His eyes flew open. She'd caught him totally by surprise. That's what an armor jock got for taking off his helmet.

"How the hell did you find me?" he said.

She tilted her head to one side. "Ident chip," she said. "Earl used to be military, remember? Some habits die hard."

Brukowski swore. Clearly, he'd never thought to check for an ident chip before he stole Earl's armor.

She adjusted her maneuvering jets to let her stand

upright, but she kept her right palm aimed at him, the laser powered on standby.

"So what are we doing here?" she asked. "Getting ready to rip the guts out of this shield generator too?"

He blinked but didn't say anything. Beads of sweat had started to roll down the side of his face.

"Or is there something else you're supposed to 'render inoperative' that you can't get to when the shield's operational?" she asked. "It better be damn important."

"It could help Tor build his empire," he said. "It could let him win the *war*."

That caught her off guard. Not that she was about to let him know that.

"What, this hunk of junk?" She snorted. Sure, the ship obviously wasn't a derelict, and Brukowski clearly knew more about it than she did, but helping Tor win the war against the *Alliance* was a pretty bold statement. "Singularium alone doesn't win a war."

At least she hoped it didn't, or her fleet was in some serious trouble. Not all the ships had singularium plating covering their entire hulls.

She could tell by Brukowski's pained expression that he was fighting with himself. How much to tell her? How much *should* he tell her?

"We're going to stay right here until I get some answers," she said. "Or until you decide to let me blow your hand off." She nodded toward the shoulder launchers on his suit. "Or until you decide to fire one of those things and blow us both to smithereens."

She sincerely hoped he wouldn't do that. Back on the surface of the ship, she'd gotten the feeling that he was ready to die if he had to in order to complete his mission. But he hadn't seemed willing to kill her. He could have shot the armor's shoulder-mounted missiles at her as soon as she touched down on the ship's hull. The missiles might not have killed her outright thanks to her armor's singularium plating.

He could have hit her with the armor's magno-beams too. Like all the other armor jocks in her fleet, Earl's armor had been fully equipped with singularium countermeasures. Those countermeasures *would* have killed her. Especially at such close range.

He dropped his hand away from the control panel. "You ever wonder why there's a transit flume in the exact *center* of this ship?" he asked.

She hadn't.

Transit flumes occurred throughout known space. Those came in all sizes, from flumes so small nothing bigger than an escape pod could get through to ones the size Gus and her fleet had used to get back to the ring ship.

Some transit flumes were stable. Others weren't, and even the most foolhardy pilots used them only in dire emergencies. Unstable flumes could deposit a ship in the center of a gas giant or in the path of a comet, and the unlucky pilot wouldn't know until it was too late.

The Alliance had an entire multi-cultural science division devoted to doing nothing but mapping naturally occurring transit flumes throughout Alliance territory. Drake had told her that the only information all pilots in the Frontier freely shared with each other was the location of stable and especially *unstable* transit flumes.

Ships equipped with the right tech could generate their

own transit flumes, but it took a hell of a lot of energy. The *Golden Void* could generate a transit flume short term, but only because Drake had upgraded the ship to handle the extra load. It was his one nod to advanced technology.

The transit flume in the center of the ring ship was the biggest Gus had ever seen.

"Was this thing constructed around the flume?" she asked Brukowski. "To protect it?"

He shook his head. "It *generates* the flume."

She was glad she still had her helmet on to hide her expression because that truly shocked her.

Tor had brought his entire pirate fleet in through this flume. Not one ship at a time, but *dozens*, including cruisers and gunships. That's why Crosscut's minefield hadn't stopped them all. There were too many coming in all at once.

That would take more power than she could even calculate. It would take—

"What the hell is powering this thing?" she asked.

"A stable contained singularity," he said.

What the *skudge??*

He sighed. "Or it was supposed to be stable. Maybe it still is and something else went wrong. They don't know. *I* don't know. This ship was a prototype, so who knows what failed during testing. It can clearly open a flume. The ship's just not where it's supposed to be. I only know I've been ordered to destroy the tech so it doesn't fall into enemy hands."

Specifically, Tor's hands.

Gus was still trying to wrap her mind around the possibility that she was standing inside a massive ship that was still generating enough power from a skudging *contained singularity* to generate a big enough transit flume to allow an entire *fleet* to go through at one time.

But why was this ship in the Frontier?

"You said it wasn't where it was supposed to be," she said. "You're telling me the Alliance *lost it?*"

He nodded. "Something like that. I don't know the details. Beyond my clearance level's what I got told when I asked. I only know the thing worked at first, then something happened, the flume encompassed the entire ship, and *poof!* It went. Somewhere."

"Wouldn't they know where it went?" she asked.

Naturally occurring transit flumes were always mapped at *both* ends, entrance and exit. When a ship generated its own transit flume, the exit coordinates were always programmed in advance. Otherwise, the flumes would be worthless.

"Nope," he said. "Prototype. Something went screwy inside. My guess is they tried to stretch the flume too far. Short distances worked, so somebody higher up the food chain got greedy."

Typical Alliance thinking.

"They overloaded the system," she said. "And the damn thing ended up way the hell out here."

Even the best contained singularity drives were dangerous as *skudge.* Overload the thing and who the hell knew what would happen.

"But what if Tor tried to use it in reverse?" she said. "Tried to use it to get his fleet into Alliance space."

"The heart of the Alliance," Brukowski said. "Don't forget that part."

"He'd end up who knows where," she said. "Him and his entire fleet." That didn't actually sound so bad.

Brukowski gave her a long, serious look. "But what if he didn't? What if this thing actually *worked* the way it's supposed to? Just think about that. The Alliance can't take that chance."

"You're assuming we can't stop him here," she said.

"*You're* assuming you can win. Against a guy who built those shield generators. That's highly classified Alliance tech," Brukowski said. "That tells me he's got somebody who can reverse engineer any high-level tech Tor runs across. He doesn't need to *steal* Alliance tech or weapons anymore. He can *build* them."

Crap. There'd been high tech stuff on Chrysallix, lots of it. Gus and Drake had destroyed most of it, and congratulated themselves on destroying the singularium refinery.

"I can't let him have this, Light," Brukowski said. "He's most likely insane, which means he'll stop at nothing to build his empire. You know it. I know you do." He held both hands out toward her. She tensed just in case he was getting ready to power up the magno-beam, but instead he said, "You have to let me do my job."

Brukowski was actually begging her. She hadn't expected that.

"I'm guessing this ship doesn't have any defensive weapons," she said. "Nothing we can use against him now."

Brukowski shook his head no. "The Alliance assigned an entire division in the military to provide security for the ship. The singularium was supposed to repel most known attacks."

Double crap.

He was out here trying to stop Tor from taking his war to the heart of the Alliance. Wasn't that what she was trying to do? Why she'd put together her fleet? To prevent Tor from waging a war that would kill billions of innocent people?

If she believed Brukowski, he was all that stood in the way of Tor getting his hands on the ring ship's tech. She certainly didn't know how to disable the tech that operated this ship. Blasting it? Not a good idea. Not inside a ship powered by a contained singularity. Those things were notoriously twitchy.

"Okay," she said. "Do it. Whatever you were going to do."

He brought his left arm up and placed his wrist against the control panel. According to Sef, that's how he'd opened the box containing the shield generator on the *Void*.

"You know what you're doing?" she asked.

He gave her a grim smile. "In theory."

"Theory?"

"No one knows what went wrong with this ship," he said. "For all we know, I could be triggering a bomb."

Now wasn't *that* a marvelous thought!

At least her suit should protect her. Unless the whole *ship* went up, then that would be all she wrote.

She really wished she'd had more time to send Drake a better message than just "I'm heading inside." She hoped he was holding his own in the battle. That the *Golden Void* was still in one piece. She hadn't had a single communication with anyone in the fleet since she'd set foot inside, probably because of all the singularium on the hull.

The control panel popped open. Gus had her visor zoom in on the electronic guts inside.

She didn't recognize any of the configurations, but her AI-enhanced sensors must have. Her visor started flashing red, and an outline had formed over a section of the electronics.

System failure flashed in the upper right-hand corner of her visor.

"Your chip triggered something," she said. "The system's crashing."

Brukowski's head whipped around toward her. "How the hell do you—""

"Enhanced AI," she said, tapping her helmet. "I had the ship's AI help with the upgrades."

Cascade Failure was now blinking.

"We really gotta go," she said.

He took his hand away from the control panel, and something sparked.

Now the display on her visor read *FAILURE IMMINENT.*

He moved his hand back to the panel. The sparking stopped, and *FAILURE IMMINENT* disappeared from her visor, replaced with *Cascade Failure in Progress.*

"That didn't fix it," she said. "How fast can we get out of here?"

"The way we came in is the closest exit."

Crap! They were deep inside the ship. They had to be. If the nearest exit was the way they'd come in…

A growling noise came from somewhere beyond the walls of the corridor, rumbling through the exposed pipes overhead.

Brukowski glanced toward his discarded gauntlets. He would have to put them back on on the run. Then there was his helmet. He'd left that by the airlock. And the fact that only one set of armor at a time could fit in the thing. Would he even have enough time to do any of that before the cascade failure reached a critical point?

A resigned expression settled over his features.

"Get out of here, Light," he said.

"I'm not—"

"That's an *order*, soldier!" When she didn't move, he said, "I'm not sacrificing myself. I'm going to fix this. I don't need you. They do. Out there. Go do what you're made for."

Armor jocks never left another jock behind. *Ever*. But Brukowski was right. She was useless here. Her fleet was fighting for their lives. She couldn't just stand here and watch Brukowski work and hope it turned out for the best.

"I'm coming back for you," she said. "Just… don't do anything stupid."

She didn't wait for him to reply.

She turned around and ran down the corridor until she could use the jets in her boots without frying him or the exposed electronics in the open control panel. Her visor was still flashing *Cascade Failure in Progress.*

She flew as fast as she dared down corridor after corridor, retracing the path she'd taken inside the ship. She spared a glance toward Earl's discarded helmet. It was the only part of his military armor he'd taken when he'd been discharged. She hoped Brukowski would get to use it one more time.

She cycled through the airlock. Spun the outer handle

301

and opened the outer hatch. She still had fuel to spare and her full complement of weapons.

She shut the outer hatch behind her and dogged it tight.

She turned toward the battle just in time to see a pirate corvette, lasers blasting away, bearing down on the *Golden Void*.

Cursing loudly, she kicked in the afterburners on her armor and jetted straight for that damn pirate. She still had a full complement of weapons and more than enough fuel to make sure that corvette had a *very* bad day.

CHAPTER 32

The pirate corvette was persistent as hell. As hard as Drake tried to shake it or blow it up, the damn thing stuck to the *Golden Void*'s tail as if attached.

At least the armor squad was having better luck aboard the Ongoni eagle ship. Courtesy of certain jocks' onboard video cameras, he could see at a glance that their march through the ship's corridors was making great headway. Their weapons chewed through one security detail after another, pausing only momentarily at certain choke points or defense perimeters to wreck the opposition and regain their momentum.

They were on their way to round up "Emperor" Tor, and it seemed nothing could stop their advance.

If only Drake could wreck the corvette with such ease and get back in the game of keeping the eagle's defenses overstretched and off balance.

"*Skudgin'* pirate!" Playing the nav console with his usual reckless grace, he swung the *Void* in a hairpin turn, then dove at the last second before what looked like a surefire collision. On the way down, he pumped another guided missile in the path of the corvette, seemingly on a point-blank trajectory.

But the damn corvette evaded his latest fire *again*, whipped around in an even tighter hairpin, and zoomed after the *Void* with energy weapons blazing.

"Who is *piloting* that thing?" snapped Drake as he swung the wheel hard to port and gunned the thrusters.

"Maybe it's more of a *what*," suggested Big Bruce. "As in a highly advanced AI system like me."

"One of *your* kind?" Drake snorted. "Then how about an AI-based strategy to *blast* his ass?"

"I'm working on it," said Big Bruce, "but if there *is* an AI in play, it seems to demonstrate significantly faster reflexes than my own."

"Well, *skudge!*" Drake cranked the wheel hard to starboard and dragged it back, pointing the ship's nose at a 45-degree angle. "I didn't come all the way *back* here to get blown to *pieces* by some minor-league pirate *skiff.*"

Just as he said it, he noticed something hurtling toward the pirate in his rearview camera, firing off sizzling beams of energy. The corvette swerved and bucked but couldn't get out of the way in time to avoid the incoming barrage.

"Captain!" shouted Big Bruce. "It's the cavalry!"

Squinting at the viewer, Drake saw the new actor was too small to be a ship and too big to be a drone. The wireframe on the nav scope showed its outlines more clearly... and made his heart leap with joy inside his chest.

An armor jock. His ass was being saved by a one-jock cavalry.

Even better, a one-*woman*-jock cavalry.

"You know who that *is*, don't you?" Big Bruce asked excitedly.

With every other armor jock hard at work inside the eagle ship, *of course* it could only be one person. Of course it could only be the one person most likely to save *any* day with her battlefield skills...and most likely to save *his heart* with everything else.

"Gus!" he shouted, just as she landed a kill shot dead center on the corvette's power plant.

The persistent pirate ship finally went up in a blast of glorious gold fire and twinkling shrapnel.

Without another second's hesitation, Drake scrambled to the comm panel and opened a channel. "Gus! Thanks for the save!"

Her voice came back over the speaker like the voice of an angel to him. "Anytime, Broken String! Not that you *needed* my help..."

"Right, right." He grinned. "But I'm grateful for it anyway, Gray Lady!"

"So what's the latest on *skudge-face* Tor?" she asked. "That giant *bird* ship wouldn't have anything to do with him, would it?"

"As a matter of fact, it would," said Drake. "That's his flagship, and it's *Emperor* Tor now."

Her snort of derision came through loud and clear. "Not if *I* have anything to say about it!"

That snort more than anything else told Drake that whatever had happened on the ring ship, his Gray Lady had come out of it just fine. More than fine. He couldn't wait to see her again in person and make *sure* she was okay. But first, they had some unfinished business to attend to.

"The rest of the armor just boarded, and they're working their way to his bridge," said Drake. "There's a big hull breach at the base of the bird's neck, if you're interested in helping them *finish* the job."

"Don't mind if I do, Broken String!" she said, already racing toward the breach he'd indicated. "I've been *waiting* to take him down a few hundred pegs!"

Just as she closed the comm channel from her end and jetted away, a bright flare of light swept through the battle-space, momentarily overwhelming the main viewer. Drake shut his eyes against the blinding illumination, then opened them again when it had faded.

"What the hell was *that?*" he asked.

"The exact cause is unknown," reported Big Bruce, "but the effect is obvious. The ring-shaped singularium vessel has *vanished.*"

"What the *skudge?*" That wasn't possible. How could something that *big* just up and disappear?

"Exactly," said Big Bruce. "I cannot presently explain how or why it occurred, but the ring ship is *gone.*"

"Well, *this* day has been full of surprises, hasn't it?"

"And I regret to inform you there are more on the way," said Big Bruce. "Specifically, a trio of Penumbra pirate fighters approaching at a particularly high rate of speed."

"Swell," said Drake. "I suppose they're all piloted by AIs?"

"I am as yet unable to answer that question," said Big

Bruce, "but I *can* tell you they have all charged and armed their weapons, and their targeting systems are locked on *this* vessel."

CHAPTER 33

The ring ship was gone. Just skudging *gone.*

The AI-enhanced sensors in Gus's helmet automatically darkened her visor, replacing it with a heads-up display that was almost as good as the real thing. No more flying in the dark like the last time an explosion had blinded her during a fight.

Not that the ring ship had exploded. If it had, the shockwave of energy from an explosion that massive would have obliterated everything in its path, including Gus and the *Golden Void,* the *Scintilla,* and even Tor's giant bird ship and the fleet ships surrounding it.

The ring ship hadn't *imploded* either. Contained singularity drives were twitchy. The Penumbra cruiser they'd fought the first time around had learned that the hard way. A breach of a contained singularity drive powering something as big as the ring ship would have pulled everything *into* it. That hadn't happened either.

The ship just flat *disappeared.*

Was this what Brukowski had been talking about when he said the Alliance *lost* the damn thing in the first place?

She sent him a message on comms. Not that she expected a response. He couldn't respond if he was still inside that ship when it went wherever the hell it went. But on the off chance he'd managed to get out of the ship in time…

His channel remained silent. She instructed her sensors to track the ident chips in Earl's armor.

Nothing. Not even the faintest trace of a signal.

Brukowski was gone.

The sudden hollow in her heart surprised her. She didn't much *like* Brukowski. They'd butted heads. He'd tried to treat her like a raw grunt still under his command. He'd lied to everyone about his real purpose for coming along on this mission. But damn it, he was still a fellow armor jock and in the end, he'd saved her. He'd stayed on that damn ship and completed his mission.

He'd kept classified Alliance tech out of Tor's hands.

"Skudging asshole," Gus muttered, but the curse had no venom in it.

She had her own mission to complete. She had a wannabe *Emperor* to corral once and for all, as Drake would say.

She jetted as fast as she dared toward the bird ship. The thing looked like the bigger, older, *meaner* brother of the *Scintilla.* Except it had a jagged hole in its hull beneath what looked like its throat.

Most of the ships in her fleet were still pouring energy blasts at the thing, shifting positions so rapidly that all the bird ship's energy blasts kept missing the intended targets. The *Scintilla* was doing a good job of teasing the bird ship, darting in so close as if daring it to hit her, then racing away, manta wings waggling up and down and spinning the *Scintilla* away from every blast of blue energy coming from the bird ship's beak.

Tor must be having a stroke inside that ship, watching his great invasion plans being thwarted by a ragtag fleet. Gus would be happy to deliver the final blow.

A directed energy beam sliced through space directly over her left shoulder. She barrel-rolled her armor as the display in her visor returned to normal, narrowly avoiding more laser fire.

A trio of Penumbra fighters swept past her, headed straight toward the *Golden Void*.

Skudge!

She needed to go after Tor. Drake *wanted* her to go after Tor, but she couldn't leave him out here alone against three fighters. Her Broken String was no slouch when it came to a battle, but even with the shield generator protecting the *Void*, going three against one, especially against ships equipped with anti-singularium weapons, was a recipe for disaster.

A war whoop sounded over her comms. Not Drake. No, this was a female voice she'd recognize anywhere.

"We got this!" Crosscut said.

Crosscut's ship, the *Delgado*, swooped down from overhead, followed by her own contingent of fighters.

"I hate these damn pirates," Crosscut said. "They just cost me the best salvage I've had in my life!"

As if to punctuate her words, the *Delgado* opened up

with a barrage of energy weapons and missiles. The Penumbra fighters peeled off their attack on the *Golden Void,* speeding away in three different directions trying to shake the missiles. Only two of them succeeded. The third ship went up in a heartwarming explosion as the missile hit home and ignited the fighter's fuel cells.

Drake's whoop joined Crosscut's. "Way to *go,* Layla!"

Between Drake and Crosscut, the Penumbra fighters didn't stand a chance.

Tor's bird ship looked like a sleek luxury yacht. The hull was a smooth, gleaming black just like the *Scintilla.* The ragged hole in the throat area looked like an open wound, jagged and leaking some type of fluid.

A force field of some type had formed over the hole. *Like a bandage,* she thought.

She didn't want to rip this bandage off. Her armor jocks were inside. While their armor was spacetight—provided none of the seals had been damaged in the fighting—the same couldn't be said of the ship's crew. She didn't want to kill everyone inside who *wasn't* behind an airtight hatch by blowing the ship's atmosphere out the hole. Plus, as good as her armor was, if she got in the way when the atmosphere exploded out of the ship, she'd end up on the far side of the battle. Just getting back to the bird ship would give the ship time to create another bandage to cover the hole.

The problem seemed to solve itself when the AI-enhanced sensors in her helmet displayed a graphic on one corner of her visor.

A hole had opened in the bandage. The hole appeared just large enough for one armor jock to enter.

An invitation? Or a trap?

Only one way to find out. She had to get inside. *Tor* was inside.

She powered on the laser embedded in her gauntlet and jetted through the hole in the bandage. Nothing attacked her. No crew were in the corridor beyond the hole in the hull. In fact, other than the ragged hole in the bulkhead on the space side of the corridor, there was no sign at all that a battle had taken place here. The shiny, dark-gray walls and ceiling looked wholly undamaged. Even the carpet beneath her boots looked unscathed.

What the skudge?

She disengaged her maneuvering jets and let the ship's artificial gravity settle her on the floor. She ordered her helmet's sensors to give her a schematic of the ship and locate the ident chips for all the armor jocks on board. Not surprisingly, they all seemed to be fighting their way toward the bridge of the ship.

Gus had never gone inside the *Scintilla*. It had seemed disloyal somehow to the *Golden Void*. Especially when Drake had seemed so enamored with the *Scintilla*. The *Void* was Gus's home now. She'd played around with its operating systems. It's where Drake's guitar was. Where his cabin with those feather pillows and down comforter were. It even *smelled* like Drake's cinnamon gum.

The *Golden Void* was like a lot of ships she'd been on. Not exactly cramped, but not exactly spacious either. Utilitarian was the best word. No effort had been made to hide pipes and conduits. Corridors were only as wide as they had to be. Cabins were only large enough to handle the basic requirements of the few crew it normally would take to fly the ship. The fact that Drake could manage to fly the ship all on his own just spoke to the level of competence he hid behind his laidback cowboy persona.

Most of the space inside the *Void* was devoted to the cargo bay and various storage areas throughout the ship. Those areas were *definitely* not designed to be anything than what they were: large, spacetight holds for transporting whatever the *Void* got paid to transport. That's why the *Void* had been the perfect ship to commandeer all those years ago when Gus had gotten the remaining members of the 83rd off Shephard's Moon after Tor had reported them all killed and took their only transport ship with him.

The interior of Tor's bird ship looked like it had been built for people with a lot of money, a lot of power, or both. Or maybe for a wannabe Emperor.

If this ship had been built specifically for Tor, she'd have to be especially careful. Drake hadn't told her much about something he called the *Scintilla's* psiflux engineering, but she did get the idea that the ship responded to thoughts. Even going so far as to change its internal and external structure according to the wishes of whoever controlled it.

If that was the case, why was there still a jagged hole in the ship's hull? Something large enough for armor jocks to get through to the inside of the ship? It wasn't like they could have boarded the thing in the usual fashion—through an airlock. The *Scintilla* didn't *have* an airlock, and she hadn't seen one on this ship either. According to Drake, doors just appeared on the *Scintilla's* hull because the pilot/owner/whoever wanted a door to appear, and the ship read those thoughts.

She contacted Benji Ochoa on her armor's comm channel. Her old 83rd Armor Division colleague had been one of the armor jocks Drake had sent inside this ship.

"Hey, Benji," she sent. "How's it hanging?"

"That you, Gray Lady?" came his reply a split second later. "You decide to join the party?"

"Couldn't let you have all the fun," she said. "What's your status?"

"Making headway," he said. "Running into lots of security, nothing we can't handle."

The heads-up display on her visor blinked to alert her to activity behind her.

She whirled, expecting a phalanx of security personnel bearing down on her, but the corridor behind her was empty.

Her visor had alerted her to something she *hadn't* expected. The hole in the ship's hull had closed up completely. No more bandage. No more ragged, bleeding wound. Just another smooth section of wall.

The ship had healed itself.

They were all trapped inside.

"You getting any weird vibes from the ship?" she asked Benji.

There was a slight pause before he asked, "Come again?"

"This ship's special," she said.

She decided to leave it at that. She wasn't sure how many of the armor jocks were aware of what the *Scintilla* could do. Most of them were damn good pilots, but Bruce Junior hadn't exactly given guided tours of the *Scintilla* back on Buddy's Bluff. Just looking at the design similarities between the *Scintilla* and this ship made it obvious they were both Ongani ships. She didn't want her squad of armor jocks to think they could *think* at the ship, and it would do what they wanted.

"Just watch your six," she told Benji.

"Always," he said.

"And don't shoot me," she added. "I'm headed in your direction."

"Copy," he said, and signed off.

She took off down the carpeted corridor toward the location of the other armor jocks. Along the way, she tried to contact Drake on the *Void*.

That communication didn't go through.

She had her AI-enhanced sensors check for interference. Her communication with Benji had gone through just fine, so there wasn't anything wrong at her end.

Ship to ship communications unavailable at this time, her sensors reported.

This damn bird ship was blocking her! Preventing her from contacting Drake to see how the rest of the fight was going.

Except she really shouldn't blame the ship. Tor wouldn't have set foot on a ship like this—a ship that responded to telepathically transmitted orders—unless he knew he could control it. He'd always been a coward at heart. He wanted everyone to think he was a big, powerful man, but deep down inside he was a coward. He got other people to do his dirty work for him. Now he was getting this *ship* to do his dirty work. This elegant, beautiful, and more than likely highly *intelligent* ship.

Gus had just about had it with Jorritz Tor.

No, check that.

She'd *more than* had it with Jorritz Tor. It was time to make that skudgehole pay.

CHAPTER 34

Earl Knox was having a very, *very* bad day.

Not only had that hardass of an *ex*-Master Sergeant *stolen* his armor, now the whole damn ring ship had disappeared! With his armor and that hardass still inside!

His armor was gone. All that lovely singularium plating the hull of the ring ship—gone! Whatever Brukowski had done inside that ship, he'd screwed everyone over.

Earl had only come on this damn mission because he wanted to get his hands on Tor. Now he couldn't even do that. Without his armor, he couldn't leave the *Silver Void*. And with Bruce-7 piloting the ship in a way no sane person ever would, whipping it back and forth, up and down, and *rolling* the damn thing while Ulrich Teppin played the weapons control board like a virtuoso, Earl was left with nothing to do but hang onto the pilot's chair for dear life and stew about all the opportunities he'd just lost.

Someone was going to have to pay for this.

Gus Light, he thought. She owed him. This whole battle had been *her* idea. She'd humiliated him at every opportunity. Dangled the opportunity to get back at Tor in front of his nose, knowing he'd follow the scent. He'd wring what was due and owing to him out of her if it was the last thing—

"*Silver Void,*" came a loud, stressed voice over the ship's speaker, startling Earl out of his daydreams of revenge. "You copy over there?"

Was that Drake? It was difficult to tell, what with the *Silver Void's* bulkheads creaking and groaning and pretty much complaining about every twist and turn Bruce-7 put it through.

This particular communication wasn't directed to anyone. Normally the ship's AI would answer a general call. But at the moment Bruce-7 was a little too busy keeping the ship in one piece to bother responding.

Teppin certainly wasn't going to respond, which left it up to Earl.

The ship jerked hard to one side, almost throwing him from his chair.

"What the hell do you want?" he said. "I'm busy getting whiplash over here."

"Just lost the camera feeds for the armor jocks on board Tor's ship," came the response.

Yup, that was Drake. The man thought he was in charge because Gus wasn't around to personally direct the battle.

"Which ones?" Earl said, just to push Drake's buttons. The only feed Drake would really care about was Gus Light's.

"All of them!"

Earl grinned. That was more like it. He'd managed to flap the unflappable space cowboy. Earl's bad mood was lifting already.

He punched in commands on the *Silver Void's* ridiculously anachronistic communications board to call up camera feeds for the jocks who had cameras embedded in their armor. Not all civilian armor had cameras. The camera in Earl's old helmet had been damaged in the same battle that had ended up costing him his military career and he'd never seen the need to fix it.

He could have been watching the boarding party all along, but it would have only pissed him off because he wasn't with them. So he'd never bothered bringing up the feeds. Now no matter what he did, the camera feeds remained blank.

"Same here," he said. "All feeds offline."

Drake swore.

Then behind him, Ulrich Teppin swore louder.

"Incoming!" Teppin shouted.

The *Silver Void* had been dodging that blue fire from Tor's bird ship like a pro. Good thing, since Earl had seen that blue energy beam slam the *Golden Void* around pretty well even with the shield generator. The *Silver Void* had one of the shield generators too and had survived a few direct hits from Tor's pirate fleet that it wouldn't have otherwise.

Had the bird ship finally caught up with Bruce-7's wild piloting strategy?

Had their luck finally run out?

Earl checked the forward viewscreen. No blue fire arcing toward them.

What the hell?

"Where?" he shouted at Teppin.

"Aft!" Teppin said. "Ships heading this way, high rate of speed. It looks like the rest of Tor's whole damn pirate fleet!"

Earl lurched over to the nav console as Bruce-7 put the ship through another spinning maneuver. He punched in the commands to bring up the aft cameras, then zoomed in.

What he saw almost turned his insides to liquid.

Ships, more than he could count, all headed their way. Fighters and corvettes, gunships and cruisers, all displaying pirate colors of the Penumbra and the Celestilons and the Order of Slaughter. Up to this point, most of those ships had been hanging back, apparently willing—or ordered—to let Tor try to take out Gus's little fleet all by himself.

Had they changed their minds?

"Do we deviate from the battle plan?" Teppin asked. "I only got two hands here, and we've got just so much ordnance left on this boat."

"Do the best you can," came Drake's voice over the speaker. "Stick to hammering Tor. Layla and I will take on the pirates with the rest of the fleet."

That would be suicide. There were just too many pirate ships all heading this way.

Earl watched the ships grow closer. So far they hadn't fired a shot.

The *Silver Void* lurched again as it changed position around the bird ship. Teppin lined up more fire according to the battle plan to keep Tor's bird ship busy.

The new position gave Earl a perfect view of the throat of the bird ship. Where there'd been a jagged hole in the hull, thanks to the combined efforts of the armor jocks, the hull was now smooth and shiny with not a single scratch in sight.

What the hell?

"You see that?" Earl said to nobody in particular. "I could have sworn we blew a hole in that sucker. Now it's gone."

Teppin shot him a look of such flabbergasted shock it would have been funny under other circumstances. Then his expression turned flat, and he turned back to his weapons control board.

Earl knew that look.

It was the look of a soldier determined to fight an unbeatable foe to the very last moment of his life.

Earl wondered if Teppin had seen the same expression on his face. He would have been surprised to know that Teppin had.

CHAPTER 35

The armor jocks inside the Ongani bird ship had most definitely handled Tor's security forces. If you could call them security forces.

Most of the dead and dying Gus ran into on her way to join up with the rest of the armor jocks had been pirates. They had worn little patches of pirate colors on what was left of their black and gray coveralls designating what faction they belonged to. Judging from the patches alone, most of them had been Penumbra.

Gus would have felt sorry for the dead pirates except she knew what the Penumbra did with the few people they didn't kill outright during their raids on peaceful settlements. She hadn't given Sef a load of bull when she'd lit into Drake's sister back on Buddy's Bluff. That was one of the reasons Gus had insisted that Sef stay behind during the battle for the ring ship.

The former ring ship. Nobody was getting the damn thing now.

Now the only objective was Tor himself, and that was one prize Gus wasn't willing to give up.

She was glad she'd turned off the olfactory sensors on her armor. She didn't need to smell the mess in the corridor.

"Distance and directions to squad," she instructed her AI-enhanced sensors.

The bird ship was big, far bigger than the *Void*. Not the city-sized mass of the ring ship where she'd flown down passageways to get to Brukowski, but still big enough that she had to jog down corridor after corridor, following the trail of blood and bodies.

Except that trail of bodies was fizzling out. Either Tor was running out of pirates to act as cannon fodder, or he'd called them all into the bridge to protect him. Fashioning himself a human shield.

At least none of the dead she'd passed had been wearing armor. Some of the pirates' weapons looked like variations of the magno-beams all the armor jocks had. If the pirates used those magno-beams on the jocks' singular-ium-plated armor and followed it up with projectile weapons, she would have seen a lot of injured or dying armor jocks.

Didn't the pirates have time to use those weapons? Or was her squad of civilian armor jocks just that good? Benji had been back when he'd been military. She hadn't known about the rest of them, but now she guessed she did.

A display appeared on her visor. Direction and distance to what looked like a last-ditch firefight.

She leveled up the power to her armor's legs and *ran*

down the corridor. She barely noticed the ceiling and walls expanding outward to give her more room to maneuver.

All eleven of her armor jocks were arrayed in a semi-circle around what had to be the last wall between them and the bridge of the bird ship.

The corridor here ended in a T-junction, but one that was much wider than any Gus had ever seen on a ship. Ships were constructed to conserve space. This junction was nearly half the size of one of the classroom amphitheaters where she'd trained as a raw recruit. The floor even sloped downward at a slight angle toward a curved wall, like the outside of a sphere.

This was Tor's theater. He must have had the ship carve this space out for him as the perfect place to address his troops. A place where he could film himself addressing his loyal subjects. If she had to guess, she'd bet the outside of that curved wall could display whatever background he wanted.

"Hey, boss," Benji said when she joined the line of armor jocks. "He's behind the wall. We've thrown everything we got at it. Combined firepower, like with the hull, and we can't make a dent."

"Even projectiles?" she asked.

If an armor jock's helmet could have an expression, Benji's would have reflected the frustration he clearly felt.

"I did say *everything*," he said. "Including one of those special grenades I found in your stash back on the Bluff."

Gus's special grenades were packed with pellets. One of those special grenades had been the only thing she'd managed to lob into the drone factory back on Chrysallix. It had been the only thing the shield generators protecting the factory weren't designed to repel because there hadn't been any energy signatures inside the grenade.

If the special grenades didn't work here, that just confirmed that Tor wasn't using shield generators to protect himself. Like she suspected, he was using the *ship* as his final line of defense.

How were they supposed to fight a ship that could repel anything they threw at it? The wall protecting the bridge didn't even have a door.

And given the way the ship had repaired the hole in its hull, even if the armor jocks *could* manage to blow a hole in the wall, the ship would just close that hole up again.

Two of the armor jocks were covering the side corridors that extended on either side of the T-junction.

"Any resistance from ship *security*?" she asked, putting extra emphasis on "security."

"Not anymore," Benji said. "Not sure there's any left that aren't behind that wall."

"On the bridge with Tor," she muttered.

She had no idea what was behind the wall. Her AI-enhanced sensors were annoyingly silent when she requested a scan of the bird ship's bridge.

Sooner or later her jocks would figure out a way to get in there. They had to. She wasn't going to get this close to Tor and fail. No way, no how. The Gray Lady *didn't* fail, not when everything was on the line.

It sure would be nice to know how many pirates Tor had

on the bridge with him. To know what kind of weapons they'd have at the ready. That was the thing about backing the enemy into a corner—they always came out fighting like berserkers with whatever weapons they had left.

Too bad that wall isn't transparent, she thought.

The wall began to shift, colors swirling through it.

"Think his 'highness' is about to give us an ultimatum?" Benji said. Clearly, he'd figured out the purpose of this room too.

Gus powered up all the weapons she was carrying. Maybe if she added her armor's weapons to those of her armor jocks—made it lucky number twelve attacking the wall—they'd get through this time.

The wall turned transparent.

Gus blinked. "You seeing that?" she asked Benji.

"If you're talking about that skudgehole and eight of his 'security,' then yeah, I'm seeing the same thing," Benji said.

And Tor was clearly seeing them.

Gus had despised the man for decades. She'd been chasing him all over the Frontier for months. But she hadn't actually *seen* him since he'd fled Shepard's Moon the night her son was born and her son's father had died.

She was surprised now at how decidedly *ordinary* he looked. He was nothing more than a middle-aged man with twin salt-and-pepper braids framing his face. Sure, his dark eyes were filled with malevolent condescension, and his head was tilted back so that he was looking down his nose at the peons that surrounded him, but he was just a *man.*

A man with delusions of grandeur who'd managed to bribe, cajole, and probably force people into following him.

He was a bully.

And he was surprised as hell that the wall to his bridge had turned transparent.

But he recovered quickly. Made it look like he'd wanted the wall to turn transparent.

"Now that you can see we're ready for you," he said, gesturing to the wicked-looking weapons his "security" personnel were holding, "I want to show you what happens when your *fleet* refuses to join my Empire!"

Screens rose into view on sections of the transparent wall. The screens displayed a 180-degree view of the ships still shifting positions and blasting away at Tor's bird ship. But more importantly, the screens displayed a clear view of Tor's entire pirate *fleet* racing toward the ships attacking the bird ship.

Gus swallowed hard. Her fleet was outnumbered at least ten to one, and some of those pirate ships were gunships and heavy cruisers. In the distance, she could see the *Golden Void* and the *Scintilla* putting up a valiant effort to try to distract the pirates, but the pirates were refusing to be distracted.

As she watched, one of the ships in her fleet, a smaller ship that had been damaged in earlier fighting, mounted a last-ditch run against a pirate gunship. The small ship roared toward the gunship, all weapons blazing. The gunship ignored it, right up until it became clear the smaller ship intended to ram the gunship. Then the pirate gunship blew the little ship apart.

Gus felt her heart clench.

She'd lost a ship. She'd lost a *crew*. People who'd come to fight for her just because she'd asked. Or because Brukowski had asked.

If things didn't change, she was about to lose everything. All the ships in her fleet, all her crew. Bruce Junior and Kymmie aboard the *Scintilla*. Earl Knox on the *Silver Void.* Big Bruce the fantastic AI on the *Golden Void.*

And Drake.

She was about to lose her space cowboy.

Well, the *hell* with that.

With a cry of pure rage, she opened fire on the transparent wall. Her shots pounded the wall at a spot level with Tor's face. He flinched, then when he realized the wall was holding, he smiled.

That smile was the very last straw.

Let me get in that room with you, she thought, *and I'll wipe that smile off your face!*

An armor-sized opening appeared in the transparent wall just right of center.

Gus didn't need to be invited twice.

She *raced* to that opening. Dove through on full power, the maneuvering jets on her armor already putting her in a barrel roll designed to avoid anything the security forces protecting Tor fired at her.

The bridge wasn't nearly as big as Tor's *amphitheater,* but it was bigger than the bridge on anything smaller than a gunship. Gus was moving so fast that combined with her armor's barrel roll, she peppered all eight of Tor's security forces with blasts from her lasers.

Then she threw one of her special grenades behind where Tor was standing, right in front of the man in the pilot's seat.

The pilot yelped and leaped out of his seat. He ran for

cover behind an organic-looking console, Tor right behind him.

The console melted into the floor the same time Gus's special grenade went off.

The singularium plating on her armor protected her from *most* of the projectiles that blanketed the bridge. One of Tor's security forces must have hit the plating covering her left shoulder joint with a magno-beam type weapon. She felt a burning sting as one of the pellets ripped through the singularium and buried itself in her shoulder.

Not skudging *again*!

Tor's security forces weren't protected by singularium plating. The pellets ripped through their uniforms, leaving all of them battered and bleeding. One man was killed outright when a pellet tore through his neck. The rest were so badly injured, they dropped their weapons.

Even Tor was bleeding from half a dozen holes in his arms and legs, and one particularly nasty hole in his belly.

The pilot was the only one who appeared mostly uninjured. A pellet had carved a new part in his hair. The wound was bleeding freely, and his eyes had the shocky look of a civilian caught in the middle of a battle he was not mentally or physically prepared for. Apparently, Tor's body had protected the pilot from any serious injuries.

Around her, the ship seemed to be healing itself from the pellets that had impacted the ship's systems.

Gus turned her gauntlet-mounted projectile weapon on Tor. From the amount of holes in his body, he wasn't wearing any type of protective gear under his own rather ostentatious outfit. He'd gone full Military Leader with olive drab coveralls festooned with fake medals and ribbons and even a braided gold sash.

"Don't move," Gus said. "Or I'll be happy to put a bullet in the middle of your forehead. I won't even lose any sleep over it."

Amazingly, Tor smiled. "I don't have to move to kill you," he said. "This ship does what I want. Or haven't you figured that out?"

Gus had actually begun to think that someone other than Tor was controlling the ship. At first, she'd thought it was the pilot, but the pilot wouldn't have made the console he'd planned to use for cover disappear right when he needed it most.

"Prove it," she said. Then she added in a low, dangerous voice. "I *dare* you, you skudging *coward*."

One side of Tor's mouth tipped down, turning his smile nasty. "You asked for it!"

Everything seemed to freeze for a long moment. Tor stood there, Gus's weapon pointed at him, a look of utter concentration on his face. Then a frown built between his eyebrows, and a look of doubt crept into his expression. Finally, pure anger twisted his features into a mask of impotent fury.

"Damn you!" he screamed. "You do what *I* say!"

Inside her armor, Gus smiled. Then she tried an experiment of her own.

Restrain this skudgehole, would you? she thought.

The organic-looking console that had melted into the floor rose up once again, only this time it formed itself into a chair complete with four-point restraints. Those restraints flowed outward toward Tor's wrists and ankles.

Tor yelped and tried to run, but Gus waggled her projectile weapon at him. "Now, now," she said. "I *really* want to punch you. And I really, *seriously* want to shoot you, but I'm willing to settle for putting you in restraints. It's up to you. Which ones don't you want because I'm good with all three."

Tor stood still, bleeding from his wounds, as the bird ship fastened the restraints and pulled him into the chair.

"I need medical attention," he said. "I'm going to bleed to death."

"Cry me a river," Gus said, starting to really feel the pain in her shoulder.

The battle wasn't over yet. The pirate fleet was about to destroy her fleet.

She whirled toward the viewscreens in the transparent wall. The pirates were still coming.

Tor laughed. "They'll come for me," he said. "My fleet's big enough to take on the entire Alliance! How do you think you'll fare against *that?*" He laughed again. "You haven't won, *Gray Lady.* You'll never win against me!"

She was beginning to wish she'd just shot him.

She needed to let Drake know that they'd taken the ship. That they'd captured Tor so those twenty-four ships attacking the bird ship could turn all their firepower on the pirate fleet.

I need Drake, she thought.

A pleasing guitar chord sounded in her mind, followed closely by Drake's voice.

"Gus!" The relief in his voice was palpable. "I've been trying to reach you. We lost vid feeds—"

She cut him off. "We've taken the ship. We've taken *Tor.*

Terminate Big Bruce's program *now* and go after those pirates!"

His whoop nearly blew out her eardrums. "That's my girl! Shifting gears now."

Girl?

Okay, she'd give him that one. She'd give him hundreds of "my girls" if he survived this battle. Her fleet was still ridiculously outnumbered.

Except now *she* apparently had control of Tor's bird ship, complete with that blue energy weapon that had been giving her fleet fits.

She turned toward the pilot. The man was still obviously in shock, but she needed him.

"Get this ship in the fight," she said, "on the *right* side."

He shook his head, nervous jerky little motions. "I can't," he said.

Gus pointed her projectile weapon at him. "You can't," she said, "or you *won't?*"

"She's not listening to me," he whined. "I haven't been able to control her ever since we got here."

"You're not the pilot?"

"I was, but—" He held out his trembling hands. "She hasn't been listening to him either." He nodded toward Tor. "Not really. She's just been doing enough to make it *look* like she was listening to him." He lowered his voice. "I don't think she likes us very much."

"Then who's she listening to?" Gus asked.

The pilot blinked. "Don't you know? I'm pretty sure she's listening to *you.*"

Huh. Gus chuffed out a bark of laughter.

"Okay, then," she said. "I guess I need to test this out."

This time she imagined she was talking directly to the bird ship. *Feel like kicking a little pirate ass?*

Even through her armor, Gus felt the ship power up. The transparent wall at the rear of the bridge disappeared, and new viewscreens flowed into existence in front of the pilot's chair.

Navigation screens. Communications screens. Weapons screens, including a screen labeled *Blue Energy Weapon Status*.

The *former* pilot stared at that last screen. "She's never called it that before."

But that's what Gus had called it whenever she thought about it.

Theory tested and proven valid. She and the bird ship were definitely sympatico.

Benji stepped up beside her on the bridge. "Want to let me in on what's going on?" he asked.

"We're going after the pirates," Gus said. "We're taking our captured ship into battle. And with this little gem on our side—"

"We're going to win the war," Benji said, finishing her sentence.

"We're going to win the war," Gus repeated, grinning ear to ear.

They were going to win the *skudging* war.

CHAPTER 36

Three days later…

"You shot yourself," Drake said.

"I did *not!*"

Drake had been teasing her about her latest injury on and off ever since they got back to Buddy's Bluff. Gus knew it was just his way of whistling past the graveyard, thankful that her shoulder was her only real injury from her confrontation with Tor on the bird ship. Things could have been *so much* worse, and they both knew it.

The medics on Buddy's Bluff had removed the pellet her special grenade shot into her shoulder through the damaged singularium plating on her armor. The surrounding muscles and tendons hadn't enjoyed the procedure, to put it mildly, and were still voicing their displeasure every time she abused that shoulder.

Drake had insisted on going with her to her final checkup, where she'd just been pronounced healthy enough to travel. Not that she needed the doctor to tell her that.

"Just take it easy for a while," Bruce Junior's personal doctor told her.

No pillow fights, Drake had mouthed at her.

For now, she'd mouthed back with a wicked grin.

Other more pleasurable pursuits, however, were definitely back on the menu. Lots and lots of pleasurable pursuits, especially once they left Buddy's Bluff behind and were finally alone on the *Golden Void.*

They needed the time to themselves. Gus had been at the forefront of all the hubbub about the war—whether she wanted to be or not—thanks to the series of reports Kymmie had filed with her news service.

Kymmie had featured Gus in all her reports on "A Secret War: The Battle for the Heart of the Alliance," as she'd dubbed it.

"Greatly outnumbered and outgunned," Kymmie's first report started out, *"a brave band of warriors preserved the way of life for every citizen of the Free Worlds Alliance when they went head-to-head against disgraced former Alliance ambassador Jorritz Tor.*

"Tor, a self-proclaimed Emperor, declared that his Frontier empire would usurp and replace the Alliance. This reporter learned that Tor was preparing to invade Alliance space with an army of vicious pirates who'd been plundering independent settlements in the Frontier for hundreds of years. Without the foresight and rock-hard determination of Augusta Light, the heroic Gray Lady of the 83rd Armored Division, who came out of retirement to spearhead the mission to stop Tor along with retired Master

Sergeant Garrison Brukowski, the Alliance would most certainly have been drawn into a lengthy and costly war against Tor's forces, with death tolls estimated in the millions, if not billions, across..."

Gus had turned the report off after that. Drake had watched the whole thing. He'd told her that Kymmie's report was accompanied by footage she'd shot aboard the *Scintilla*. But not *all* the footage she'd shot.

There'd been no vids of the ring ship, even though Kymmie had told Gus she'd managed to capture the ring ship not only sitting there big as life in Frontier space, but also the moment when the ring ship disappeared.

Gus hadn't watched any of Kymmie's subsequent reports. Hearing herself described as a hero had always made Gus feel uncomfortable, and it certainly did now. She wasn't a hero. She'd just been a warrior out for revenge. Drake had his Smiley Face Gambit. Now Gus was apparently the star of the *Kick Tor's Ass* Gambit. The only difference was that Drake hadn't lost anyone during his. People had died because of hers. It was going to take some time for her to come to terms with that.

They were halfway to Bruce Junior's trading post when Gus's comms pinged.

"I want to buy you a drink," Kymmie said without preamble. "I have some news you're going to want to hear."

Gus tried to beg off, but Kymmie had said it was important.

"Go," Drake said, giving her a little kiss. "Have a drink. You deserve it." He unwrapped a stick of cinnamon gum and stuck it in his mouth. "I'll take care of Bruce." He gave her a wink.

The spaceport had really spruced up since the first time Gus had set foot on Buddy's Bluff, back when two Fluke ships hung low in orbit around the planet. Most of what Gus remembered from those days was the overpowering mud and muck. Now the outpost was looking like a real city. It even had a couple of bars that were far more inviting than the one Gus used to frequent on Depak Station.

Kymmie was already waiting for her in a back booth. "You remember Ulrich Teppin?" she asked after Gus sat down and they both ordered drinks from the automated system at the table.

Teppin was the ex-military tech who'd served as the weapons officer on the *Silver Void* during the battle.

When Gus nodded, Kymmie leaned forward, arms resting on the table. "I need to bring you up to speed on what's been going on in the background. Some of this stuff I probably shouldn't tell you, but I figure you need to know some of it and you *deserve* to know the rest."

According to Kymmie, Teppin had contacted his former C.O. as soon as the *Silver Void* made it back to Buddy's Bluff. Teppin told his old C.O. that Gus had captured Jorritz Tor, and that Teppin and the rest of the men Brukowski had brought on this mission had Tor in custody.

Teppin told the man that they intended to take Tor to the prison on Melody Station, where he'd be kept until the Alliance came to get him. Brukowski's men had all volunteered for guard duty. As Teppin put it, they were "highly motivated" to make sure Tor received the justice he so very richly deserved. It was the least they could do in memory of Master Sergeant. Teppin was only waiting for Tor's doctors to give the okay to transport him off planet, then they'd be heading out to Melody Station.

"Here's where it gets interesting," Kymmie said.

Teppin had also told his former C.O. that a reporter had traveled with the fleet into battle. Teppin didn't know what Kymmie had seen or recorded, but he had an idea that she must have seen at least some advanced and possibly classified tech. He didn't feel right keeping that information from his former C.O.

"He gave me a heads-up about the call," Kymmie said. "He didn't have to, but Teppin's a good guy."

Less than an hour after that, Kymmie had received a highly encrypted communication from a military intelligence officer. The call hadn't come as a surprise. In fact, once she'd heard about Teppin's call to his old C.O., Kymmie had been counting on it.

"The guy didn't tell me his name," Kymmie said, "so I'm just going to refer to him as Agent Zero."

Agent Zero had been adamant that she refrain from reporting about any advanced Alliance technology, *especially* the ring ship or its disappearance.

Kymmie was no longer a newbie in the news business. She had a feel for just how far she could push Agent Zero before she'd put herself in danger. She also knew military intelligence could quash all her reports with a simple threat to her news service. But she wasn't going to agree to Agent Zero's demands without getting something in return.

She ended up getting *two* things out of the Alliance.

"They even let me put it on the record," she said. "I have recordings stored in multiple places, including here on the Bluff. You'll see why I'm telling *you* this in a minute."

The first thing Kymmie got was an exclusive on the prosecution of Jorritz Tor. She'd be the only reporter given access to the Alliance's strategy sessions prior to trial, and the only reporter allowed inside the courtroom once the trial started.

The second concession from the Alliance involved Gus.

"I made you the star of every story for a reason," Kymmie said. "Don't get me wrong. You deserve it, you and Brukowski both. Even the Alliance recognizes that. The military's going to do right by you *and* the men who died in battle."

The military would be conveying the highest honors on Brukowski and his men. They'd also make sure their families were set for life financially. Kymmie said she'd agreed to simply say that the men had been lost defending the Alliance without going into any details of how they'd died.

As for Gus...

"They agreed to expunge all charges against you," Kymmie said. "The official line now is that your actions on Shepard's Moon—yours and Drake's—were fully sanctioned by the Alliance." Kymmie raised her glass in a toast to Gus. "You're a free woman, with all the rights and privileges thereof. Congratulations!"

Gus could hardly believe it. She'd be free now to travel inside the Alliance if she wanted to. She could use Alliance communication channels. Alliance databases. She'd even have access to all her funds on deposit with various financial institutions inside the Alliance. That was a whole lot of cash. She'd put most of her military pay into those accounts year after year.

For once, Gus hadn't known what to say. Thank you seemed insufficient, and she told Kymmie that.

"I wouldn't have a career without you," Kymmie said. "When you brought me in for that story on Shepard's Moon? I know you chose me because you hoped I'd embarrass the Alliance into helping the planet's government, but you could have called any reporter. They would have chomped at the story. You called *me*. And you called me again for this story. *I* owe *you*, Gus Light, and I'll never forget it."

Gus left the bar in a daze.

She was a free woman. She'd gotten used to the idea that she'd be spending the rest of her life in the Frontier. Now that didn't matter. She could go anywhere she wanted. Anywhere *they* wanted to go in known space. It didn't matter now if someone caught her in Alliance space and tried to make trouble for her. Without the threat of military prison hanging over her head, she could just spit in their face.

She'd pinged Drake on her comm unit.

"Meet me at the *Void*," she'd said. "You're not gonna believe this."

CHAPTER 37

The only fly left in the ointment was Exchequer, which meant they had to deal with Drake's sister. Gus's sudden windfall would make that easier.

That, and what the bird ship had in one of its many holds.

To put it mildly, Sef hadn't been happy that one of the ships she'd leased from Honest Gordian had been destroyed in battle and that others had some fairly significant damage. And an unhappy Sef had been making everyone's life miserable.

She'd been in space traffic control when the fleet arrived at Buddy's Bluff. From what space traffic control told Gus, Sef hadn't *left* space traffic control the entire time the fleet was gone.

Neither Gus nor Drake were in any sort of a mood to deal with Sef the minute they got back to the Bluff. Not after they'd just finished sending the last of Tor's pirate fleet packing.

The rest of the battle had been rather anticlimactic. As soon as the bird ship started firing at the pirates, the pirates had stopped putting up any kind of a fight. Whether the pirates didn't want to face the wrath of the bird ship's blue laser fire, or whether they realized that whatever deals they'd made with Tor had gone up in smoke now that he'd been captured, including their shares of the promised bounty—all that lovely singularium on the ring ship's hull —the pirates had beat a hasty retreat through the transit flume Tor used to ambush the *Golden Void* in the first place.

No honor among pirates. The look on Tor's face as he'd watched his pirate fleet disappear into the transit flume one by one, leaving him behind, had been priceless.

After the pirates had skedaddled and the fighting was finally over, Gus and the rest of the armor jocks had decided to stay on the bird ship for the trip back to Buddy's Bluff. Drake had wanted Gus back on the *Golden Void*, but she was worried Tor would try to make the bird ship follow *his* thoughts again if she left the ship while he was still on board. Besides, the rest of the armor jocks were staying on the bird ship too, dividing their time between guarding Tor and rounding up the rest of the crew who were still alive. Most of the crew, including the poor beleaguered pilot, said Tor had threatened to ruin their families if they didn't serve him. All of his surviving crew were only too happy to get off the ship once they got to Buddy's Bluff.

Gus and Drake had finally reunited after both ships landed at the port. Drake had made sure the *Golden Void's* berth was as close to the bird ship as he could get. Only the

Scintilla was closer. The *Scintilla* had refused to land at any other berth than the one right next to the bird ship no matter how many times Bruce Junior tried to direct her to another berth. Bruce Junior guessed the two ships were the equivalent of siblings who'd been apart too long.

Gus still had most of her armor on when she'd gotten off the bird ship. She'd taken her helmet off once Tor's pirate fleet had fled and the fighting was over. She would have taken off the rest of her armor, but it was easier to wear it than to carry it, like she was carrying her helmet.

Drake had taken one look at the blood staining her armor's left shoulder and gone pale. He'd insisted she go directly to the medics. She'd insisted that she needed to store her armor on the *Void* first. When they saw Sef stomping toward them on her impractical high heels, they both went back into the bird ship instead.

They stayed there until Sef gave up and went away. They'd been avoiding her ever since, but now they had a plan.

After Gus and Drake had a little celebratory alone time on the *Golden Void* to celebrate her unexpected freedom, they'd tracked Sef down. She wasn't in space traffic control anymore. Instead, Bruce Junior had let her use a private little office at the back of his trading post. She was currently making arrangements—or trying to make arrangements— to return the surviving leased ships back to the Honest Gordian's.

She scowled at Gus and Drake when they walked in.

"Phisto," she said as soon as she ended her call, "do you have *any idea* how much you've cost Exchequer?"

"Hello to you too, sis," he said.

347

Her scowl got deeper. She was probably wondering why he had a shit-eating grin on his face.

"This is no time for niceties," she said. "You *guaranteed* those shield generators would protect the ships!"

They'd never had enough shield generators to protect all the ships in the fleet. Sef knew that. She was just being difficult. Gus might have rankled at her tone if she didn't have something up her sleeve that would take the wind right out of Sef's sails.

Drake exchanged a look with Gus. "Now might be a good time," he said.

Sef glared at him. "A good time for *what?*"

This was going to be fun. "To split the bounty," Gus said.

Tor's bird ship was a hell of a big ship. It was also a resourceful ship. Once Tor was fully restrained and his remaining crew rounded up, the ship had told Gus—through a series of snippets of the songs Drake always played on his guitar, of all things—about certain cargo holds the ship had kept hidden from Tor and his crew.

The cargo holds were massive, and they were all filled to the brim with singularium.

Gus has asked the ship how she'd gotten it, but the ship had remained stubbornly silent. It had communicated its clear intent, again through song, that Gus could have all the singularium she wanted. Then the ship had sent her a snippet of a joyful type of music Drake *definitely* wouldn't play on his guitar while the word *Freedom!* appeared over and over in Gus's mind.

She and Drake had discussed what to do with all that

singularium. They'd already decided on how to split some of it up. Had, in fact, already given some of it away. They'd also decided how much to sell to Bruce Junior, so they'd have some ready cash. Ready cash wasn't really a factor now, but they didn't want to give Exchequer a windfall either. Just enough to get Sef off Drake's back.

It took some time to get Sef to understand that singularium was more valuable than straight, hard cash.

"The Alliance wants this stuff," Drake told her. "*Bruce* wants this stuff. Hell, Honest Gordian's would even take it as payment for their lost ship."

Sef had called up market information for singularium on a little device she took out of the jacket of her business suit. Her mouth dropped open a bit in surprise before she caught herself and remembered that she was supposed to be pissed at her brother.

She still grumped that the amount wasn't nearly enough to compensate *her* for her time and her worry that *none* of the ships would make it back.

"How about I throw in one of the shield generators?" Drake said. "And don't forget, all those ships now come equipped with little Bruces. That has to count for something!"

"Not nearly enough," Sef said. "What else can you put on the table? Remember, I have to sell this deal to Exchequer, and they're not happy."

It was like listening to someone haggle with a used ship dealer, but Drake was pretty damn good at it. Sef drove a hard bargain, but in the end she agreed to take the amount of singularium they were willing to give her.

And all the little Bruces.

And a case of the Bluff's best liquor. The good stuff.

When Drake and Sef left to go get the booze, Sef gave Gus a surreptitious wink behind Drake's back.

She'd been playing Drake all along.

Gus shook her head. Siblings. She was happy that the only brothers she'd ever had were her brothers in arms.

Gus got out of Drake's bed and pulled on her clothes. They'd been engaging in a little afternoon delight on the *Void*. They'd be leaving Buddy's Bluff in a few hours, and Gus had a few things she needed to do first.

Things she needed to do alone.

"Leaving already, darlin'?" Drake asked.

He smelled of cinnamon and sex and all the wonderfulness that she'd been afraid she'd never see again. The last thing she wanted to do was leave him behind, but she had someplace to be.

She leaned over and gave him a long, lingering kiss. "I'll be back." She kissed him again. "I promise." She cocked one eyebrow. "Besides, don't you have some last-minute checks to run? Or did you have Big Bruce handle everything?"

He kissed her back. "Read you loud and clear. I'll keep myself busy."

The berth housing the transport ship that had brought Brukowski and his men to the Bluff was on the other side of the spaceport. By the time Gus got there, Julio Ortiz and Earl Knox, of all people, were already there saying goodbye to Benji Ochoa. Benji would be going back to Melody Station as one of the armor jocks keeping Tor under lock and key.

She knew that Brukowski's men would rather have set off for Melody Station days ago, but Tor's injuries had been too severe to move him right away. Nobody wanted him to take the easy way out by dying before he went on trial.

Tor had already been loaded onto the ship. Good riddance to bad rubbish. Gus didn't want to see that bastard again. Ever.

"I'll be wearing my armor the whole time, don't you worry," Benji told her. "Just in case that skudgehole tries something."

With Benji Ochoa on the job, she didn't have a thing to worry about, and she told him so. There'd be no last-minute rescue attempts either. Kymmie had done a crackerjack job of making it clear that Tor was a malevolent despot wannabe dictator out to bring everyone in the Alliance under this thumb. She'd promised Gus that by the time she was done, everyone in the Alliance would know that Tor was lower than pond scum. He wouldn't be anyone's hero or martyr to a lost cause, just a pathetic, delusional old man.

Along with Julio Ortiz and Earl Knox, Gus watched Benji's transport take off. Watching him go was harder than she'd thought it would be. She'd taken a lot of razzing during her time with the 83rd, but there'd been the kind of camaraderie among the armor jocks she hadn't found anywhere else.

"Can't believe you decided to stay behind," she said to Ortiz after Benji's transport was out of sight. "The Bluff isn't exactly Melody Station. You're leaving the good life behind."

"Oh, I don't know about that," he said. "Watching all you armor jocks take on the bad guys while I was stuck in a pilot's chair got me thinking about the old days."

Ortiz hadn't brought any armor with him to Buddy's Bluff. Maybe that's why he and Earl seemed to be buddy-buddy now. Earl had lost his armor when Brukowski stole it and the ring ship disappeared with Brukowski and Earl's armor inside. Something Earl had complained long and hard to Gus about. He'd actually blamed *her* for dragging him along on her harebrained mission.

Right up until she gave him his share of the bounty— enough of the singularium in the bird ship's secret cargo hold to not only square up his accounts with Bruce Junior but to buy the necessary supplies so he could build a new suit of armor, with singularium to spare.

"I'm gonna build *two* suits," Earl said now.

Gus's eyebrows climbed halfway up her forehead. "You? You need *two?*"

"One's for me," Ortiz said with a grin. He slung an arm around Earl's shoulder. "We're gonna go be a tag team. Big Earl and the Teez. Whaddya think?"

Gus shook her head. "I think the known 'verse won't know what hit it."

They shook hands, then each man hugged Gus—carefully—and slapped her on the back—also carefully. She watched them walk back in the direction of the trading post, talking and gesturing and laughing as they went.

Earl Knox was laughing! Imagine that.

She only had one more goodbye, and it wasn't with

Bruce Junior. She had an idea they might be seeing him again sometime in the future. He did, after all, run one of the best supply posts in the Frontier. Especially now that the Fluke were no longer an issue.

No, this goodbye was going to be a little harder.

Because it was one she'd never expected she'd have to say.

CHAPTER 38

The bird ship had looked big in space. In its berth on Buddy's Bluff, it looked *massive.*

All sleek ebony, without even a single rivet or break in the metal on the hull, the ship loomed over Gus, dwarfing her with its mere presence. It looked more like a bird now than ever, with its wings angled backward along its sides and its beak lowered toward the deck.

Gus knew there'd been a hole in the ship's hull below its throat. But looking at it now, the ship seemed as pristine as the day it had been made.

Made? Or *born?*

No one knew how the Ongoni had created this ship. The Ongoni were a secretive species. They didn't allow outworlders in their space, much less on their planet. As far as Gus knew—hell, as far as Bruce Junior knew—the bird ship and the *Scintilla* were the first Ongoni ships anyone who wasn't Ongoni had seen in known space. The person who'd parted with the *Scintilla* to settle his debts with Bruce Junior had implied there were more ships like the *Scintilla*, but even Bruce Junior hadn't really believed it.

And this ship, this wonderful, beautiful, *sentient* ship, had allowed Gus to commune with it.

There was no other word for it. Bruce Junior and whatever shipwrights had looked over the *Scintilla* might claim that the ship was a product of *psiflux engineering* and communication with it was through *telepathically transmitted thought engrams,* but Gus thought trying to pin scientific concepts on something so obviously yet differently organic was way off the mark. All she knew was that she'd felt closer to this ship than anything else she'd ever gone into battle with in her lifetime. *Including* her armor.

That was a hell of an admission for a lifelong armor jock to make.

She'd bonded with her armor, no question there. But she'd always thought of her armor as an extension of her physical body. The armor made her faster, stronger, and far more deadly than she was as Augusta Light, human soldier. Even the AI-enhanced sensors in her helmet were still just part and parcel of her physical self.

The bird ship had been part of her *mind.*

It had read her thoughts, and she had read its thoughts. Or at least the thoughts it had allowed her to see. It had trusted her to take care of it. She had trusted it to take care of her. Drake had told her that piloting the *Scintilla* had been one of the most intimate things he'd ever experienced. After her own experience with the bird ship, Gus understood that now.

But it was time to say goodbye.

And gods, but it *hurt.* It was like saying goodbye to a part of herself. She hadn't felt anything like it since she'd been forced to leave her infant son behind on Shepard's Moon.

She rested her right hand on the ship's sleek hull, feeling an odd sense of déjà vu. She'd traced her fingers along the hull of the *Golden Void* back on Depak Station when she'd practically hijacked Drake to take her to Shepard's Moon so she could save her son. Well, if she was honest with herself, there'd been no *practically* about it. She'd paid off his debts and marched herself and her armor on board like she owned the ship.

They'd fought like cats and dogs back then. But they came to respect each other. Drake had even backed her up in battle, and somewhere along the way, they'd fallen in love. She could no more say goodbye to Drake and the *Golden Void* than she could cut out her own heart. But this goodbye—saying goodbye to this wonderful ship—was *hard.*

Her fingertips tingled, and images began to flash through her mind as the feelings those images invoked bombarded her heart.

The night her son was born. The joy of holding him for the first time in her arms.

Hoping against hope that his father, terminally injured in battle, would regain consciousness long enough to see his son.

The devastation that threatened to consume her when that didn't happen.

The despair the *bird ship* felt when the *Scintilla* was stolen.

The long decades the bird ship had searched for the *Scintilla*. The humans the bird ship had allowed inside herself to ease her loneliness.

The men Gus had taken to her bed for a quick tumble between the sheets to ease her own loneliness after she'd been forced to leave her newborn son behind.

The bird ship's revulsion when it realized it had been deceived by Tor.

The hatred it felt when Tor threatened to destroy the *Scintilla* if the bird ship didn't do as he said.

The hope the bird ship felt when it first read Gus's thoughts and realized she hated Tor as much as the bird ship did.

The love Gus had felt when she saw her adult son on Shepard's Moon and realized he'd made a wonderful, meaningful life for himself even though she would never be a part of it.

The love the bird ship felt when it recognized the *Scintilla* and the *Scintilla* recognized it.

Gus reeled, the deck seeming to sway beneath her feet, as the images disappeared from her mind with an almost audible *snap!*

She blinked and shook her head. The bird ship had never told Gus its name—*her* name, for the ship was decidedly female—but she'd just told Gus something far more important.

The *Scintilla* wasn't the bird ship's sibling. It was her *child*. A child that had been stolen from her. No wonder the *Scintilla* had insisted, in its own way, that it be berthed right next to the bird ship. They were mother and child.

Gus couldn't let them be split up again, not when she could do something about it.

She just hoped Drake would understand.

"You gave it away?" Drake stared at her, mouth open in shock. "*All* of it?"

Gus shrugged, then winced as her shoulder complained.

"You just got it back!" he said.

She'd found Drake lounging in his captain's chair when she got back to the *Golden Void*. He had his ancient guitar on his lap and was singing one of his favorite old cowboy songs.

Or he had been until she told him what she'd done. Now he was leaning forward, elbows on his knees, the guitar forgotten.

"I didn't give it *all* away," she said.

She still had enough money in various accounts inside the Alliance to last the two of them a good long time, provided they didn't splurge. Or have to buy a bunch of ships and ammo to fight another war. Then they'd be strapped for cash again, but Gus figured Sef and Exchequer owed them. She wasn't above knocking on Sef's door to collect.

Besides, she hadn't technically given her money—and the rest of the singularium—away.

She'd bought two Ongoni ships their well-deserved freedom.

Gus sat down on Drake's lap and brushed his hair back

away from his face. "I couldn't turn my back on them," she said. "Not after they saved our bacon."

She'd purchased the rights to the *Scintilla* outright from Bruce Junior. That had been the easy part of the deal. The hard part had been settling the squabble between Bruce Junior and Layla Crosscut over the bird ship.

Bruce Junior had claimed the ship was his since it was berthed in his port and its last "owner" had abandoned it since he'd be spending the next several lifetimes sitting in an Alliance prison. Crosscut had insisted that if the bird ship was considered unowned property, it was *hers* because she had claimed salvage rights to all unowned property in the area in space where the ring ship had been including the bird ship.

The Alliance could probably lay claim to the bird ship as well since it was no doubt purchased by Tor with earnings from his illegal activities. If anyone took the bird ship into Alliance space, the authorities would probably seize it.

Gus had decided not to mention that. It was hard enough dealing with Crosscut and Bruce Junior as it was.

What she did tell them was that *she* should be considered the bird ship's rightful owner because she was the last one the ship had communicated with and *she'd* been the one to capture Tor.

"The ship's *my* rightful bounty," she'd said. "Unless either one of you wants to fight me for it."

Crosscut had bluffed and blustered. Bruce Junior had just gone pale. He'd seen what she'd done to Earl in their little "staged" fight for the benefit of the Fluke.

"*But,*" Gus had added, "since we're all friends here, I'm willing to be reasonable. How about we discuss what you might consider fair compensation for the release of your claims." She'd paused, then said again, "Since we're friends."

She'd started negotiations by offering to split the remaining singularium in the bird ship's hold equally between the two of them. Bruce Junior said that was fair, *provided* she was talking about a hell of a lot of singularium. Gus figured he'd been planning on selling the bird ship for a king's ransom since it was basically one of a kind.

Crosscut had demanded a 60/40 split, and she wouldn't budge. "I lost an entire *planet's* worth of singularium," she'd said.

Gus had just given Crosscut an *I call bullshit* glare. The ring ship had been big, but it wasn't *that* big.

But rather than argue that ten percent swing, Gus had taken Bruce aside and told him that she'd make up the difference by throwing in some additional cash. When he'd started to balk, she'd reminded him exactly who'd gotten rid of the Fluke for him. He'd swallowed hard and accepted the deal.

It turned out to be rather a *lot* of additional cash. Bruce had been surprised to learn that Gus was good for it. After all, he'd gone with Drake to beg Exchequer for funding for the war because Gus and Drake were pretty much broke.

Gus just told him she'd gotten a sudden windfall and left it at that. He probably thought the Alliance had paid her a bounty for Tor. Gus had already decided that *if* the Alliance wanted to pay someone a bounty for Tor's sorry ass, they should split it among the civilians who'd volunteered to join her in the fight.

As soon as the singularium had been offloaded from the

bird ship, Gus had told the bird ship that she and the *Scintilla* were free to go. Then she'd stayed at the port to watch both ships lift off. Neither ship had any crew on board. They didn't need people anymore. They had each other.

And, apparently, they also had something else.

Before they blasted out of sight, a distinct guitar riff had played in Gus's mind. She didn't recognize the song, but it was something far more upbeat than Drake had ever played. He'd mentioned that his guitar had gone missing for a while when he'd been on the *Scintilla*. Gus liked to think that the ship had learned how to play its own style of music by learning to play Drake's antique guitar. At least the *Scintilla* had given the guitar back to him.

Rock and roll among the stars, played by two sentient beings traveling wherever they wanted to go. Together.

Kind of like her and Drake.

After she explained everything she'd done and why, Drake gave her a broad grin and hugged her, mindful of her injured shoulder. He seemed to have gotten over his shock at her sudden decision about the money and the singularium with his usual space cowboy casualness. She had a feeling he was used to money slipping through his fingers.

"You're a soft touch, Gray Lady," he said, stroking the side of her face with a gentle hand.

She arched an eyebrow at him. "I also have a pretty *strong grip* when I want to, Broken String," she said, placing an emphasis on the right words to make sure her innuendo came through loud and clear.

They'd been cleared to take off from Buddy's Bluff whenever they wanted. The ship was fully supplied with food and fuel. She would need to repair the singularium plating on her armor, but that could wait. The boxy shield generator was fully operational and already set up to protect the ship, Tor's pirates had gone back to wherever they came from, no doubt licking their wounds, and Tor was on his way to a nice prison cell on Melody Station. They could afford to take some time just for themselves. Head out into the vastness of space with no particular destination in mind.

"Feel like letting the kid take over?" Gus asked, leaning forward to nuzzle Drake's ear.

Drake cleared his throat. "Hey, Big Bruce!"

"Yes, Captain?" came the AI's voice. "You rang?"

The words were accompanied by a raucous blast of music with a definite heavy beat.

"Um… what's that?" Gus asked.

"Music!" Big Bruce said. "The *Scintilla* introduced me to a whole different kind of music."

Gus and Drake exchanged an incredulous look.

"You've been *talking* to the *Scintilla*?" he asked.

"Oh, yes!" Another loud chord reverberated from the ship's speakers, rattling the strings on Drake's guitar. "She's a wonderful ship. She just discovered music thanks to the Captain. She said no one ever played music for her before. Now she's writing her own. I downloaded all the music I could find in the Bluff's databanks so I could share it with her. What do you think of this one?"

The music changed to an even louder song, although this one had a more recognizable melody.

"Isn't it wonderful?" Big Bruce said. "The *Scintilla* *loved* it!"

Gus stifled a snicker. Big Bruce was sharing his favorite music with a sentient ship.

"I think our kid just discovered girls," she said to Drake, keeping her voice pitched low enough for only him to hear. Pretty easy since Big Bruce's favorite music was threatening to blow out her eardrums.

"Think you can dial it down a notch, pardner?" Drake asked.

The AI didn't respond, unless the fact that the music got even louder as the song segued into the chorus. Everyone in the spaceport could probably hear it.

"*Bruce Azazel!*" Gus shouted to make herself heard. "Turn it down. Please!"

The music immediately dropped to a more conversational level.

"That's another thing!" Big Bruce said. "I've decided on a last name. In honor of my new favorite musician! You should like it, Captain. He's from Old Earth. Not quite as old as *your* music, but still an antique!"

Gus had a bad feeling about this, but she needed to ask. Bruce would be expecting it. And he had, after all, taken it well when he had to say goodbye to all the little Bruces when the leased ships left Buddy's Bluff on their way back to Honest Gordian's.

"Don't keep us hanging," she said.

"Ozzyborne!" Big Bruce said. "I'm now Bruce Azazel Ozzyborne. What do you think?"

Gus gave Drake a quizzical look. She wasn't familiar with the music of Old Earth, except for the cowboy songs Drake sang. If the music Big Bruce had just been playing was any indication, Ozzyborne had never played anything like "back in the saddle again."

Drake shrugged. He clearly hadn't heard of this Ozzyborne either.

"Sounds good," he said. "Now if you think you can *handle* it, Bruce Azazel *Ozzyborne,* want to take us out of the port and into the great beyond? *Without* blowing out our eardrums?"

"Absolutely, Captain! What's our destination?"

Drake grinned at Gus, and she smiled back.

"Out there," she said. "We need some private time, so just take us somewhere where we won't run into trouble."

"You're giving me the *wheel?*" Big Bruce sounded as excited as a teenager who'd just been given the keys to his parents' spaceship.

"You realize he's gonna have us following his girlfriend," Drake murmured.

"Probably," Gus said. "Would that be such a bad thing?"

Drake gave her waist a squeeze. "Not at all, darlin'. That's what I'd do. Follow you to the end of the known space and back again."

"Same here, cowboy," she said. She leaned her forehead against his, reveling in the feel of him. She never wanted to be parted from him again. Whatever came their way, whatever their future held, as long as they were together, that's all she wanted. "Same here."

EPILOGUE

Garrison Brukowski, Gary to the drinking buddies he'd never see again, Bruiser to the guys he'd served with in the 83rd Armor Division, was royally screwed.

No food. No water. No comms. And no hope of even figuring out where he was.

Was this what death was like? He had no skudging idea. Would he still be bleeding from a thousand little cuts on his hands and face if he was dead?

Oh, he knew where he was in the immediate sense of the word. He was still on the ring ship. His last clear memory before the universe went insane was telling Gus Light to get the hell off the ship before it blew.

But the ship hadn't blown. It was still here. *He* was still here.

Only where was here?

He'd come back to himself in the same corridor of the ring ship where he'd opened the panel to the brains of the classified tech he was supposed to "render inoperative." Ha. Such an innocuous term. He was supposed to kill the brains in this section of the ship, which was supposed to kill the brains for the entire ship, thanks to the way the artificial neural network had been designed.

Only somehow, the ship had decided it would rather kill *his* brains instead.

He had the mother of all headaches. His head actually felt overstuffed, like his brain was trying to fight its way out of his skull. Even moving his head just a little brought on a fit of vertigo so severe he felt like screaming.

The ring ship wasn't supposed to be sentient. It was just a damn *tool*. Something the Alliance had developed to give it an edge against its enemies, whoever they might be. Give the Alliance the ability to send an entire fleet almost anywhere in known space.

Known space, now that really was a laugh.

The ring ship was powered by a contained singularity drive, the biggest one ever harnessed for use on a ship. The Alliance was big, pardon the expression, on having the biggest everything. As far as Brukowski could tell, there'd been a power surge from that singularity, as if the brains of the ship had *un*contained that little contained black hole and sucked everything inside. Ship, tech, *and* one covert military intelligence operative named Brukowski.

Then the singularity spat them all out on the other side.

That wasn't supposed to happen. The spitting out part.

Yet here he was. Still alive. Still breathing. Still in agony.

What the hell had the Alliance created?

Or maybe they hadn't created it at all. Maybe the ship *wasn't* sentient. The skudging scavengers had been removing singularium from the ship's hull. According to the specs Brukowski had studied, plating the hull with all that very expensive singularium was supposed to make the ship invulnerable to attack. But what if it had a different purpose? What if it was supposed to help *contain* the huge contained singularity that powered the ship? And by removing some of the singularium panels—a tiny percentage of the overall number of panels on the hull—the containment field couldn't work the way it was designed?

Then when Brukowski had awakened the ship's brain, a brain that had been slumbering for decades, the singularity drive kicked into gear and took the ship… somewhere.

Only that didn't make sense. This wasn't the first time the ship had just up and disappeared.

Brukowski couldn't think straight. His head hurt too much. All he knew for certain was that the ship had never been built for a human crew. There was nothing inside he could use to sustain his life.

That meant he had to go outside.

He was still wearing most of Knox's armor. He'd dropped the gauntlets and gloves to free up his hands so he could use the chip embedded in his wrist. There was a charred bit of flesh on his wrist now where the chip had been. It must have shorted it out.

Funny, but his wrist didn't hurt. Just his head. He didn't even want to think what that meant.

It would be a hell of a long walk back to the airlock where he'd left the armor's helmet, but what else did he have to do?

He picked up the gauntlets and gloves and started walking.

He lost track of how long it took for him to find the airlock. Vertigo threatened every time he moved too fast or turned his head too quickly. He almost missed a couple of junctions where he needed to take a different corridor. Maybe he should have left breadcrumbs on the way in. Then he'd at least have something to eat.

By the time he caught sight of the right airlock, the one with Knox's helmet next to it—thank goodness Light hadn't taken the helmet with her when she'd left the ship—Brukowski's head was pounding hard enough he was surprised it was still attached to his neck.

He lowered the helmet over his aching head and attached it to the rest of the armor at the shoulders, then put on the gauntlets and gloves. The armor powered up like it should, although it informed him he only had twenty percent available fuel left. He hadn't been worried about using too much fuel when he'd raced to the ring ship in the middle of the battle. Back then he'd been more concerned about not taking a missile hit. Now he wished he'd been a little more conservative.

At least all the spacetight seals on the armor hadn't been compromised, even if the helmet did still smell nasty inside.

Onward and outward, he thought, then he fought the urge to giggle.

Maybe he had brain damage. He never giggled.

He cycled through the airlock, made sure the magnets on his boots were engaged, and stepped outside.

To nothing.

Oh sure, the space around him glittered with the distant light of billions of stars in millions of galaxies, but he didn't recognize any of them. Had he been the poetic sort, he might have been moved to create rhymes to try and capture the immensity of it all. The cold, distant beauty of being all alone yet surrounded by such natural wonder.

No planets. No satellites. No moons or asteroids or even a passing comet.

Once again, he felt like screaming.

He'd succeeded. He'd kept the ring ship and its technology out of Tor's hands. Brukowski had even been ready to die for the cause.

But not like *this.* Not attached by magnetic boots to the hull of a dead ship until the fuel in his armor ran out and the oxygen recyclers quit and he suffocated to death.

He could take the helmet off and let the vacuum of space kill him, but he'd seen deaths like that. He didn't want to go out that way either.

Just for the hell of it, just to confirm what he already knew, he had the armor's sensors scan the area of space around him. Maybe they'd find a small asteroid he could get to. Someplace where he could sit and watch space around him while he died. Better than dying on the hull of the ring ship. It had tried to kill him.

A moment later a small red display blinked to life on one corner of the helmet's visor.

Brukowski tried to focus. His eyes didn't seem to work right, and it took a moment when he did see the words for them to make sense.

A ship.

There was another ship out there in all that emptiness.

The ship was as black as the space around it, its surface non-reflective. It was almost a null presence, certainly nothing he could have seen on his own. According to the sensors in his helmet, the ship was small, barely larger than a shuttle. If it was under power, its power signature was so low his sensors didn't register it.

The ship was just hanging there, like it was watching him.

He had the armor's sensors calculate the distance between the ring ship and his unexpected neighbor, then he tried to do the math to determine if he had enough fuel to make it to the other ship. The ring ship was still exerting a small gravitational pull, and he had to figure that in as well.

The sensors in his armor were no help at all. Either Knox had never needed to calculate something like that, or the part of the armor's systems that handled complex special calculations was busted. The pounding in his head kept distracting him. The harder he tried to concentrate, the more his head throbbed.

By the time he came up with three different answers to the same set of calculations, he decided just screw it.

What did he have to lose? He could stay attached to the ring ship and sit there and die, or he could try to make it to the little black ship. The little ship might not let him inside, but then again, it might.

He disengaged the magnets on the bottom of the armor's boots and pushed off the ring ship's hull. He risked using just a bit of fuel for the maneuvering jets to line up his trajectory, then he considered whether he should use the suit's thrusters. He should just float over, using the minimal power from the maneuvering jets to propel him along. He didn't want to come in hot. He couldn't *afford* to come in hot. He didn't want whoever—or whatever—was in that ship to think he was attacking.

But he couldn't wait for that. Now that he wasn't attached to the ring ship, his stomach was doing slow rolls every time his head throbbed. The stench inside the helmet wasn't helping.

Brukowski had survived a lot of long shots in his life. The biggest one was waking up alive in the belly of the ring ship when he should have been dead.

Did he have another long shot in him? Or had he already used up more than a lifetime's worth of good luck?

Well, there was only one way to find out.

He concentrated on the null spot in space that was the little black ship, said a prayer to a deity he didn't believe in, and fired the armor's thrusters.

ABOUT THE AUTHORS

A prolific, versatile, and award-winning writer, **Annie Reed** has written more short fiction than she can count. She's a frequent contributor to both *Pulphouse Fiction Magazine* and *Mystery, Crime and Mayhem*. She's received a Silver Honorable Mention from Writers of the Future, and her stories have appeared in numerous annual year's best mystery volumes. She's even had a story selected for inclusion in study materials for Japanese college entrance exams. Her *Unexpected* series of short-story collections showcase some of her best work.

Her longer works include the superhero origin novel *Faster*, novellas *The Wizard Behind the Curtain* and *In Dreams*, and mystery novels *Pretty Little Horses, Paper Bullets*, and *A Death in Cumberland*.

Annie writes mystery, science fiction, and fantasy under her own name and writes suspense as Kris Sparks. She also writes the sweet romance *Liberty Springs* novels under the name Liz McKnight. She can be found on the web at anniereed.wordpress.com.

Robert Jeschonek is an envelope-pushing, *USA Today* bestselling author whose fiction, comics, and non-fiction have been published around the world. His stories have appeared in *Clarkesworld, Galaxy's Edge, StarShipSofa, Pulphouse,* and many other publications. He has written official *Star Trek* and *Doctor Who* fiction and has scripted comics for DC, AHOY, and others. His young adult slipstream novel, *My Favorite Band Does Not Exist*, won the Forward National Literature Award and was named one of *Booklist's* Top Ten First Novels for Youth. He also won an International Book Award, a Scribe Award for Best Original Novel, and the grand prize in Pocket Books' Strange New Worlds contest. Visit him online at www.bobscribe.com. You can also find him on Facebook and follow him as @TheFictioneer on X (Twitter) and @bobscribe.bsky.social on Bluesy. Subscribe to the Blastoff Books Newsletter: http://newsletter.blastoff books.net/.

www.ingramcontent.com/pod-product-compliance
Lightning Source LLC
Chambersburg PA
CBHW070400260626
47161CB00001B/205